EVERY BODY HAS A STORY

A novel

Beverly Gologorsky

Haymarket Books
Chicago, Illinois

Published in 2018 by
Haymarket Books
P.O. Box 180165
Chicago, IL 60618
773-583-7884
www.haymarketbooks.org
info@haymarketbooks.org

ISBN: 978-1-60846-907-9

An earlier version of an excerpt from *Every Body Has a Story* appeared
in Hamilton Stone Review, April 2016. Excerpt from *The Niagara River,*
copyright © 2005 by Kay Ryan. Used by permission of Grove/Atlantic, Inc.
Any third party use of this material, outside of this publication, is prohibited.

Trade distribution:
In the US, Consortium Book Sales and Distribution,
www.cbsd.com
In Canada, Publishers Group Canada, www.pgcbooks.ca
In the UK, Turnaround Publisher Services,
www.turnaround-uk.com
All other countries, Ingram Publisher Services International, IPS_Intl-
sales@ingramcontent.com

This book was published with the generous support of Lannan Founda-
tion and Wallace Action Fund.

Printed in Canada by union labor.

Cover design by Mimi Bark, mimibark.com

Library of Congress Cataloging-in-Publication data is available.

10 9 8 7 6 5 4 3 2 1

Things Shouldn't Be So Hard
Kay Ryan

A life should leave
deep tracks:
ruts where she
went out and back
to get the mail
or move the hose
around the yard;
where she used to
stand before the sink,
a worn-out place;
beneath her hand
the china knobs
rubbed down to
white pastilles;
the switch she
used to feel for
in the dark
almost erased.
Her things should
keep her marks.
The passage
of a life should show;
it should abrade.
And when life stops,
a certain space—
however small—
should be left scarred
by the grand and
damaging parade.
Things shouldn't
be so hard.

As always, for: Georgina, Dònal,
and especially Maya

for
Tom Engelhardt, with deep appreciation

and

In Memory of
Charlie Wiggins

PART ONE

1.

Lena stands, as always, at the window in the train door gazing at the old East Bronx apartment buildings, the elevation not high enough to avoid glimpses into a grayness that can't be altered by light bulbs. She knows this grayness, grew up within its grip like a pigeon on a windowsill. Never a smooth ride, the elevated train bounces along the track, shaking awake a few of the sleepy rush-hour passengers. Suddenly a woman's gaunt face peers out at her from an open window, her expression fierce, certain, frightening. She turns away, refusing to remember.

2.

Lifting her head from the dizzying columns of numbers on the screen, she checks the clock on the wall, nearly six, and shuts down the computer. The head bookkeeper left at the stroke of five. It's Friday. The weekend begins and not a minute too soon. She needs to hurry yet finds herself staring up at the porthole window, out of which nothing whole can be viewed. A few drinks, she hopes, will revive her. The gaiety of the next hours will demand that. On the phone yesterday, she asked Dory if this was really how she wanted to celebrate her birthday. Stu planned the whole evening, Dory responded. Subject closed.

She slips out of flats into suede pumps, stuffs her reading glasses and phone in her purse, locks the office door, and crosses the small lobby with its worn carpet and faded flowery couch. The hotel is on the edge of seedy, though the head bookkeeper swears it was once quite fancy.

Belting her coat, she joins the midtown crowd. Despite the heels she'll walk from Lexington to Seventh Avenue where, like a hooker, she'll wait on the corner for the car to pick her up. It's a cold, blue dusk, a cloudless sky, no sign of snow. Zack pays serious attention to weather forecasts. Snow means construction work stops. A man whose admitted ambition is to get home each evening, he craves bad weather like a prisoner his freedom. Since they bought the house he's even more domestic, or maybe it's difficult for him to believe it exists unless he's in it. Well, she doesn't adore her job either. Who does? Except Dory, who loves her work.

Fur-coated women trailing perfume jostle past her, swinging their brand-name bags. Such an easy life. What would it feel like?

There's always the daily lotto ticket. Her father bought one, no matter what. And if he didn't have the two bucks, the guy trusted him to pay, which he eventually did. He never won a thing. Of course he didn't. Anyway, it's not in her nature to pin her hopes on games.

In the amber-lit club, waiters weave between the tables, balancing trays. Statues of the Buddha lounge in corners, their enigmatic smiles eternal. Silver and gold sparkling balls flash lights on the ceiling, revealing half a face here, a glint of teeth there, the sudden gleam of jewelry on an invisible ear, the dance floor as disorienting as an accident scene. Stu will pull her there to gyrate to music her fifteen-year-old daughter would love. He likes dancing with her, always has. Once upon a time, the four of them were an item, went everywhere together.

They follow a hostess to a small round table. She drops off four menus and disappears.

"She didn't give us a chance to order drinks," Stu complains, barely changed from the slim, handsome youth all the girls trailed—to Dory's consternation. His mischievous green eyes and slightly lifted brows remain ready for play, though the loose boyish smile never quite breaks through anymore. Unlike Zack, who grins a lot.

"Birthdays have memories."

"Dory, you're going on forty, not eighty," she says.

"It was when they were living in the projects . . ."

"Years to forget."

"Lena, let the girl finish her story," Zack says amiably.

"It was your birthday, Lena, sixteen. The four of us went out drinking at the Café something or other on Simpson Street, got shit-faced, and ended up on Orchard Beach, remember?"

"Yes, so?"

"What a great night that was."

But it wasn't. Barely a breeze off Long Island Sound. Lots of people on blankets, laughing, drinking, making noises of every sort. Zack and Stu wanted a little loving and tented a blanket on the sand. She became weirdly self-conscious and asked to go home. Stu tried to make her stay, whispering that it would be no fun to break up the gang. She insisted on leaving, and Zack stood up, ready to oblige. Stu called her a prude, accused her of ruining the night. Dory's memories have a way of cleansing scenes where Stu is concerned.

"I'm more attached to Lena's eighteenth birthday," Stu says. "The girl goes to the ladies' room and doesn't come back. Dory finds her asleep on the toilet. Soused, of course."

"Actually, I had the flu . . . Of course, the drinking didn't help." They laugh.

"Stu, what about the night I had to lug you off the bus singing the national anthem?" Zack says.

" I wasn't drunk. I was high."

"Lord, it does sound like we spent our youth stoned," Dory says. "Now, we're upright, sober, whatever, except for occasions like this. I mean, how many nights do we go out clubbing?"

"Not enough," Stu responds sourly.

"Does it really bother you?" Zack asks.

"Yeah, it does. It's a giving up . . . a loss of . . . I don't know . . . fun, and for what?"

"We have fun, don't we?" Dory searches Stu's face, her small, delicate chin uplifted.

"Depends." He's searching the room for a waiter to lasso.

"Fun changes as we take on responsibilities," Zack says.

She and Dory exchange looks.

The waiter arrives. "Drinks?"

"A bottle of Asti Spumante champagne," says Stu, and the waiter heads for the bar.

"A bit pricey, no?" she ventures, annoyed.

"Hey, it's a birthday, isn't it?"

"It's okay, Stu," Dory begins, "we don't need to spend . . ."

"No, not okay. We have to toast."

No one says anything.

"How is Miss Z.?" Lena asks.

"Who is Miss Z.?" Zack wants to know.

"One of Dory's charges at the nursing home."

"She still waits at the door for a sister who will never appear, but hope springs. . . ."

"I'd shoot myself before ending up like that," Stu says.

"Miss Z. is not demented," Dory responds. "It's how she chooses to spend her time."

"Who knows, Stu, maybe you'd be happier without reality," she quips.

"Reality?"

The waiter reappears, uncorks the sparkling wine, fills the glasses, then deftly opens a menu in front of each of them before vanishing.

"To Dory, who deserves only the best." Stu lifts his glass.

"To my forever best friend, many happy years to come."

"To our everlasting friendship," Zack chimes in.

"This stuff tastes good," Stu says. "Waiter, another!" he calls out, pointing to his almost empty glass and ignoring the partially filled bottle on the table.

"Did you win on a number?" Zack jokes.

Stu gazes at the dancers. "I'm taking the new floor position at the plant."

"I thought you weren't going to abandon your work team," Dory says, careful not to show surprise. "What happened?" It's clear, though, that she's hearing the news for the first time.

Stu shrugs. "Drink up, mates. Another bottle is on the way, and we need to get to the dancing."

After dropping off Dory and Stu, they head for home, as her mind wanders through the last few hours. She tried to enjoy herself. She really did. She even danced, but it felt like a performance. Stu was working too hard at celebrating and Dory was clearly upset, though she tried her best to hide it. Why hadn't he told her about the job change? Zack's staring at the road, his youthful face not the least bit tired-looking.

"Do you think Stu's fucking around?"

"He's not," Zack states.

"How do you know?"

He shrugs.

"You mean it's a guy thing, recognizing cheating?"

"He tells me stuff."

"Then how come you didn't know about the job change?"

"I did. He asked me to say nothing until he made up his mind. They're only keeping one member of each welding team, so he kissed ass to be that one."

"That's awful."

"Would you rather he be let go?"

"Of course not, but why didn't he share the news with Dory?"

"Dory's very high-minded. She'd be disappointed in him for selling out his crew, which is what it amounts to."

"Well, they were unusually quiet in the car."

"Quiet is good."

She settles deeper into the seat.

"At the construction site, quiet isn't allowed. The noise is constant. I think I'm losing my hearing. The guys socialize by ribbing, joking, griping, pushing, and poking each other—no fun when you're up that high. Maybe the others don't mind, but I can't finish the day fast enough."

None of this is news to her. Again and again she listens to similar complaints, and they never lead anywhere.

"You remember the Stubbs story. The fool jumped from one beam to another and didn't make it. Wouldn't that stop anyone else from doing the same? No. They need to prove it can be done. I take the elevator down and then up to the other top floor beam. They call me lady. Lady, do this. Lady, do that. It's what I deal with every day."

"I'm sorry you have to live through that." She speaks softly, almost sensually, to stop him from going any further. It would take him forever to find another job, and what would that be if not construction?

He grins. "The universe is selfish. No man can have both the best job and the best woman. Anyway, angel, for you I'll keep balancing on those cold fucking beams."

He waits for a response. He always does. She's done this so many times, every which way. And truth to tell, she's too tired of the subject to do it now.

Except for the streetlight on the corner, the road leading

to the house is dark. It's a newly renovated area in a once downtrodden part of the East Bronx. The houses were built and sold quickly at a manageable price. Aluminum-sided Cape Cods, apart from different colors and trims, look alike, each with a small backyard and an even smaller front lawn. Hers, however, sports a maple tree that flames gorgeous in autumn. Several of the men who live on the road also work in construction. She wonders if they, too, complain to their wives about their jobs.

Upstairs, Rosie, barefoot, in cutoff pajama bottoms and a T-shirt, comes out of her room.

"Hi. What's up?" Zack says.

"Mirabelle's mom couldn't take us to dinner."

"What did you and your brother do for food?" Lena asks.

"Ordered pizza."

"Good thinking." She revels in her daughter's gorgeous mass of curly, dark hair.

"Don't sound so surprised. I'm not an infant."

"I know that."

"I wonder," Rosie turns and strides back into her room.

"She hates me," she whispers half to herself.

"For now," Zack says.

"Easy for you to say, it's not you she sasses."

"Lena, she's a cookie-cutter version of you."

"That's crap."

Zack grins and opens the bedroom door.

Though tired, she's wide awake. Zack's eyes are closed. He can sleep at will. Not a worrier, he's a man who refuses to anticipate problems. At times it annoys her, but it was that same laid-back, affectionate nature that drew her to him twenty years ago. An only child of parents who rarely touched each other, she grew up in a household where no one spoke unless absolutely necessary. Her parents slept in twin beds pushed as far apart as their small room would permit. She often wanted to ask her mother what happened, but it felt too dangerous.

In the never-complete darkness, her head propped high on pillows, she stares at the wall hanging they bought in Mexico on their honeymoon. That first night, right before dawn, the hotel began to shake, the ground an angry ocean. Grabbing whatever they could, they joined the others being shepherded outside. The quake, more exciting than scary, was proof that the unexpected happens.

She slips out of bed, tiptoes to the window, and opens the blinds on the small backyard, where a card table, several folding chairs, Casey's bike, and an outdoor grill fill the shadowy space. Growing up, no one they knew owned property. Everyone crowded inside project apartments stacked on top of each other, windows facing other windows or dirty brick walls. Now, they own a house. Still, is this all?

"Lena," he stage whispers. "Come back to bed."

His voice startles her. "In a minute."

"I think the food disagreed with me."

"Can I get you something?"

"Your body." They'd made love earlier that morning, but he's tireless when it comes to sex.

She says nothing, doesn't turn around.

"My body needs yours to heal."

She continues to gaze at the navy-blue, sequined sky, defiance and compliance warring inside her.

"Lena? I can't fall asleep without you."

She snaps the blinds shut and gets back into bed. His arm wraps around her, his skin warm against hers, his mouth close to her ear.

"I watched you at the window receiving holy messages. I was jealous."

She doesn't move. When his breathing slows, she slides up to sitting. In a darkness even more open to her now, she can just make out the velvet knitting bag from her childhood. A neighbor taught her how to knit when she was eight or nine. Told her to be careful. A ball of yarn can get away from you and quickly unravel.

3.

F rom the window Dory watches as Stu's car backs out of the garage. She doesn't want him to go. They've just come home. He pleaded his need for that last drink, the one he didn't have at the club, the one that wouldn't taste as good in the living room, though he didn't quite say that.

The house is too big to be empty, too empty to be alone in. Only when Stu's at home does she take pleasure in the careful décor of each room. Swallowing two aspirin for the headache that's insisted on itself all evening, she pads across the pale-blue carpeted floor to the den and stretches out on the couch. He should've told her about the new job. He's good at avoiding conflict and knew she wouldn't make a fuss at the club. The other night when she mentioned how preoccupied he seemed, a perfect moment to tell her about his work situation, he said nothing. He'd been drinking but wasn't drunk. He rested his head against hers, the smell of whisky evident, and whispered, "Life is difficult, we always need more money, my back hurts." Then kissed her cheek and went to bed. Long marriages ebb and flow. She knows that. Relationships change. Of course they do. At work she hears stories about marriages that make her wonder how people survive their lives.

The spell of dizziness and urge to retch strike suddenly. A

virus or food poisoning, she has no idea which. One hand over her mouth, using the wall for balance she makes it to the bathroom, but there's nothing in the medicine cabinet that would help. She needs something to stop the vomiting before she dehydrates. The dizziness is profound. She can't black out.

In the bar mirror, between whiskey bottles hang the faces of his late-night companions, not one of whom he cares to engage with. He's heard enough about lost jobs and unemployment to last past his lifetime. It's what the guys at the plant chew on day after day.

What's done is done. He's made his move without a nickel more in his pay. Six welders on his team let go so he could stay, which isn't going to win him any friends on Monday. He'd love to give the owners the finger and walk out, but then what? Then where?

Get in the car, Stu, that's where. Find a bar with better faces, that's what. He drops a bill on the counter and takes off.

Where he's driving will be the next surprise, and he likes surprises. They remind him there are forces out there stirring the shit. Where he's not heading is home. He's on Boston Post Road, the old Route 1 that wobbles through the Bronx. There are bars somewhere along here. It would be kind to call Dory, let her know he's alive and on his way to oblivion, except she wouldn't be happy to hear that, now, would she? Anyway she's probably asleep, fine woman that she is, a woman who truly demands respect, who loves him without question, a woman he lately can't breathe around.

He switches on the radio loud enough to turn other drivers' heads, if there were any around to turn, but everyone's home with loved ones, cuddling ass to ass or belly to ass, or however couples find comfort in the dark. He and Dory share a king-sized space. He finds it restful not having to inhale her sweet-smelling hair that doesn't turn him on anymore.

Okay, he's thinking like a drunk. Stop thinking. Fortunately, he spies a familiar neon sign in a window and speeds toward it, and the place is open, son of a gun. His car is only the third in the small lot.

He remembers to drop the car keys in his pocket—see, Dory, not that drunk—and hurries inside through the cold. Music comes from an old jukebox in the rear, where a hunched-over sack of a man sits. A woman on a barstool spins around to look at him. He returns her smile, surprised to see her slip off the stool and walk behind the wooden counter. Place could fit in his living room. He's come up in the world.

"Wild Turkey on the rocks, and how are you this night?"

"I'm good."

Amazing. Spitting image of Lena: dark hair, pale skin, wide black eyes. No, wait, Lena's eyes . . . greenish-brown, at least when he's sober. She doesn't have Lena's never-wavering small, square chin either. And what color are Dory's eyes? Gray. Okay, passed the good husband test. Good husbands comment favorably when their wives return from the beauty salon or cook special meals for them. By normal standards he's a good husband. Except he's not normal in the normal way, is he? Two swigs and the glass empties. He taps it on the counter for another.

"So how late are you kept busy by this place?" he asks her, wanting to see if maybe she sounds like Lena as well.

"Another half hour and I shut it down." She refills his glass.

No, she's a smoker, the gravelly, hoarse voice nothing like Lena's.

He sips at the drink. He's a bit spacey now, a feeling he likes. It removes hard surfaces, doesn't levitate him exactly but provides a more cloud-like stillness. He remembers the hash pipe he and his buddies passed back and forth in the sandy tents once upon a time, not a promising memory for him to revisit right now.

"So can I buy you a drink?" he hears himself ask.

"Nah. It'll keep me awake," she says.

"Lots to do when you're awake."

She stares at him, considering, then turns away. A brushoff, thank god. He takes down the rest of the drink. "Have a nice tomorrow," he says, laying a twenty on the counter. Big shot.

The prickly, burning numbness in his arm enters his consciousness. It's wedged under his head. He lets the cold piece of flesh drop to his side then squeezes the fingers open and shut. His legs sprawl across the seat. Whatever cramped position he collapsed in has left its marks. He hoists himself to sitting. A cold wind blows through the open window. Daylight.

Drunk and asleep in a car. Not a good sign. He scrambles out, jumps up and down a few times to get the blood flowing and suddenly realizes he's not wearing a jacket. Did he leave it in the bar? Crap. A quick search and he finds it on the floor by the rear seat. How the hell did it get there? It reeks of whiskey. Did he spill on himself? Has he really become that kind of drunk? His father always smelled of booze even after a shower, which was weird. He slips his not quite thawed arm into the warmth of his jacket, slides behind the steering wheel and turns up the heat. The bar's neon sign is dead. His is the only car in the lot.

He stares at the few leafless trees in the center island that divides the boulevard. He knows which side will take him home, though not necessarily where he wants to go. Zack tells him he needs a vacation from marriage, not a separation from Dory. Then again, Zack would never leave Lena. He listens to her prattle on without batting an eye. A few too many sentences from Dory and his insides clutch. He takes a deep breath.

Dory, I have to get away from marriage for a while. Don't know why. Don't know where. Don't know how long. I'll call you as soon as I figure things out. Can he handle saying that? After twenty years? Maybe.

Questions will surely arise. Why now? Is it something I've done? Are you sick? What's changed? Could he say, "I've always felt this way?" But is that true? It would be so much easier if she'd just get fucking out-of-her-head raging mad and chase him out. Instead, she'll stand there, with brimming eyes in her quiet, disappointed, pretty little face, and the thing is, he's dying, sort of.

The flickering green digits on the dashboard read 6:35. The old TV news query plays in his head: "Do you know where your children are?" Except they don't have any, and if they did, would it have changed anything?

He pats his jacket pockets. Phone, where are you? Leans his head back on the seat as if that would jog his memory. Where did he use it last? The first bar? The second bar? Did he even have it to begin with?

He'll go home, tell her the truth: I got drunk and fell asleep in the car. Will he add that he's thinking of leaving her? He'll run it by Zack first to hear how it sounds. Or maybe he just needs to try harder to feel what he doesn't feel anymore.

The car rolls slowly toward the corner where the journey home begins.

4.

Inklings of daylight disrupt the cold pewter sky as the taxi from the ER reaches her house. She checks the garage. Stu's car still not there. It isn't the first night he's stayed out. She used to worry crazily. Not so much anymore. There's a pattern. He drinks, then falls asleep in the car, which is better than driving drunk.

What a nightmare the past hours, though they dealt with her pronto, feeding her some thick syrupy stuff she could barely swallow. She was alone in a cubicle with a bucket, waiting for a doctor when the retching stopped. It took a while longer for the dizziness to vanish, but it did, thank everyone. The ER doctor gave her a prescription to settle her stomach and said the onset troubled him. His eyes were intent and made her nervous. What was he seeing? He wanted to schedule a brain test just to rule out . . . he doesn't quite say what.

Run her head and neck through a magnetic tunnel? No way. She's seen it a million times with her charges. Enough tests and they're bound to find something, a congenital anomaly, an aberration, who knows, except no doubt it's something she could live with for the next fifty years. Hospitals always want to test, especially if the patient has insurance. It's part of the institutional DNA. She knows; she works in one. She plans to file away the night's events and not access them again. A strong will can do wonders.

After taking the longest shower of her life, she mists her hands and body with perfumed spray and slips into a silky Japanese lounger that belonged to her mother. Her father brought it back from Korea, a time he refused to talk about. A subway conductor, he was a man who believed the streets offered the best education. She would stand with him at the front window of the train, peering into a darkness that would light up for a few seconds, offering glimpses of mysterious rooms, doors, strange-shaped corners. At the end of his shift, they'd hit the diner for a banana split or whatever her heart desired. When he died of a coronary at fifty-five she was only fourteen. She still misses him. He'd love to know that the job she began at eighteen, doing menial tasks at the nursing home, developed into a supervisory position.

Not a bad achievement, she assures her too-thin face in the dresser mirror, then ties back her long hair. Squeezing a dollop of cream into her palm, she rubs her hands together, massaging her neck and chest. She glances at the old photo of Lena's kids, Rosie and Casey, in the wooden frame. Eight-year-old Rosie, ever the actress, her chin tilted upward, arms reaching for the sky, even then the child's need to challenge invisibility. Casey, not yet three, and already in her shadow. He doesn't seem to mind. Lena has high hopes for the girl's future. Rosie would be the first of them all to go to college.

From the living room window, a glass of Chardonnay in hand, Dory sees not a soul. Dirty clouds wander the sky. Rain, no doubt. Stu would be amused to see her drinking this early.

Anything she does that's even slightly unexpected produces that loopy half-smile, proof she's not perfect. Of course she's not. Would perfect accept him as he is? But it's the him she grew up with, the him who owns her secrets, who carried her to her honeymoon bed in Montauk. They left the hotel only for short walks, laughing at having traveled so far for a bed. It's the him who held her night after night after her mother died, who worked his ass off countless extra hours to get them this house, and who has never resented their not having children, though he didn't want to adopt. It seemed like such an expensive proposition at a time when they were saving like robins to buy a place of their own. It's that him she adores. Ah crap!

The phone rings and she grabs it. "Hello."

"Dory, I know it's only seven but . . ."

"Lena?" She's relieved . . . it's not the police reporting Stu in an accident. "What's up?"

"How are you?"

"Fine, why?"

"Last night's revelation . . . Stu's job?"

"Oh, it's okay. He hates conflict. He was trying to save himself from the million questions he knew I wouldn't ask in company."

"Is he still asleep?"

"Didn't get home yet. Went out drinking after our outing. Don't be shocked. It's happened before. I know the drill."

"But Dory . . ."

"What?"

"You know what I'm saying."

"No, say it."

"I don't know . . . I suppose it's your business . . . except if it were Zack you'd be peppering me with questions and advice."

"It's not Zack, and I've got this covered."

"If you say so."

"Put your mother instinct to better use."

Lena laughs. "Okay, you win, I think."

"Stu just pulled into the garage," she lies. "Talk to you later."
Still, it won't be long before he returns, and she's got to throw
all the soiled towels and bedding into the washing machine,
then scour the den, floor, and bathroom sink, erase every rem-
nant before he gets back.

5.

Zack pays the cashier, who looks younger than Rosie. The cold wind whistles past his ears as he strides toward the car. Lena refused to go out for breakfast. Rosie went shoe shopping. Casey was, as always, glued to his computer.

Eating alone doesn't suit him. A lot of guys would turn somersaults for time away from family or to be with other guys. Not him. He doesn't enjoy the push-and-shove of testosterone-fueled talk. Except for Stu. Maybe that's because Stu's one dissatisfied man who makes him feel great about his life. Not a nice thought. Nor does he like being alone at home without Lena and the kids. Alone, his mind dwells too long on the negative, like now.

At the site, the head guy's pissed at him for turning down last week's extra hours. First, the assholes fire a bunch of guys, then they want overtime from him. The honcho, a burly man in his fifties, regards anyone who refuses extra money in a downsizing job force as a dimwit. Worse yet, Zack didn't offer acceptable excuses. No doubt the union will get an earful of Zack's stupidity, laziness, lack of concern for his fellow workers, or all of the above.

In the car last night he wanted to tell Lena about the overtime snafu, but she would've thought him a fool. She wants him to succeed, whatever the fuck that means. It's simpler to keep the complicated work situations to himself. That way he can avoid the look of disapproval that always flits across her gorgeous face because, really, the only thing he ever wants to do is please her. He finds the phone deep in his pocket, calls home. It happens sometimes, that sudden need to make sure she's where she says she'll be. It's not jealousy, it's fear. Before she picks up he notices a text from Stu.

Stu circles the neighborhood, looking for a parking space. Even after he got home, showered, had breakfast, and apologized for being out all night, he was too antsy to stay still. He offered Dory afternoon drinks at the bar of her choice. She wasn't up for it. Actually, she seemed distracted. Did he probe? Of course not. Was he unhappy? Not that he would notice.

He pulls into a space in front of the Bronx Zoo. Years ago, dead of night, high on hash, he and Zack had sneaked in to serenade the inhabitants of the monkey house. Then nearly died laughing when the monkeys began screeching. Man, that was another time. Young, filled with the heat of forward movement, ready for something, for anything, please just point the way. In those days, he exhaled hope, not alcohol fumes. No guarantees about anything anymore, except maybe worry. No one at the plant dares make plans even for the next day, let alone the next week, month, or year. He's a bastard for what he did to the guys on his team, no argument there, but someone was going to stay. Why not him? For which he has no answer. At work he'll remain mute. Anything he might say will and should be held against him. He'll just shove around that acetylene torch like a fucking johnson and do his best to maintain some cool.

Climbing never-ending hills to Fordham and Grand Concourse, he thinks it best not to arrive at the bar and begin drinking before Zack, though goddamn it if he isn't thirsty. He slows his stride, glances into shop windows. "Cheap, everything cheap," reads one sign. A jewelry shop features women's wigs; a hair salon, an array of jewelry; the men's clothing store, lotto tickets. Nothing, but nothing is what it's supposed to be. Like his life. His mom had one desire: to get him out and away from his dad. She believed in him, thought he'd have it all someday, whatever all meant. She never said. Well, he can't ask her now. She's gone.

The last time he visited this bar, the room was bigger. Whatever's changed, the bartender's sour expression tells him not to ask. Still, he notes an unpainted plasterboard wall that's cut off a part of the rear space. Probably an immigrant family on the other side of it. People will live anywhere when things are bad, and these days loads of people are down on their luck. That fact is not disputable. Money makes money, and luck favors the few who already have it. Maybe someday—but he doesn't believe this—there will be an intergalactic juxtaposition that upends the pyramid, and the people at the bottom will become the lucky ones.

A drunk on a barstool gives him the furtive eye. Is he one of the drunks? The question flits through his head to an early dismissal. No sign of Zack. He orders a bottle of Bud. Sip it slowly, he warns himself, and heads for the table farthest from the bar. A therapist told his teammate Jock, who was trying to quit smoking, to leave his cigarettes in the mailbox. Behavior modification. Walking down four flights to smoke would dampen his desire. Thing is, he did walk down, until the pack was empty. Jock's gone from the plant, and he prays never to bump into him again because what could he say to a man with four children? Bad karma.

Apart from the missing panels above his head, it's too dimly lit to see the rest of the misery. The place must've been built before the last century, the old wood floor warped and shiny from wear. Lived in, he'd say, homey. As a bar it has character, he decides, even if it has no class. He was surprised Zack agreed to leave his family on a weekend. He isn't even sure what he wants from this sit-down. Zack does steady him, though he can't say why. Maybe it's his refusal to stew over things that can't be changed, like death. Weeks ago, his mind in turmoil, he shared his confusion about making a move for the floor job that would break up his team. Zack, who has no rush in him, took his time, listing all possible solutions until they whittled that list down to one: go for the job. Which is ironic, given how Zack avoids change at all cost.

He sees him stop at the bar, his slim torso lost in a thick ski jacket, a woolen hat pulled low over his forehead, a man in disguise.

"Afraid someone would recognize you," he quips as Zack approaches, beer in hand.

"It's cold out there."

"Is there a message in that remark?"

"Yes, definitely. I'd rather be at home."

"Too fucking bad, my friend, because you are my friend, and this is what we do for each other."

"Could you be a little more specific? "

"I prepare an I'm-about-to-leave-you speech to give to Dory. Arrive home apologize for being out all night, but she's too distracted to concentrate and flits all over the place doing god knows what. It's not like her."

"Bad day, bad dreams, someone at the nursing home died. Too many possibilities that have nothing to do with you, Stu."

"Fuck! Did Lena tell you something happened?"

"She told Lena you were out all night after the club."

"I'm not in the mood to be judged. I need a real drink." Bourbon will burn through the blockage hardening inside him. Truth is, Dory's home waiting for him, probably cooking a delicious dinner, wine on the table. It's too much to absorb. Maybe tomorrow he'll have a sit-down with Dory, but he doubts it's going to happen. Just thinking about it feels dangerous, though he can't say why, which is the real problem.

At the bar, he orders a double bourbon, neat, and looks out the dirt-streaked window at a gray brick building, pure Bronx, with its worn façade and a faded aquamarine mermaid reclining over the entrance. Makes him think of the stone gargoyles along the courtyard eaves of the buildings near the projects where they all grew up. Nothing you want to meet coming home late at night. He takes a slug of the drink and decides he doesn't want to talk about Dory after all.

"So, my man, how's it going by you?"

Zack shrugs.

It's not his usual style to press Zack for details, believing as he does that stories unfurl as necessary. Still he asks, "What's that supposed to mean?"

"God knows."

"Between you and Lena?"

"Not yet."

"Stop with the mystery shit. What is it?"

"I didn't take the overtime my boss offered. I've just fallen below zero on their keep scale. Even without this, everyone at work is suddenly as sure as his name the building site we're supposed to report to next month is never going to happen. They're placing bets on when we'll be told and the layoffs begin.

Then again, these guys bet on what's in a lunch bag."

"At my plant, it's what the men yak about, too. Layoffs, layoffs . . . bitch and moan about what's coming next. Very depressing."

"Don't say anything to Dory about this or Lena will find out. I don't want her to worry."

"How sweet."

Zack grins. "Are you saying I'm a nicer guy than you?"

"Your edges are rounder, that's all."

"What does that mean?"

"That I'm sharper than you?"

"Quit playing . . ."

"That's what I do, I play. How else does anyone get through this fucking life? Singing outside the monkey house, remember that?"

"Of course."

"Have we reached an age where those were the good old days? I mean, what about now, man?"

"They were good old days, but I don't miss the car sex." Zack shakes his head. "Beaches, backseats, and front seats, I couldn't do that anymore."

"But they were days of expectation, right? What would happen, what could we make happen, what we didn't yet know would happen? That expectation's been doused, blown out like a candle."

"How eloquent."

"Don't tell me you don't miss any of that because I won't believe you."

Zack looks at him. "Okay, what I miss most is taking everything for granted."

"Too bad that's untrue. If memory serves, you've never worried, not then, not now. I mean terror-worry, Zack. The kind that's in the body. The back hurts all the time, the bowels move too often or not at all, you can't stomach food, your limbs feel heavy, you want to cry but the liquid's gone. And the worst part is realizing there's nothing you can fucking do about it all because circumstances are so beyond your control you don't even know where to begin. The Buddhists have it made. They clap their hands and accept. Me, I walk through the hours not wanting to know what I know. There is no fucking light at the end of the tunnel because it isn't a tunnel, it's my life. That, my man, is terror-worrying. You don't get to have that. Your DNA doesn't allow it."

"Jesus, Stu. Okay, you've lost your connection with Dory, but that's temporary. These ties come back, they really do. A word, a glance, some gesture will light the old fire. And your job, hell, you just got a new position. They're not going to boot you, not yet, maybe for even longer than not yet."

"Let's get high and lose our minds for a couple hours."

"Can't. They're at home expecting me to return the way I left. Come have dinner with us."

"Lena wouldn't want an unexpected guest."

Zack says nothing, which he finds strangely upsetting.

"Anyway, Dory's waiting," he adds, not even sure if that's where he's headed.

6.

Instead of tackling the laundry, Lena takes the Sunday papers to the couch and begins flipping through the pages, but it's Dory's attitude about Stu that's on her mind. If it was Zack . . . but it wouldn't be.

Rosie bounces down the stairs. "Where's Casey?"

"In his room watching something on his computer."

"Is Dad back?"

"He's still out with Stu."

"Where did they go?"

"You'll have to ask him."

"I loaned Mirabelle two of my textbooks and I need to use them to finish some homework before Monday. I won't be gone long, but you know Mirabelle, she has a thing about talking."

"Do you have to go right now?" She pats the couch for Rosie to sit. "It's the weekend. Nice if you'd hang out with us."

"Us? I've been home all day. You must've felt my presence, or is that only happening now?"

"I don't want to argue."

"If I stay home, I'll be on the phone anyway. You and me, we're not in the habit of chatting idly, are we?"

"Rosie, if you want to chat, idly or not, I'm all ears."

"Well, I don't. See you later."

"When?"

"Oops, forgot something." Rosie rushes upstairs. And finds Casey sitting cross-legged on the bed, watching an episode of *The Office* on his laptop. "I need your help."

"What," he responds, his eyes still on the screen.

"I lied to mom. I told her I'd be at Mirabelle's. You have to answer the cordless if it rings in case it's Mirabelle and tell her I used her as an excuse."

"Call and tell her yourself."

"I did, jerk. Something's messed with her cell phone. I'll try again, but just in case . . . I need a cover." She stares into his wide eyes. "I'd do it for you. You'll want me to later on, I promise. I'll never forget that I owe you."

"I'll try to get to the phone first."

"Not good enough. That's why I brought the cordless up here. And why do you like that program?"

"It illustrates how ridiculous people can be with each other."

"Who do you know like that?"

She can tell that Casey's sorting out an answer in his usual methodical way. She drops the cordless on his bed.

"Where are you going?"

"I'm meeting friends somewhere."

In the vestibule, she grabs her down jacket off the hook and slings a small backpack over one shoulder, knowing her mother's watching.

Seeing Rosie half out the door, Lena's about to remind her to be home by ten, but decides it's best to say nothing. Mothers and daughters, dicey at times. She suddenly remembers her own mother at the center of a triangle of benches, undressing before a small circle of gaping tenants, her dress already puddled at her feet. She tried to stop her. "Too tight, too tight," her mother muttered, pushing her away with shocking force as she finished peeling off her underpants and bra, revealing robust breasts, dark brown nipples, rounded hips, her long, shapely legs for all to see. The need to run away thwarted only by the horror that nailed her to that spot, the vision of her mother's voluptuous body imprinted on her brain. She was thirteen, two years younger than Rosie, that tender age when shame, humiliation, anything odd is almost unbearable. A police car, siren blasting, sped into the projects. A young cop, who looked as embarrassed as she was, tried and failed to get her mother's dress back on. Her arms still flailing, two cops wrapped her in a blanket and placed her in the patrol car. She got in as well, largely to escape the onlookers.

At the hospital, her mother was whisked away. No one told her anything, though she kept asking the nurses for information. Never a shy child, she grabbed the arm of someone in scrubs and demanded to know if her mother was dead, which suddenly seemed frighteningly possible. Not long after, a thin older woman came over and in a voice lower than a whisper told her that her mother had been admitted to the psychiatric ward.

Zack always dismisses her concerns about sanity as melodramatic, says history doesn't follow that generationally, that her mother had been unstable since forever. She likes hearing him say these things, but they also cut off discussion.

The steam comes on with a loud hiss then quiets to a hum. The wind presses on the windows desperate to get in. She reaches over to switch on a lamp, a halo of amber light. With the image of her mother still fresh in her mind, she wishes now she'd reminded Rosie to be home on time.

7.

Rosie hurries to the bus stop. It irks her—her mother on that couch as if there were nothing in the world larger than the house. Her mother isn't stupid, but she's a woman without dreams. A house, two kids, obedient husband, and the same-old same-old are more than enough for her. Well, not for Rosie. Life on the edge, that's what she wants, never less than what's possible. Her work will be meaningful. The Peace Corps, maybe, or Doctors Without Borders. Marry when she's forty, or maybe not. Children? Probable but not required. Once, foolishly, she tried to explain her future to her mother, who listened with a barely hidden smirk, as if Rosie were only saying what any teen would say. It annoyed the crap out of her and killed any urge to make her mother understand the ways in which they're different, so different.

The bus speeds through the night. Rosie sits near the window. The outside world a black-and-white blur, a negative of its daytime self. It's the same route she takes to school. When her parents bought the house, she, like Mirabelle, refused to change schools.

Siri is waiting and she can barely sit still. She loves remembering the moment they met, nearly six months ago, a good day, she'd say, if anyone asked, except no one but Mirabelle knows about him, so who would ask? He was sitting alone in the school cafeteria, reading a book. Its title, *Seven Kinds of Ambiguity*, intrigued her almost as much as his handsome face. She asked what it meant. It was a philosophical novel, he explained, that challenged the role ambiguity plays in how we think, talk, and write. After school that day they walked for hours. He told her he was sent to America to help care for his elderly aunt and uncle. One afternoon a week he food shops for them; Thursday evenings, he accompanies his uncle to the chiropractor. On weekends, he works in an Indian restaurant, mostly delivering takeout. He's two years older, which pleases her.

She exits the bus near the Whitestone Bridge and walks on, bathed in the blue glow of its lights. If her mother saw her here with only the FDR expressway and a field of dried grass and brittle bushes for company she'd freak. Beyond the field, she can just make out the row of attached brick houses not far from the church. She's trekked this path before, though always with Siri. Now, weird shadows appear wherever her eyes land. She begins to jog.

He's there in front of the old stone church, wearing a hooded jacket. Several men in tattered blankets sleep on its wide steps. Weeks ago, Siri discovered the grotto behind the church filled with tombstones, marble benches, statues, and lanes that end suddenly. The first time there, it was a bit eerie. Siri whispered that he wouldn't let a soul hurt her, which made her laugh. Back home, he said, that would not be a joke. When he talks about Pakistan, which isn't often, his merry black-lashed eyes go serious; his gentle tone turns earnest.

"You okay?" he whispers.

"Why not?"

They're sitting on the wide marble gravestone of the beloved

Randall family, their backs against a stone bench. Is it illegal to sit on the dead, she wonders? Under the puffy down jacket his arm wraps her waist tightly.

"I came, you know," his tone confessional.

"Me, too."

"Really, just from my fingers?"

She laughs. "Yes."

"First time?"

"First time with you."

"What?"

She laughs again. "Kidding."

"What does it feel like for a girl?"

"No different than what you feel, I guess."

"Wow, that's great."

"Have you done the real thing with anyone?" she asks.

"Real thing?"

"You know . . . penetration."

He kisses her nose. "You are the only one."

"So you're a virgin, too?"

"Still, yes. Is that bad?"

"I have no idea."

"Are you cold, Rosie?"

"Yes."

"Want my hands to rub at you?"

"I can't. I have to go home."

"Rosie, thank you."

"I don't like it when you say that?"

"Why?"

"I'm not a prostitute."

He looks at her. "Is that what thanking you means?"

"Sort of."

8.

Dory hurries through the automatic doors into the lobby. She asked the cleaning staff to use Clorox on the floors. Nothing else kills the institutional stink. She waves to a new face behind the poor imitation of a reception desk, then strides past the cracked vinyl couch, the two stained, upholstered chairs, and through another set of doors into the locker room, where she changes into ugly, comfortable shoes. She slips on her not unfashionable pink uniform. Snug, it falls lovingly over her hips. A tremor of sadness runs through her. Stu's passion has gone underground. It's been weeks. She misses the rhythms of his body as well as the sweet aftermath, his woody scent, her gently aching limbs. "What's happening?" she whispered one recent night in bed. "Too damn tired, can't get it up." His words muffled by the pillow. Okay, she understands . . . the new job . . . the choice he made . . . he's upset, drinking more, which doesn't help the blood flow, but still . . .

She walks up two flights of stairs to her floor. Her coworkers are steady, sturdy women. "Lunch is almost over. Mr. Todd isn't moving from his room. Missed breakfast." Janet, the day nurse, calls over her shoulder on her way to the dining room. "Want to try to get him out?"

"Sure. Give me a minute."

43

She checks in at the desk, sees that there's a new admission today. Passing abandoned walkers, folded wheelchairs, a few discarded stuffed animals that await new owners, she notices the latest coat of paint is already flaking off the walls. How's that possible?

"Mr. Todd, why are you in here instead of out there eating?" He's perched on the side of the bed, his bare feet on the floor. His dark eyes peer at her from beneath thick brows and a full head of long white hair he refuses to cut.

"Where were you for breakfast?" he accuses.

"Had a headache, slept in. Are you feeling all right?"

"I'm perfectly miserable but not unhealthy."

"Health is everything, isn't it?" A remark that feels close to home.

"You're young." He says it dismissively.

"So were you, once."

"Well, that's gone."

"What is it you'd like to be? Younger? Healthier? Elsewhere?"

"Dead."

"Oh, Mr. Todd, you don't mean that."

"But I do."

"Think of all you would miss!" Except he has no one special. "If you join the others and eat something it'll raise your spirits. Nutrition and socializing can do that." She sounds like some do-good asshole mouthing new-age claptrap she'd hate to have anyone say to her.

"Where did you hear that crap?"

She laughs. "I can't remember. Come on, Mr. T. Come with me. I need coffee, keep me company."

"That's a better line."

Once he was clearly a hearty man who could put away a

six-pack, but now the paper-thin skin of his hands and face reveal the skeleton beneath. A corrections officer for thirty years, he must've been rough and tough, but he rarely talks about it. She moves his walker to the bed. He pushes it away. "I can walk without it. It's only here because if I fall I can sue you."

"Can I link your arm?"

"I need to put on shoes."

She waits. Of course he can't find his shoes. Of course they're way under the bed. Of course she has to bite the dust to get them. Damn. Next staff meeting, dust and Clorox are on her agenda. She stands up, brushes herself off, and hands him the shoes, the backs of which are collapsed. He slips them on like scuffs. His eyes challenge her to make him wear them as shoes. She refuses and walks out, but slowly, and he does follow her to the dining room.

The cafeterias on each of the institution's six floors are alike. Kitchens in the center, five tables, each with eight seats, pale green walls, small, bare windows, a vase with plastic flowers on the serving counter, and food odors that mingle with the musty scents of age. The sixth floor houses the Alzheimer's clientele. Her second-floor charges are more reachable, even when some choose not to be. It's as if they've pulled down a curtain to protect the past from the present. She used to pry; she doesn't anymore.

With Mr. Todd a few steps behind her, she finds an empty table. Most of the other diners have already wandered off to the TV room, crafts, or their bedrooms. Some will walk the hallways or even get on the elevator, head for the ground floor, and leave. Who can blame them?

"Stay here, I'll get some lunch for you. And coffee for me." He eyes her suspiciously as if, now that she's got him in here, she'll disappear.

"You don't know what I want?"

"Tell me."

"Cold cereal with real milk."

"Easy."

They're shutting down the food service, but she manages to snag the cereal, milk, and coffee, which she brings over on a tray.

"The coffee tastes awful," she says.

"You're honest. The rest of them act like this is paradise."

"Oh, that it is not. Indeed it's not. Tell me, do you ever miss the work you did?"

"No. I didn't like it there either. Why were you late this morning?"

"I told you I had . . ."

"That wouldn't keep you away."

She studies his large face, eyes steady on her, and to her surprise hears herself telling him about her hours at the ER, and how they wanted her to have an MRI, and how she refused it. That she was late today because she needed to catch up on lost sleep.

"Well, you're a smart cookie. Never trust them is what I say. It's their job to make you jump through hoops. Tests, they especially love tests. Tried to put me on the operating table for a new something in my heart, but I told them I'd rather die on my own, thank you very much. Then again, you're young. You can still be helped. Maybe. Are you feeling better now?" His tone suddenly warmer, his eyes still steady on her.

She strokes the deeply veined hand on the table. "Nearly all better, thanks. Can you open the cereal box?"

She watches him fumble a bit with it, then does it for him. Janet gestures to her from the doorway. "I have to welcome a new admission," she tells him.

46

"Another lucky person."

The elevator doors open to release a tall, willowy woman in her late eighties, wearing a long, tailored black skirt and white blouse, her silver-streaked dark hair pulled into a bun. Her bright blue eyes gaze out of deep sockets.

"Welcome, Miss Dyan. Let me show you to your room," she begins, as she does with each new admission.

The woman doesn't move, an angry expression etched on her face.

"First days are difficult."

"I can't stay here," she declares fiercely, clearly a woman used to being obeyed. But stay she will; she has no choice. On the cusp of losing her memory, forgetting to take her meds or shut off the oven, living on her own has become too dangerous.

"We'll do what we can to make you comfortable," she recites, deciding the usual orientation is out for today.

"You're the new one. Lucky you." Mr. Todd pauses in passing.

"Please, Mr. Todd, be more welcoming."

"There's no way to disguise what's here," he says as he continues to walk.

"Would you like a cup of coffee?" she asks the woman.

"I'll wait here on the bench for you to bring it to me."

"Why not," she murmurs, heading back to the cafeteria, where her nearly untouched cup of coffee remains on the table.

9.

Lena waits for her boss to arrive. She's been summoned to his office but doesn't know why, which is slightly unnerving. It can't be her work. She's meticulous. Handling money is a serious business. Making up the hotel payroll demands scrupulous attention. People's salaries matter. She checks and rechecks, true of all the duties she carries out.

His office is twice the size of hers. One huge window overlooks the UN building, its glassy façade reflecting the clouds as if it owned the sky. On his desk, a gold-framed photo of his wife, two boys, and a German shepherd, behind them a house shaded by tall trees. She guesses Connecticut. She doesn't doubt the rumor that he's messing around with one of the hotel maids. Maybe his wife's relieved. Maybe she's tired of having sex with him. Maybe everything between them is as stale as his excuses, but who else will support her in the style she's accustomed to?

He struts in, briefcase in hand. A slender man in his fifties, wisps of hair covering a balding pate, a drinker's red cheeks, and eyes with no spark behind rimless glasses. "Hello, Lena. " He slides behind the large desk, half of him disappearing. "Sorry to be late. I had to attend to my other hotel first. It took longer than expected." He removes a folder from his briefcase and places it in front of him. "Look, this is all very difficult, but I don't want to waste any more of your time. We have to let you go. Not just you, of course. We're closing the other hotel and shutting down the two top floors here. We're going to need less staff." He looks past her.

"I'm stunned" is what comes out of her mouth.

"The board made the decision over the weekend."

"Why me?" She dares him to tell her. A white heat of anger and fear already consuming her.

"We don't need two bookkeepers now. And ... well ... you're the assistant."

For a moment they stare at each other. "Two weeks' severance, a letter of reference, and you'll be eligible for six months' unemployment. That's it, Lena. I'm sorry."

He looks down at the folder. She's dismissed but still glued to the seat because once she leaves, it'll be true. So she sits. A wall clock ticks. Somewhere in the distance the muted sounds of traffic, a siren. Footsteps pass the closed door.

"As soon as you can get your things together.... We'll pay you for today, of course." But his eyes remain locked on the folder.

She wants him to look up at her, to acknowledge her plight, a smile, a short wave of the hand, even a call to security, but he flicks the folder open. He's done with her.

When the elevator reaches the lobby, she hurries to her office, glad the bookkeeper isn't there. Her eyes scan the file cabinets, wall schedules, and her desktop. Nothing here she wants. She empties the desk drawers of a pair of shoes, two sweaters, some hair clips. She fills one small plastic shopping bag. Ten years' worth of nothing.

The taxi driver intends to make every light going north on Amsterdam Avenue, swerving in and out of lanes to avoid vehicles, people, and heaven knows what else. Buildings pass in a blur, erasing the bleakness of the streets. The speed feels good, right, dangerous, daring, the ride mimicking the turmoil inside her. She closes her eyes against the rush of cold air hitting her face through the driver's half-open window and takes short, deep breaths in anticipation of the sudden crash that's bound to come.

When the taxi slows to a stop she's shocked, disappointed, reluctant to get out. The driver turns his expectant face to her and points at the meter. She pays and gives him a tip, both of which have become unaffordable.

The cold bricks of the tall symmetrical buildings greet her with indifference. She has no desire to walk through the projects. Instead she heads down a street of small shops, cars parked on either side; supply trucks clot the area, double-parked everywhere. Lining the curb, piles of see-through garbage bags. People go by without a glance in her direction. Pieces of conversation float past: "I feel stronger since I've been taking it." "The abdominal pain was ferocious." "She's full-time on oxygen now." Around here, it's all about personal tales of survival. No talk of politics or Wall Street or the economics of anything but getting by. What's she even doing in the old neighborhood? Why didn't she go straight home?

The last time she walked these streets, three years ago, was to attend Matt's funeral. His death still unacceptable, another among too many soldiers sent home in body bags. Once upon a time, she and Zack, Dory and Stu, had all hung out with Matt at his parents' restaurant, where his mother, Tina, served not just pizza but a semblance of normalcy on difficult days. Tina was once her go-to person in times of confusion, the one who sat with her at the restaurant after visits to her hospitalized mother; it was Tina who often fed her dinner as well. Matt would appear, carrying his drawing pad, to lighten the moment, his voice teasing, joyous, a boy refusing to be brought down by circumstance.

It's still there, just where it's always been, the faded, weather-beaten, green-striped awning stenciled "Tina and Jerome's Pizzeria." It's a small place, four booths and a short counter. A silver oven takes up the rear wall. The smells of basil, garlic, and hot dough are heavy and familiar.

A young man wearing a white apron liberally sprinkled with tomato sauce is behind the counter.

"Hi," she says a bit hesitant. "Where's Tina?"

"Tina," he calls into the back. "Someone to see you."

She orders a slice of pizza and a cup of coffee, both of which he promptly places on the counter.

Tina stops at the back doorway, her small face prepared for trouble. She doesn't smile. "What are you doing here?"

"I was in the neighborhood . . ."

"Come sit down."

Carrying the pizza and coffee, she follows Tina's large body, clad in loose black slacks and a rose-colored blouse, to one of the aging booths.

"Is Zack okay? And the boy? Your girl? No more children, right?"

"Everyone's fine, and no more children."

"And Dory? With that handsome man?"

"She's great and he's still handsome."

With some difficulty, Tina slides into the booth opposite her. "Yes, what happened?" The voice calm, always calm, no matter what Tina's thinking.

"I was fired from my job a few hours ago." So that's why she's here. To rehearse, to try out the words she'll have to repeat to family, friends.

Tina's dark, intelligent eyes take her in. "So big deal."

"Well, it's not exactly nothing."

"You'll find a job. Who cares? Don't suffer."

That's another reason she's come here. Only life and death move Tina; the rest, as she often says, is bunk.

"They're closing floors in my hotel and letting staff go." Somehow, she desperately needs to explain.

Tina sighs. "Soon they'll be short-handed and hire. Never pin your hopes on bosses."

"How's Jerome?"

Tina takes a moment to consider her response, something she always did when the news wasn't good.

"He passed last year, right here in the restaurant. We were together forty-eight years. I didn't expect to miss him this much."

"Oh, god, Tina, I didn't know. Someone should've called . . . I'm so sorry . . . I . . ."

"People get old and die, but only people. Your coffee mug is as old as I am, and if someone doesn't drop it, it will last like the river and the trees."

"You're so sure of what you say. It's good."

"You will be, too, when you reach my age. But it's not worth it, getting older to be wiser."

Tina's aging, of course she is. The wrinkles, the jowls, the gray hair, but old like the people Dory cares for? No, it's not how she sees her. "No one would guess your age."

Tina studies her somewhat swollen hands resting palms down on the table. "That's not what's important."

Dear god, please don't let her announce some incurable

illness. "Is something wrong?"

"Wrong, no, I wouldn't say so, just inevitable."

"What are you talking about?"

"The frailty ahead."

"You're a strong woman."

"Strong has nothing to do with it. Yesterday I lost the keys to the front door of my apartment. Gone. Disappeared. I probably dropped them in a grocery bag I was carrying, then threw the bag down the incinerator. My mind used to focus easily on details like that. Now, from one minute to the next I struggle to keep up with that younger self. So listen to me. Take a week off. No one will starve. Sleep late. Go to a good movie. Walk around a park. See the sights. Play with your children. They're healthy, alive."

Lena's eyes flit to the framed oil painting that takes up half of the adjacent wall. Tina moved it here from her apartment after Matt died. Crazy zigzag lines, weird multicolored splashes. What was Matt seeing? She remembers him in a paint-smeared tank top, his hair long, curly, wild, in front of an easel in the middle of Tina's living room. Around him, paint tubes, rags, brushes, turpentine, all kinds of smells. For months, no one else could use the area. Zack said Matt was being selfish. She thought him audacious, taking the space he needed. She was shocked when Matt joined the marines.

She has to ask, has to know how long finality lasts. "Do you think about Matt a lot?"

"On days when I'm feeling him in my belly, I sit down and write him a letter, then remind myself I don't have his address and drop it in the drawer with the others."

"Tina, I didn't mean to . . ."

"Talking about Matt's good. I don't want closure. It's not about time passing, either. It's about finding ways to live with

53

it. You'll get another job," Tina abruptly changes the subject. "More coffee?"

She shakes her head "Maybe I'll look for something different," she says more to herself than Tina.

"Like what?"

"A guide on one of those tour buses that ride around the city? I know New York. I could do that." The restlessness inside her is physical.

"It's your world. I no longer understand half of what goes on. Customers want me to buy a smart phone so they can text me an order that I'll never be able to access. I'd rather hear it over the phone."

"Tina, you're quick, you'd be able to do that."

"But I don't want to. Some people window-shop endlessly. Not me. I only shop to buy what I need. I don't need a smart phone. Lena, don't wait years to come see me again. Hear me?"

"I promise." But her words are lost, as Tina gets up to help several people who have just entered the restaurant.

Despite the cold, she walks into a small park nearby, where Rosie played when she was little. The wind whips a few dried leaves off the branches. The place seems eerily quiet.

Inside the playground, she takes out her phone.

"Why are you calling me at work?" Dory asks.

"I was fired."

She hears an intake of breath. "That sucks."

"It was a shock. I had no idea."

"Bastards."

"I just left Tina's."

"Tina's? My god, whatever for?"

"Can you take a break?"

"No. Meet me here in the lobby at five. We'll go drinking."

"Sounds right." She has three hours to kill.

She sits on a swing, pushes high off the ground, as the winter sun begins its slow descent. Without Tina, there'd be no reason ever to visit these streets again.

10.

It's not quite five when she reaches the nursing home in a rundown neighborhood near Washington Heights. A large man seated behind a small reception desk pays her no mind. She ignores the sign-in book. Framed photos of cats, dogs, and horses line one wall. The lighting is dim, the windows sooty, the couch sagging. Still, after spending two hours walking around the Bronx Botanical Gardens, she's glad to sit. Tina used to take Matt and her to the gardens for pizza-and-Coke picnics. It was far enough from the South Bronx to feel like an adventure. Today, though, the gardens bored her and the overpowering scent of lilies in the greenhouse drove her out. It's sad to no longer experience the joy of small events.

Dory strides through the lobby in black slacks and a yellow turtleneck sweater, her shiny mane of pale red hair tied back with a black velvet ribbon.

"There you are. Sorry about your job, but you look elegant in your suit."

"That and two bucks will get me where?"

"True." Dory slips into her white down jacket with its black fur-trimmed hood.

The automatic doors open and shut behind them.

The cold wind stings their faces. They walk quickly, passing boarded-up shops, dirt lots filled with broken appliances, and buildings she can't believe people still live in, except they do. Many streetlamps aren't working and car headlights startle the ashy darkness.

"Are you freaking out?"

"I'm upset to lose the paycheck but strangely not the job. It feels like a door opening onto an unfamiliar street."

"Change takes time to absorb. I see it with new admissions. Some are never ready. They clam up and clutch a doll like it was life itself."

"They're old, I'm not. It's different." A spark of annoyance alights in her.

"Right. You're free to discover."

"Are you being sarcastic? I have responsibilities."

"Which stops you from doing what?"

"Going abroad," she says sarcastically. "Taking an easel to the park, spending the spring months painting what I see." Matt, again.

"Since when has that been your desire?"

"Since this minute. I might apply to be a guide on a tour bus."

"You don't mean that."

"Why not?"

"You'd make more as a waitress."

"It's not about the money."

"I get that. What did Zack say about you being fired?"

"Haven't told him yet."

Dory stops short. "Why?"

"I don't know. Keep walking, it's cold."

"Sure you do. We always know."

"Why is everyone else so wise?"

"Who else?"

"Tina told me take a vacation and not suffer."

"Why haven't you phoned Zack?"

"Because I know what he'll say, and I don't want to hear the predictable, 'Honey, come home. I'll cook dinner. You relax.' In short, nothing, he'll say nothing."

Across the street is a small bar. "Let's go in, I'm freezing," Dory says.

She glances at the grimy windows filled with fading beer posters. "Is it safe?"

"Whoever's waiting in a dark corner will have to take us both on," Dory replies. "Remember that night long ago? My god, the poor guy . . . we screamed like banshees, scared him out of his pants."

"He shouldn't have been lurking in that hallway."

"Why not? He lived there."

"Great memories," she murmurs.

"Hey, a little levity, always welcome."

Except for the bartender, no one else is inside. It's a small room with a few red formica tables across a narrow aisle from the bar. The table is so small their knees touch, and she flashes on that long-ago day in the funeral limo, a man stroking her knee with fat fingers, the pleasant sensation shaming her.

"This place looks older than my charges," Dory whispers.

"Do you think all neighborhood bars have bad lighting and not enough heat?" She wraps her coat around her shoulders.

"Two scotch, neat, with water on the side," Dory orders.

The bartender, heavy around the middle, with slim shoulders and a disinterested expression, deposits their drinks on the water-stained bar.

"So, again. Why didn't you go home? Why aren't you being comforted in the arms of family? What's there that . . ."

Her hand goes up. "Stop. I don't want to process any of it right now. Let's talk about what's going on with you." She searches Dory's face, her silky skin pale in this light.

"Why would anything be going on?"

"Stu staying out nights, the job change . . ."

She shrugs. "He's having a hard time at work, but he won't talk about it, just drinks it away. If I try to stop the drinking, well, I don't know that I can."

"You've never been one to accept crap and not try to change the situation."

"You're one to talk. You won't even call home."

"That's different. I'll tell everyone in due time, just not this minute."

"I'll deal with Stu in due time, just not yet."

"It bothers me to see you sucking it up . . ."

"Enough, Lena, don't go there."

"Okay, but I see you as tougher than me." She slips her arms into the coat and resettles in its warmth.

"Well, maybe I am, maybe I can wait it out. Anyway, ponder this. We haven't fucked in weeks." Dory finishes her drink.

"I'd find that a relief," Lena says, surprising herself.

"We could trade."

"If you could even contemplate life without Stu . . ."

"You're right. I don't mean a word of it." Dory shuts her mouth tight.

"I didn't mean to upset you. I only learned today that Jerome died, and Tina told me she's afraid of getting old."

"Sad. But Tina will never get old."

"I said as much. She was a rock to me. Sometimes I wonder if I should've married Matt and gotten her in the bargain. Sounds crazy, but Tina acting like something's out there waiting to snatch her away spooked me."

"Babe, you just lost your job. You feel vulnerable, which is the true female curse."

She glances out the dirt-streaked window at the empty, busted-up sidewalk. "Amazing, what we can't or won't or don't know how to deal with," Dory muses.

"Like Stu?"

"You promised. Hey, we can't get a buzz on one drink. Another round," Dory calls.

The bartender fills two narrow shot glasses to the brim. Dory retrieves them, depositing one in front of her. "Three neat is the magic number for buzz. Remember?"

How could she not? Their younger years were spent in bars, at movies, and on beaches. After a few drinks induced an aura of well-being, the next stop was finding a private space to make love. It was all about sex then and she didn't even know it.

Dory downs her shot in one gulp. "Go on, you too." Lena drains the glass. "Good girl." Dory leans across to the bar with two empty glasses. "Again, please." He obliges without a word. No judge, he.

"Dory, take it easy."

"Drink up and we'll go slow on the next round."

"This is going to cost a fortune," she says.

"Yup."

Again, she drains the glass, her throat no longer registering the initial shock of bitterness. What if they didn't go home? Stayed out all night, watched the sunrise—from where?—then breakfast at a diner?

The door swings open with a bang. "Mikel, how the hell are you?" A booming voice followed by a burst of cold air, the door left ajar.

"Hey, shut the door," Dory calls.

"Oops, sorry." He's too exuberant for such a cold, dark night, she thinks, taking him in. About her age, broad-shouldered, in a handsome beige car coat, leather gloves, silky white scarf, the latter an interesting touch. He leans over the counter in a proprietary manner. "The usual, my friend. How's every little thing?"

"Nothing new," the low baritone voice of the bartender is as surprising as his name.

"Ah, Mikel, there's always something new. Life is where you look."

Dory whispers, "I would've sworn John or Bob, but Mikel?"

"Mothers are always optimistic."

Dory laughs. "You should call home. They'll have the police out."

"Do you ladies need help?" He overhears and flashes his badge.

"Fort Apache," they say in unison.

"Ladies from the Bronx. Anywhere near the 49th?"

"Not anymore, thank the lord," Dory says.

"Do you need a cop?"

"It was just an expression."

"Can I get the next round?"

"No thanks, we're good," Dory declares.

"Want to share names?" The man smiles. Nice white teeth.

"She's Lena, I'm Dory."

"And you?" Lena asks, taking in his thin wedding band. Marry young, fuck around forever, the old neighborhood motto. Not Zack, though, she reminds herself. Why not?

"Arthur," he says.

"Arthur?" Dory tries not to giggle.

"What's funny?"

"He's Mikel and you're Arthur," she explains, realizing she's saying nothing. Call home, she tells herself, but a spacey, laziness swirls inside her head.

He drains his shot glass. "You sure I can't get us another round?"

"One more," she agrees, ignoring Dory's head shake, "then we have to go."

He sets down three full shot glasses and pulls up a chair. A handsome dude, Rosie would say, with his black patent leather hair and dark shiny eyes.

"That white scarf is an original touch, " she says, a ventriloquist giving voice to her thoughts.

He unwraps it, tosses it over her shoulder. "Looks good against all that dark hair." His eyes subtly investigate her.

She wraps the scarf around her throat. The silkiness beneath her chin is compelling.

"So what do you know about my precinct."

"Nothing, really. It was years ago." Dory says.

"I remember tripping and bloodying my nose when I was seven or eight. A cop brought me into the precinct and gave me an ice pack." There were, of course, the other times Lena doesn't mention.

His laugh is strangely high-pitched and feminine.

"Aren't cops always with a partner?" Dory interrupts.

"I'm a detective. I'm driving north. Want a ride home?"

Dory catches her eye, indicating no. She ignores it.

"That would be super. We have to leave real soon."

"I'm about ready, have to deal with nature's call." He finishes the drink, then disappears into the dark back of the bar.

"Are you crazy?" Dory whispers, pulling the scarf off Lena's shoulder and depositing it on his chair. "We're not friends of cops, remember?"

Yes, she does remember: two teens on an empty, dark board-walk, two cops with groping hands, laughing, taunting. Who are you going to call for help? But that was a different time in a different place.

"Let's get out of here before he returns," Dory insists.

"That would be rude. Besides, it'll cost a mint for a cab and we're in no condition for mass transportation. He's only being nice."

"No stranger is just being nice."

"You invited him over."

"I did not. He heard me say police."

"Same thing."

"Lena, we're drunk. I'll pay for the taxi. Driving with a guy we don't know is stupid."

"But he's a detective, he's . . ."

"Oh give me a break, he's a man. Please, Lena, let's go."

"Not before thanking him properly."

Dory sighs. "Your judgment sucks, but we'll say goodbye."

"So, ladies . . ." He wraps the scarf back around his neck, which looks sexy to her.

"Thanks for the offer, but there's a few stops we have to make before getting home, so you go on without us," she hears Dory say, wondering if the evening's adventure is over, wondering, too, if he's written anything on the back of the card he's hand-ing her. If she were alone, she just might go dancing with Arthur. He'd be good at it, she's certain, guiding her across the floor, her head resting on his shoulder . . . because she's very tired . . .

The taxi drops her off first. She gets out at the corner of her street. It might alarm her family if she pulls up in a cab. It's late.

Her phone's been off. She walks along the snow-banked edges of the road. It's so cold it seems breathing's dangerous. She feels a surge of sympathy for Zack, working outdoors all day. Warm light spills out of houses onto small lawns. Four shots of scotch on an empty stomach, oh, woe tomorrow. Arthur's card, what did she do with it?

Everyone is in the living room.

"Where have you been?" Rosie scolds.

"We couldn't reach you," Casey adds.

From the couch Zack wears an expression she can't read.

"I assume you all had dinner." Oh, god, she's slurring.

"Mom, what's going on?" Rosie, again.

'I'm a little drunk," she admits. "Just a little. Dory and I had a few."

"Dad has some bad news," Casey says solemnly.

Work accident runs through her sodden brain, but he looks intact, hands on his lap, legs stretched out, eyes gazing at anything but her.

"What?"

"Dad was laid off," Rosie says, the privilege of knowledge in her commanding tone.

She laughs.

"Oh, shit, you are drunk," Rosie says. "Go to bed. We'll talk tomorrow."

"You go to bed," she says, still stifling laughter.

"Mom, you're scaring me," Casey says.

"Sorry, honey. It's just funny. I mean sad-funny. Never mind. I'm going to take your advice, Rosie." Without looking at Zack, she walks ever so carefully up each step to the bedroom.

Their voices reach as she undresses. Go to sleep, all of you, she mutters into the pillow. Tomorrow she'll remain in bed. She can. She's not working. Except that's what her mother did, remained in bed. We have a situation here, she tells herself, and pulls the comforter over her head.

"It's snowing," Rosie shouts.

PART TWO

11.

The summer heat presses against the car windows. Clouds burden the sky. People are indoors with A/C or out in their bedroom-sized backyards. She pulls up in front of her house, tired from yet another day of job interviews out of too many days to count. Rain begins to splatter the windshield.

She hears loud voices and raucous laughter, and flashes on an old cartoon of a levitating house, floors shaking, furniture floating, windows expanding explosively. She pushes open the door. Lots of people making lots of noise. It's a party no one's told her about and in her house. She eyes the debris of paper plates and cups on unprotected surfaces, food-filled dishes that don't belong to her, empty beer bottles strewn everywhere. Around here parties get wild.

A few table fans whirr to no effect.

Always a good actress—in school the best parts were hers—she leans against the front door. "Wow!"

Zack calls out, "It's a party, enjoy."

She stands there, a smile pasted on her face, thinking she needs a scotch, neat, and quick. Zack shoulders her into the crowd, then walks off before she can ask him what's going on. Mumbling hello, touching arms, she weaves through clusters of people, social conditioning stronger than bewilderment.

Most of them she's met casually at the supermarket, school, somewhere, but she can't remember who is who. Women in their thirties and forties in sun dresses or shorts and wedged shoes, summoned from their backyards. In fact the resemblance among them feels a bit eerie. The men, too, dressed for summer in cutoffs or shorts, tank tops, baseball caps, making it difficult to see their faces. Does she care? Only that she, too, would like to slip into something comfortable. She settles for removing her dress jacket and stepping out of her pumps.

"Mom," Rosie whispers, "good entrance. Everyone thinks you're glad to see them."

She's about to say, I am, but fooling Rosie isn't that simple. She smiles at her daughter's unblemished face, the doe-like eyes, so misrepresentative of the child's temperament. "You think so?"

"Yeah, now you have to talk to people."

"Rosie, why are these neighbors here?" She tries to keep the alarm out of her voice.

"Dad follows some instinct none of us share."

"It looks like he went door to door inviting every neighbor. I hope people brought their own booze."

"Whatever," Rosie says and sidles over to chat with a man in his forties. She has no idea who he is, but it's clear he can't take his eyes off her daughter. "Rosie, I need another minute."

"Here I come." Her daughter sashays over.

"In the kitchen, please."

And she follows Lena in.

"When did Dad invite these people?"

Rosie shrugs. "It was spur of the moment."

"Why? Tell me."

"It's nothing. It's just a party," she says with a bit of disdain.

"I don't want secrets."

69

"Christ, Mom."

"Tell me." The mother's no-shit stern voice.

"Honestly, I don't know what hit Dad this morning, but he said we had to have a party. We needed to lighten up our lives. It would be potluck and he'd take care of inviting people. Happy now?"

"Why didn't you call or text me?"

"Did you get the job?"

"No, and I don't want any more surprises."

"Forgive us our trespasses."

"Don't be snide."

"You love spoiling anything nice others want to do."

She stares at Rosie. "Oh, god, now isn't the time for this."

"Then we agree." And Rosie saunters back over to the older man who is way too pleased to be speaking to a fifteen year-old.

As she moves to retrieve the scotch under the kitchen sink, her private stash for nights when sleep refuses to come, Zack taps her shoulder. "That bottle's empty."

"What the fuck's going on?" she says.

"I put out everything we had. Someone brought bourbon. It's on the table." His eyes are a bit glazed.

"Have you lost your mind?"

"I thought you'd be pleased?" He stands there, T-shirt sticking to his chest, grinning, daring her to disagree.

"You must be kidding. We have no money for parties."

"Rosie and Casey were sure you wouldn't want it," he goes on blithely. "I told the kids you don't like giving parties but since they were doing the work and the neighbors were bringing the food ... well ... here we are." He's not really looking at her, and he doesn't seem drunk. So what's going on? She helps herself to the drink he's holding, downing some kind of bitter, burning whiskey.

"You go out there and party, angel."

"Zack, I need answers."

"Answers will come soon enough."

"What's wrong?"

"Wrong? What in Christ's name could be wrong? Lighten up." His tone—loud and aggressive—is unusual. He walks away. Embarrassed, she reminds herself that these are not her real friends. So who cares? The whole scene is ludicrous. Has Zack gone nuts? She's heard of men his age who suffer brain aneurysms that suddenly change their personalities, but he hasn't complained of headaches, hasn't stopped eating, and god knows, hasn't lost interest in sex. He's being willful, that's what, and stupid, and she needs to catch her breath.

She finds a paper cup in the living room, fills it halfway with bourbon, drops in two ice cubes, grabs a slice of cheese from some neighbor's carefully arrayed plate, and squeezes onto Casey's chair. He, like her, probably can't wait for everyone to leave.

Drinks in hand, people sprawl on the couch, chairs, the coffee table, the staircase; some lean on walls, others move around her house like they've been here a thousand times. It's all a weird buzz.

Zack clinks his glass with a knife for silence. "Ladies and gentlemen, my wife is thirty-nine. In one year she'll be officially middle-aged, but I'll always be a year older. And what does that mean? What does any of it mean? Huh?" He rocks back on his heels, then looks around as if he actually expects an answer.

A cold fist of fear lodges inside her.

"Okay, here's what I think. No, what I believe. No, what I'm proposing.

"I propose we dance. It's a big room. It should be used. Why else buy a house? We can be as noisy as we want. No one upstairs or downstairs will complain. Move the limbs. Free the mind. Let's do it."

Zack turns the music up to blast, making it impossible to hear anyone. Casey looks at her with alarm.

She goes to the stereo and lowers the volume.

Zack jacks it up again. "Everyone dance," he orders.

"Zack," she shouts, "People want to talk."

"Hey, what's wrong with having a good time in my own house?" He's shouting, too. "I own this house. Not really, of course. Like all of us, it's only mine as long as I pay the rent. Oops, I mean the mortgage. Otherwise it's the bank's, or maybe the mortgage company's. Who the fuck knows who owns what? I don't. I do know that we have to use the space, man, gyrate like you mean it. I'm waiting." He's still shouting, though someone has again turned down the music, revealing a sudden church-like hush in the room. Her stomach's in free fall now, her face flushed. She goes to Zack, though she'd like to run in the opposite direction.

"Casey, bring your dad some water. Zack, come sit with me." She takes his arm.

"What the fuck, Lena." He throws off her hand. "This is still my house. I want to dance. Rosie, come dance with your dad."

"Dad, what if I make you a sandwich?"

"Hey, everyone, what's happening, where's the problem?" Zack shouts.

His eyes suddenly look bloodshot to her.

A flash memory of her mother undressing in the street.

People get it, thank god, and begin leaving. She goes to the door to say good night—it's the least she can do—but says nothing more, only shakes her head as if to commiserate with her own problems. No one comments to embarrass her further and she feels a shiver of gratitude. Stepping outside with the last guest, she watches as some get into cars, others stroll home. She, too, would like to take off, walk for miles. The rain has stopped; the humidity's without mercy. It's a starless night. The only light comes from nearby houses.

She finds them at the kitchen table. Zack wears a look of bewilderment; Rosie and Casey are mute but watchful. They're waiting for her to make sense of the last disastrous hour and allay their anxieties, apparent in Casey's unblinking eyes. Rosie seems more curious than frightened; this is a father she doesn't know.

"Mom? What are you going to do?" Casey asks.

"Nothing, honey, there's nothing to do. Dad had a bad day, a few drinks, and everything got mashed together. It happens."

"What bad day, Dad?" Rosie asks softly.

He says nothing.

"Zack, whatever's on your mind, tell us." Her voice is soft, too, though in her head she's lining up possibilities: cancer, ALS, MS . . .

His eyes flit from one to the other. "I want to go to bed."

"Mom, he can't do that. We have to know what's going on," Rosie pleads.

She gazes at Zack, at a loss. "We'll talk in the morning. You go to bed, too. We'll straighten up tomorrow."

"Not fair," Rosie complains. "Dad will tell you and we'll have to spend the entire night not knowing."

"Can't help it," she almost whispers, thinking she could easily fall asleep before he says a word.

She follows him upstairs. He drops on the bed without undressing, sneakers and all.

She switches on the small A/C they brought over from the

old apartment, which makes way too much noise. Some hot nights she has to switch it off to fall asleep. She pulls off his sneakers, then slips out of her clothing and into a short gown. He sits up and grabs her arm.

"What?" She shakes free.

He's gazing so intently at something behind her that she can't help turning around, but it's just the same old wall with the framed photos of the children, the one they've lived with for the past four years. "Zack you're officially scaring me, do you know that?"

"Yes."

"What do you mean, yes? For shit's sake, what's going on?" Suddenly, the intensity in his expression is replaced by a vacant stare. She decides it's better to reassure him. "You'll find a job," she says. "So will I. It will happen, it has to. It's just a bad patch we're going through."

"This is not our house."

"Of course it is."

"Uh-uh. We no longer own this house. We've been officially foreclosed. We'll be evicted in thirty days if we don't make plans to move out. They, whoever the fuck they really are, are taking away our home."

The words hit her like shrapnel, causing pain everywhere.

"Do you hear me?"

She nods.

"Well, now you know," he adds, as if to say, not my problem anymore.

"We need to figure out a way to make a payment," she says automatically.

"Too late." He responds, a note in his voice that sounds almost gleeful, which scares her more.

"What does that mean?"

"It's a final notice."

"You were notified before?"

"Many times." He doesn't sound upset or sad, just absent.

"And you didn't tell me?"

"I planned to make a back payment. Too late now."

"Stop saying that."

"Today's letter had the eviction clause."

The words conjure up the two families down the road who were forced out. Furniture left on lawns for the garbage truck, neighbors pretending to ignore the sad scene, undoubtedly fearing for their own homes. Where will they go? Who will have them, a family of four? Cold, hard terror short-circuits her brain. "We'll borrow money. Go to a lawyer. Appeal. We won't accept being thrown out of our house."

"No one will lend us anything."

It's as if he's purposely putting up obstacles. "How long haven't you paid the mortgage?"

"Almost a year. And a lawyer costs."

"A year . . ." she whispers. Who is this man? What did he think he was saving her from? Or was he expecting something, god knows what, to make it all go away? Damn him, waiting till the roof fell in. . . .

"I need sleep," she mumbles, closing her eyes, because she can't continue talking, because her head feels like a smashed apple, because this is a nightmare from which she might wake up in the morning.

Lemony stripes of early sunlight rouse her from a fitful night. Her eyes scour the room. All the familiar objects. The white rocking chair and dresser, the brass lamp reflected in the floor-to-ceiling mirror, the hand-carved magazine rack beneath the window, the white silky drapes it took her weeks to sew . . . No, it isn't possible to give this up.

Zack's asleep, his face oddly peaceful. When the children were infants, she often stood at their cribs while they slept to make sure they were breathing. Sometimes Zack had to tug her out of their room. Secretly she believed her hovering presence insured their lives. Now, she feels no such magic.

Grabbing her cell phone from the bedside table, she tiptoes into the bathroom, closes the door gently, and locks it. Then she surveys everything . . . the aqua-painted shelves Zack built to hold his shaving gear, her makeup kit, soaps, lotions, perfume. He tiled the walls and floor, aqua and white, gorgeous, simply gorgeous. She remembers choosing the shower curtain with its undulating swans, the globe light fixture with its tiny star-shaped cutouts. She inventories each item, etching them into her brain. Is it leaving all of this that's so devastating, or having to start over? She flashes on their camping equipment tucked away in the basement, a tent and air mattresses they could set up in Harriman State Park. But winter will arrive. And what if they still have no jobs? What if they have to live in their car? She's seen those families on TV. Bundles piled high, blocking rear windows; people with gloved hands, eating straight out of cans. It could be the 1930s. And what about school? What if her children are forced into foster care? Another number on a case file in the dreaded system? Fear seeps through her. Some people have parents they can turn to, not her, not now, not ever really.

She punches in Dory's number, her mouth dry.

"Lena? What? I'm still waking up."

"We're being evicted. Zack hasn't paid the mortgage for

almost a year. We have thirty days." The words thicken in her throat but she refuses tears.

"Wow." Dory mumbles sleepily. "How could you let it get this far?"

"Zack never told me. He takes care of the bills. It's what the men in his family have always done. I take care of everything else. It's never been a problem. No one's turned off our electricity or cable. Whatever money he got from unemployment or the pittance from the union must have gone for everything but the mortgage. Evidently, people don't telephone anymore to say that they're going to take your house away. It's done by letter. Zack picks up the mail. A man who believes in miracles, he just waited for one to come along to do whatever-the-fuck . . ."

"How much do you owe?" Dory interrupts.

"Thousands."

"Look, there must be some way to fight this." Dory's voice is stronger now. Maybe she's formulating a plan. Isn't that what best friends do?

"If he'd told me sooner, before we owed so fucking much, we could've borrowed something." She's praying for help, anything at all.

"Let me talk to Stu. See how much extra we have."

"Sweet, but no. His job is only a bit more secure than my future. You guys can't bail us out. I just need to vent or choke."

"Do the kids know?"

"I dread telling them. Parents are supposed to protect their children, prepare the way for their futures. Did Zack think of that?"

"Rosie's pretty mature, she'll understand. Casey's young, but he's so sweet, he'll want to be assured everyone is going to be okay."

"That's just it. What does okay mean? Where can we go, a family of four? I told you about the two foreclosed houses on our road . . ."

"Whoa, Lena, that was them. You only learned last night."

The impossibility of their situation slams her anew. "Dory, I need to go. I'll call you later." She clicks off. And stares down at the tiles that are so much prettier than the warped bathroom floor under the leaky roof where she grew up.

It rained so hard that long-ago day. She rarely allows herself to remember. She was in the shower, washing her hair, when a large chunk of ceiling plaster crashed into the tub, just missing her. She grabbed a towel and ran into the living room, soap still in her hair. Not that anyone was there to help. Her father was at work. Her mother, only recently released from her fourth stay in the psychiatric unit, hadn't left her bed or spoken since returning home. After each admission, her father would say, "Your mother's having one of her breakdowns," as if it were willful. And some part of her, she remembers, agreed with him.

And she also remembers how, after rinsing the soap from her hair in the kitchen sink and putting on jeans and a sweatshirt, she had prepared her mother's dinner. She carried in the tray—an omelet with peas, she remembers that, too—and switched on a bedroom lamp. To her surprise, her mother, usually prone, was perched on the edge of the bed, her face pale in the dim light. While setting out the food, she began to describe the moment in the shower. It was a way to fill the silence. Her mother reached up to stroke her wet hair as if to check out her story, or was it a touch of affection? She never could decide. Then, with a fierce, certain expression on her face, her mother whispered, "Go away. Please." She knew then, as she knows now, that something awful was about to happen, something she felt entirely unable to stop.

Rosie, banging on the door, interrupts her thoughts. "Need to get in. This second."

As they pass each other, she looks away.

"What's the matter?"

"Nothing."

Rosie disappears into the bathroom. Despite what Dory thinks, Rosie's not going to take this well.

Zack is still asleep. She shakes his shoulder. "Wake up. We have to tell the children."

"Let them go to school," he says groggily.

"Jesus, Zack, they're on summer vacation."

"What's the rush?" His eyes remain closed.

She can't decide. He could be right. What's the rush? Why not wait till there's a plan of some sort. "Get up. It's late." Though for what, she has no idea.

He slides his legs off the bed and sits there, still dressed in yesterday's clothing. "I need a shower." He peels off socks and shirt on the way to the bathroom. She hears him bang on the door. Maybe their next house will have two bathrooms.

She frees the table of some of last night's debris and pulls breakfast stuff out of cabinets and the fridge. Zack needs to be strong with the children. She drops onto a chair.

"Hi, mom." Casey lays a quick hand on her shoulder, then begins making his breakfast the way he likes it, not too much yogurt, spooned into a cup, a half-teaspoon of jelly on rye bread, no butter, god forbid, his movements smooth and predetermined. How to tell this boy that they're being ousted from their home?

"Mom, why aren't you getting the coffee?"

"I am." She forces herself up. She needs to do what she does every morning. Act normal, whatever that means. She watches the interminable drip-drip of liquid into the carafe. People say one door closes and another opens. People say a lot of shit.

Rosie, barefoot in short-shorts and T-strap top, strides in and goes straight to the fridge to take out the juice; her body more womanly each day.

"So, Mom, what exactly did dad tell you?"

"Let's wait for him to get down."

"All this delay is killing me."

"Rosie, in life . . ."

"I know, I know, don't bore me, you've said it a million times, be patient. I can't. I take after you."

"Not true. I'm patient."

"You are not, right, Casey?"

"I don't know."

"Dad, what happened last night?" Rosie asks, before Zack reaches the kitchen table.

Her throat tightens. She pours two cups of coffee, sets one down for Zack and takes a chair.

His wet, curly hair uncombed, he doesn't look the least bit refreshed by the shower. His ancient jeans with kneeholes are ludicrous on a man his age. He's preparing for homelessness, she thinks. He takes a few sips of coffee. "Ask your mom."

"Jesus, Zack!"

"Mom, come on . . ." Rosie's large eyes blaze with need and curiosity. Casey, too, looks at her, worry written on his face. She roots around in her mind to find an encouraging way to tell them.

"Do you kids know what foreclosure means?"

"What?" says Rosie. "You're kidding!"

"You know we haven't been working. There's been a real shortage of cash, and Dad hasn't paid the mortgage . . ."

"Dad, you didn't pay the bills? What's going to happen?" This directly to him. Good girl.

He squirms in his chair. "Well, it's not entirely clear. There are still avenues to pursue, we just haven't gotten there."

"What are you talking about?" Rosie asks.

"We have to make back payments, but as your mother said, without jobs . . ."

"Mom, tell us." Rosie pleads.

"They're going to foreclose on our house."

"That can't happen." Rosie shakes her head as if to ward off the words.

"Dad and I are trying to figure out how to make some payments so we won't be evicted."

Casey's watching in an unblinking way that scares her. She reaches out and he flinches.

"Evicted? Like in *The Grapes of Wrath?* That book was about long ago. They can't do that any more, can they? Aren't there laws against it?"

Rosie's tone begs for an answer and not the one she has to offer. It's breaking her heart.

"They can," says Casey suddenly. "It's what happened to the people down the road. The cops made them leave and their houses are still empty. How come?" he asks his dad, who wears yesterday's bewildered expression.

"Zack, say something."

"You never know what will turn up," he responds, then grins, and both kids look at her.

"Nothing will happen today or tomorrow or even next week. There's time."

"Time for what, Mom?" Rosie, again.

"To figure things out . . ."

"You know what I was thinking," Zack says suddenly. "If our house burns down before we're evicted, we have fire insurance. They'd have to pay us off or build another house."

"Zack, for god's sake!" He can't incite the children this way.

"I said what's true," he responds stubbornly.

"Zack, we think all kinds of thoughts we don't give voice to."

"Mom, we need to get money." Practical Rosie.

"I know, and we'll try to do that."

"But how?" Casey asks in a tone of deep concern.

"I don't know yet. Finish your breakfast. I'll start making phone calls." She heads for the couch with no idea who to call. None whatsoever. Zack's dead parents smile benevolently down on them from a photo on the breakfront.

12.

She's out the door before her mother has a chance to ask where she's going.

Too restless to wait for a bus, she begins walking the mile to the elevated train. The sun is baking hot. She decides to snag a car ride for the A/C, which is bound to be on. But as a car approaches, she hesitates. Her mother isn't always right. Lots of people hitch. Then, with more determination, her hand goes up. A car stops. The window rolls down. A man older than her father, she guesses, checks her out. "Where you headed?"

"The train station."

"Hop in."

She does, and decides this is the first step toward everything in her life that's about to change.

The A/C is on, the car messy, sand on the floor, beach gear strewn about. A man his age driving barefoot, is that normal?

"Going out to do something nice?" His easy tone says she's a child.

"Meeting a friend in the city."

"To do what?"

"A movie," she lies. "Do you live around here?" She courts a casual voice.

"Nope."

"Kids at home?"

"As a matter of fact they're with their mom."

"Oh, a divorced dad."

He glances at her. "Not yet, but on the way."

"I guess I should say sorry."

"Depends," he mumbles.

"I see."

"Do you?" In his voice she hears humor.

"I do. I'm the product of a broken family. It gets better with time."

"What gets better?" He sounds interested.

"You know, the situation, picking up, dropping off, holidays, all of it becomes more . . . I don't know . . . tolerable."

"Hope you're right."

"It does depend on the age of the children," she adds for good measure.

"Well, Katy's ten, and . . ." He falls silent.

She says nothing, not sure how much further to spin this tale.

"Hey, I'm driving into the city, I could drop you off."

"Thanks but no thanks, I'm meeting my friend at the station." How easily the lies come. Besides, riding with him is bound to get boring.

She climbs the warped stairs to the ancient outdoor platform with its wobbly, wood-slatted floor and graffiti-covered ads. The sun burns steadily. She ducks inside a phone-less telephone booth for shade. Her family life is falling apart. No doubt about it. Eviction could split them up. She and her dad in one place, Casey and her mom in another. Might be interesting. On the other hand, they could end up in a shelter, but not her, no way, she's not going there. She'll quit school, get a job, nanny, waitress, whatever. She considers phoning Mirabelle to tell her about the eviction, but Mirabelle's you're-worrying-too-much attitude will piss her off. Siri, however, will be sympathetic. They'll find a small flat. Isn't that what they call it in Pakistan, or maybe London? Or they'll rent someone's furnished basement and keep house for a while. They'll...

The elevated train asthmatically climbs the inclined track and screeches to a halt. She waits impatiently for the old doors to tremble open. The A/C inside is weak to nonexistent. It's Sunday morning, only a few riders. Across the aisle, two tough-looking dudes eye her. Nothing new. She passes guys like them daily. They hang out near her school. Usually she smiles daintily in a good-girly way, then averts her eyes.

"Where you going, pretty girl?"

The guy has tiny gold-hoop earrings, a red bandana around his forehead, a vest open over a T-shirt. His upper arms are thick and tanned.

"Downtown," she says.

"Times Square?"

"No."

"Hey, share."

"Thirty-fourth Street."

"The girl's going to Macy's," he tells his friend, who couldn't care less.

She takes out her phone and begins scrolling.

"Yo! Don't like what you see?" Bandana guy again, his face animated, his green eyes sharp, his dark-blond curls his prize.

"I don't know if I like it or not. I'm not interested."

"Girl isn't interested. What do you think of that, mate?"

Mate doesn't smile.

She looks around the car. Two old women.

"You're alone with me and my dude here."

She stares back to let him know he's not scaring her, though he is. A bit, anyway.

"Staring isn't polite. Didn't your mother teach you manners?"

"More than yours, asshole."

"The girl has courage." One giant step and he's across the aisle sitting beside her. Up close his face looks gentler, younger than she thought, though much older than Siri.

"What exactly do you want, because truth is, I'm seriously not in a talking mood? My family's about to be evicted." She can't believe she's said it.

"Hey, you all will find something else. A new place is clean, shiny. Don't despair. I've been there."

"Are you being poetic?" her tone as sarcastic as she can make it.

"That's what I do. Rap, poems, talk a lot of fast thoughts. I have a gig in Queens tonight, want to come?" A sweet smile flits across his face.

Queens? Nowhere near the destination she's planned, though the idea of doing something entirely new appeals to her.

"Maybe another time. I have someplace to go right now."

"Your choice," his smile opens into a surprisingly lovely grin.

"Do you have many gigs?"

"I'm wanted on every corner. And I have a You Tube channel. I'll give you a CD for nothing, well, not for nothing, for being so upstanding."

"Upstanding?"

"Lots of beautiful girls aren't courageous, they just preen to be seen and wait to be queen."

"Can you talk normal?"

"Maybe. Are you interested in what my mama calls me?"

She smiles. "What does your mother call you?"

"Sonny. And you?"

"Rosie."

"I knew it was a flower. I told myself Daisy or Iris, but Rosie's good. I'll call you Rosy-Posy, cause that's what I do, rhyme and rap and rendezvous."

"And how do you do that?"

"I don't know, it happens. I'm talented. Everyone owns talent. We have to find yours, Rosy-Posy."

Again she smiles. She can't help it. He's morphing into an interesting, handsome guy who's capable of lifting her spirits.

"I get off at Jackson Avenue, next stop," his voice filled with mock sorrow.

"South Bronx?"

"Hunts Point and below is the true burn-'em-up South Bronx."

"My mom grew up in the projects."

"No wonder you're special. Rosy-Posy, so here's what I impart, your number here, close to my heart." He produces a pen and his arm. "Write it." His friend is already waiting at the door.

She considers . . . decides, jots down her cell phone number.

"You will surely hear from me." Two fingers brush her cheek.

As the train leaves the station he taps on the window, hand on heart, big smile on his too-handsome face.

She exits the subway strangely elated by the encounter, amazed at how the unexpected can intervene to change the moment. Walking along the narrow, hot sidewalk of 28th Street, she passes tiny shops selling Indian fabrics and Indian spices. The restaurant where Siri works is what her mother would call a hole in the wall, but she's not her mother. She descends three worn, concrete steps into a cool, dark chamber, where she sees no one. Siri told her he arrives early to straighten up before the place opens for lunch, but he's nowhere to be seen. A large man rises from a dark corner, startling her. "Yes, please, can I help you? We are not serving yet."

"I'm looking for my friend Siri. We go to the same school." She feels a need to explain the connection. For all she knows, this could be his uncle.

"He's up from the cellar any minute, take a seat. Water?"

"Yes. It's very hot outside. Thank you so much." Her mother's teachings of politeness ever there, she sinks down onto a thickly padded wicker seat near a glass-topped table, with an upside-down plate and a slim, white vase with one daisy; the soft velvety petals tell her it's fresh.

The man places a glass of water in front of her, then turns and says, "Sirhan, your friend from school, she's sitting here."

"Rosie? What happened?"

She catches the genuine concern in his voice as he enters through the front door and places the carton he's carrying on a table.

"Can we talk?" she asks.

He leads her to the back, parts a heavy, beaded curtain, behind which is a small room with shiny, sequined pillows scattered along a vinyl banquette. "We can talk here."

Relieved that the man doesn't follow them, she quickly relates the sad tale of the coming eviction and her desire not to live in a shelter where, she adds, young women like her are raped. She reveals as well her idea that they should set up temporary quarters together. "I would get a job and help pay the rent, of course." Even as she says all this, she realizes it's not what she wants after all, which is weird, considering it's why she's come.

"Rosie, the news you bring is bad, very bad, indeed. But I cannot believe my aunt and uncle will approve the plan you have. If they don't, they could send me back to Pakistan. I don't want that. You shouldn't either." His eyes, pleading and sad, are steady on her. Is it sadness for her or for himself?

Suddenly, none of this matters. "I need to go home now," she says.

"Wait, Rosie. Are we still going to the movies?"

"Call me. I have no idea what my life will be like by Friday." She parts the curtain and walks quickly out of the restaurant onto a blinding sunstruck street.

Her phone rings. It's a number she doesn't know. She answers anyway.

13.

Stu scans the whiteboard above the bar. It's habit. The pub menu never changes: chef salad, burger, minestrone soup, and once in a while chili, in tiny print near the bottom. Whatever he orders will taste wrong, but he doesn't care. He's glad to sit here and take a beer with his overdone burger. In the evenings Manny's Pub is three-deep with workers from the nearby plant. At noon, it's empty.

Once upon a time he would've announced to the men that he was heading off to Manny's for a beer. Today he didn't say a word. He left them at chow time, like prisoners jostling for seats at the long metal lunch table, undoing paper bags, cursing plastic wraps, but keeping their complaints about work to a minimum. Strange suits now roam the floor, listening, watching, calculating, noting down procedures. Ask the foreman who the assholes are and he shrugs his bony shoulders. Nerve-wracking. The plant has gone from one hundred fifty workers to seventy-five, but who's counting? Still, even after all these months, the guys haven't entirely forgiven him for fucking over his team. Then again, if worse happens, what he did or didn't do won't matter a bit.

Right now, none of this bothers him. He's excited, maybe even elated, though he can't tell because it's been so long since anything other than the next drink got him high.

It was Dory's text this morning: Zack, Lena, and family being evicted! It came to him immediately. Of course, he'll check it out with Dory first, but she'll agree. He feels it in his bones. Rosie and Casey could share the guestroom, Lena and Zack could have the basement. It's nearly finished. He'll help Zack build a tiny bathroom down there. It'll do. It won't be forever, but for now, what better could they ask for? They'll lick their fingers with his brunches, five fancy ways to serve eggs plus French toast, plus Bloody Marys. And on Saturday nights, add music to the drinks, maybe a TV movie, their own little party. Why would anyone say no to that? Lena does have a way of spoiling his fantasies, but would she rather live in a shelter with two kids, for godsakes? Even if they scrape up some money, it'll only buy them another month in their house, tops. The answer to their emergency is a free place to live while they seek work. No-brainer.

He drains the Sam Adams. Okay, man, be honest. His offer isn't completely kosher. She's his best friend's wife, but what's wrong with enjoying her presence, basking in her proximity? Of course, a few too many drinks, and dangerously revealing words could ooze from his sodden brain. And the kids will be there. Actually, it's scary, the thought of her living so close, her scent, the sudden cleavage as she bends over the sink, her eyes, mostly those eyes, which are bound to be dewy grateful for being given a home. Truth is, he can't trust himself. Truth is, he's a certified bastard. Ask anyone at work. But man, he has only one life, and it hasn't been going well for way too long. Why shouldn't he take what he can where he can?

Ideally, and this is the dumbest thought in his still sober mind, he'd like to ask Zack's opinion. How crazy is that? I want your family to live with us, but I'm scared I might jump your wife. Zack, I'd like to offer your family a place to live, but my feelings toward Lena . . . Can't say that either. Can't say any of it to anyone, ever!

Though the offer isn't really about him, is it? A family in need, and not just any family, but their best friends. Could he let them end up in the gutter, homeless? Of course not. What kind of friend would do that?

Who's he kidding? And maybe they've already found their own way out of their dilemma. Maybe they've chosen to live with some never-before-mentioned aunt in the boonies. And what could he do about that? Doubt, always waiting to jump him, raises its demonic head. From elation to confusion in two minutes. How does he do it?

He sighs. Manny looks up from behind the bar, then goes back to his racing form, which he reads with a magnifying glass. Too fat by far, he's owner, bartender, janitor, and numbers-taker on the side. Always present but never a participant, he's not someone you chew the fat with. Once he asked Manny where he lived, which got him a minute-long stare. People don't usually ask me anything personal, Manny then said, leaving him to wonder if he'd crossed some line. He taps the empty glass on the bar for another beer, which Manny produces in no time at all.

14.

It's already four and she's phoned no one, because who in the world that she knows would have that kind of money to lend? Instead, she's been on the couch for hours, staring at the room or gazing out at the maple tree in full leaf, a view she's about to lose. For a while after her father died she'd wake up each morning and have to remind herself that he was gone. It was as if she hadn't quite absorbed his presence, so his absence was difficult to take in. It's the way she feels now about the house: the colorful scatter rugs placed smartly across the living room floor, the two brass lamps that arrived slightly scratched but that she loved too much to return, the leather club chair from their first apartment, dented and scuffed from wear, but so comfortable.

Rosie tears through the front door, an air of excitement about her, and drops into the chair. "You haven't changed out of your robe. That's not helpful," Rosie scolds, her face so alive.

"Go bother your father." Where is Zack, anyway? Why isn't he at her side, trying to sort out the next steps?

"Is that what I am, a bother?"

"What is it you want me to do?"

"Do? Mom? What's the matter with you? You need to talk to us."

"We talked at breakfast."

"That was hours ago. We have ideas too . . ." Rosie's voice suddenly taking on the challenging tone she's come to know so well.

Can she say they're drowning, that she hasn't a clue how to save them? "Where were you all day?"

"I went into Manhattan, walked around."

"By yourself?"

"Of course, I'm not a child. That's when I decided I should live with Mirabelle, and Casey could live with his good friend Robbie, and you guys, well, I couldn't figure that one out."

"We don't split up the family."

"Then you better come up with a solution fast." Rosie studies her. "How come you didn't notice when I left the house?" The suddenly plaintive note catches her off guard. It dawns on her that she expects, actually prefers, Rosie to be strong, combative, feet planted solidly on the ground.

"I must've been in the kitchen getting coffee."

"No. You were on the couch. Didn't you care that I was leaving?"

"I always care."

"Are you horribly disappointed? Does the eviction give you an empty feeling inside like you lost your best friend, or . . ."

"Rosie, what happened? Did you and Mirabelle have a fight?"

Rosie stares at her. "I'm going to take a shower. It's so damn hot."

The loud, determined knock at the front door sends Rosie to the vestibule instead. "Mom! It's Dory and Stu," she calls.

She hoists herself off the couch. The last thing she wants is to be sociable.

"Hi," Dory says. "We brought food." Dory's carrying a pizza box, Stu, a six-pack.

"Dory, you should've called first," she chides quietly, following her into the kitchen.

"We're not company," Dory says.

She leans close to whisper. "I'm not ready to have our lives laid out like that pie."

"Have you and Zack discussed the eviction with the children?" Dory whispers back.

"Of course."

"We've come here with a solution. Rosie, find your father and get Casey to the table, too." Dory, who knows where everything is, sets out paper plates, utensils, glasses. Her take-charge personality and innate optimism is what Lena usually counts on, but right now it grates.

Stu hands Zack a beer as he comes up from the basement.

"I should go change into something . . ." she begins.

"Hey, you're fine, covered in silk," Stu remarks.

"Lena, it's okay." Dory fishes in her bag for a bottle of aspirin, and pops two in her mouth. "Headache, awful nuisance."

Casey shuffles in, shyly nods to no one in particular, and sits.

"Thanks for this," Rosie says, as if she's the mistress of the house, and why not? Her mother's missing in action.

Stu places a slice of pizza on each plate. "Ladies, join me in a beer?"

"Mom, can I?" Rosie looks at her.

"No."

Stu twists open the cap, places the beer in front of Lena. She takes a long pull. It's cold, bitter, sharp, just right. She wouldn't mind several more. Pizza, however; that's hopeless. Zack's expression of satisfaction on biting into a slice irritates her.

Rosie, for whom silence is doom, says, "Why are you here? I mean, is this a charity visit? You know, bring food to the needy family?"

"That's not why we came. Stu, it's your idea, you explain."

"It's simple, no problem. You can move in with us. The guest room for Rosie and Casey, the basement for you two. Zack and I can build a little bathroom down there." Stu speaks directly and only to Zack, then takes a long swig of the beer, nearly emptying the contents. Lena wonders if he's embarrassed about making the offer, or worried they'll accept.

"I wouldn't have my own room?" Rosie's voice rises in alarm.

"Does your house have Wi-Fi?"

"Of course," Dory assures Casey.

"The problem will be crowding. You'll have six people living in close quarters," Rosie explains, as if that should be enough to put an end to the conversation.

Her daughter's not only reading her mind but also sizing up the situation correctly. A momentary fantasy of dropping the entire eviction problem in her feisty daughter's lap leaves her slightly light-headed.

"Besides," Rosie continues, "I can't share a room with Casey, not simply because he's a boy, but because we have very different lifestyles. Right, Casey?"

"Better than a shelter," Casey says.

"Dad, you haven't said anything yet," Rosie scolds.

"The decision is up to your mother," Zack replies and all eyes turn to her, but she has nothing to add.

An uncomfortable hour filled with small talk later, no decision made, she stands at the rain-streaked window watching the silver Honda drive off. Zack disappears upstairs. Rosie leaves for Mirabelle's. Casey is somewhere. Dory's parting whisper replays in her head. "It could be fun. It could even be helpful." Helpful? To her and Zack? To Dory and Stu? And what about Dory's pristine house? Everything always in place. Lovely, yes, but clearly, no children live there. Hers will put their feet up on the couch, insist on watching stupid TV programs, and open the fridge every ten minutes to retrieve food, the debris of which will be found in other rooms.

In truth, though, it's her reluctance that's the issue. The offer leaves her restless, anxious, as if she's being given a present she's afraid—no, terrified—to open. Growing up, she felt like such an outsider at home, an intruder whose presence caused more trouble than joy. The rooms didn't recognize or embrace her, as a home should, as her home does her children. She can't live that way again, as a guest.

There's no point getting dressed now, but she hikes upstairs and finds Zack on the bed, hands behind his head. A slight smile flits across his face when he sees her. Why isn't he more upset?

"I'll have to tell Rosie and Casey that their allowances are suspended until we get jobs. Maybe Rosie can find some babysitting to do."

"You and I never had allowances," Zack reminds her.

"So what? I want better for our children, don't you?"

"They'll manage. They're not out on the street, starving. We still have unemployment and some savings."

"Which will be gone soon enough."

"Did you give any more thought to Stu's suggestion?" his tone so matter of fact he could be asking the time.

She drops into the rocking chair. "Dory and Stu are sweet to offer us a place, but it's not the answer. We have to find jobs and pay the bank."

"It's too late."

"I don't accept that. I told you I'll find a job."

"Where?"

"Where will *I* work?" The idiocy of the question drives nails through her skin. "What the fuck? What about you? You don't have to wait for another site."

"What else can I do?"

"Who cares? Flip papers, hand out flyers, sell fruit."

"I can't do those things."

"Yes, you can, you must. I'll clean houses, wash dishes, anything that brings in money." A blue-gray light filters through the blur of rain. She inhales the sachet scent of the bedroom. "I'm not taking four years' worth of home and piling it into some storage space where it will fade or smell so bad I won't want any of it anymore."

"We'll take a few small pieces with us, and the rest will be stored. It's only furniture."

"Only furniture?" rips from her throat. "Don't you have feelings for this home we've made that will be smashed to pieces? For Chrissakes!"

"Even if I find some jerk job, we can't make enough money soon enough to halt the eviction." The sudden weariness in Zack's voice catches her attention, as do his unshaven cheeks. Letting himself go, rolling downhill, how soon will he hit bottom? She stares hard at him.

"What?"

"I don't want to move," she says quietly. "I don't want to break up a home. I don't want to displace the children or us. I don't want to be someone's guest. I want to stay here. That's what I want." The last words exhaled on a shaky breath. She clasps her hands tightly, trying to slow her breathing, trying as well not to blame him, though she does.

He slides off the bed. "We'll stay."

"Don't humor me."

"I'm not. It's something I've been thinking about. The guys on my old site will put their bodies on the line. They like playing hero. They'll circle the house, construct a barrier. We'll set up a few tents, call a local TV station, get some PR." His hands chop the air, his expression intense.

Has he lost it, again?

"My guys won't let the eviction people cross the line. They won't get near the house. It'll be weeks before they try again. By then we could have jobs or find some money somehow. Believe me, all we need is time."

His eyes are moist and feverish, the way they were at that bash for the neighbors. He's imagining putting off the inevitable with another party of beer and food. How crazy is that? Still, where's her plan? Looking past his eager gaze, she notes the Mexican wall hanging, the women climbing that hill forever, carrying their heavy baskets. It was their honeymoon, for godsakes, why didn't they buy something more hopeful?

He takes her hand, squeezes it, urges her to agree, the way he once urged her to marry him. She was eighteen. It was a moment of heart-stopping indecision. Stay in that awful apartment, her mother dead and a father who only wanted her gone? College never an option, her prospects slim. If she turned down his proposal, the future would remain open for anything, every bit of it unknown. So she said yes, and everything became known. Until now.

"Go on, organize a hardhat posse, keep those bastards from our door. Why the fuck not?" Maybe the authorities will go away and it will buy them some time, but the surge of frivolous hope is vanishing as rapidly as it arose. The idea's ridiculous. The cops will arrive, barge through, rough up and arrest the bunch of them, including her and Zack. And then what?

15.

Rosie strides to her friend's house through the humid, drizzly streets. Dory and Stu left without a decision. The eviction isn't far away. She needs to know what her life's going to be like come September. One thing she does know, moving into Dory's won't happen with her aboard. Still, she's curious. Why didn't her mother accept Stu's offer? Her father wanted to but deferred, naturally. She'll never live with a man who doesn't have a strong will of his own. It's why her relationship with Siri couldn't progress. What kind of love listens first to an aunt or uncle? He should've insisted on rescuing her from the possibility of living in a shelter. Sonny would've done it, of that she's certain. His phone call just hours after they met was a surprise. He was assertive, flirtatious, funny, and sweet. They talked for a long time. He wants to see her. Hesitant about making a date so soon, she reminds herself the only way to experience the world is to take risks. Otherwise nothing new and different can happen.

Her mother fears chaos; she doesn't. No wonder her mother's youth was spent bar-hopping with her dad, Stu, and Dory, which led to early marriage, kids, a mortgage. Next: get old and die. Not her agenda. By the time she's her mother's age, her experiences will fill a trunk. She'll have traveled to a thousand countries, met too many people to remember. There are so many things she wants to do that sometimes it hurts to think about them.

Mirabelle's two-story house, white and blue with a back porch and a landscaped lawn, is the last on the road. Unlike her noisy abode, it's almost deathly quiet. Her mom walks barefoot on wall-to-wall carpeting and speaks in whispery tones, as if someone is sleeping nearby. Her father works at home in the basement. Rosie rarely sees him. Mirabelle prefers Rosie's house, likes to converse with her mother, which Rosie only allows for brief periods, ever mindful that Mirabelle could inadvertently reveal what her mother shouldn't know.

The two of them are stretched out on Mirabelle's full-size bed, propped on loads of pillows, the plaid bedspread bunched on the floor. Her friend's icy-blue eyes remain on her as she discloses the eviction and that her parents seem completely nonfunctional. Mirabelle doesn't look moved. "I might have to live in a shelter with the other homeless."

"Don't be dramatic. You'll live in our guest room."

"It's compelling," she agrees, knowing Mirabelle would say exactly this and envisioning that bedroom with its bay window, dressing table, and half-bathroom. "Your parents may not want a long-term guest."

"My mother has no opinions, at least none she shares with me. And my father won't even realize you're here. Not to worry." Mirabelle's short, stubby blond dreadlocks frame a pudgy face, but she doesn't believe in diets. "After you move in, we'll get tattoos at that shop down in the Village I told you about. I want a swan with a hint of water, just below my belly button."

"Ouch."

"It hurts the same no matter where you put it. Having it there is a gift for very special people . . ." Mirabelle's voice trails off.

"Tattoos are not on my immediate to-do list."

"So what is, my sweet girl?"

"It's finished with Siri. He turned out to be a wimp. I met this handsome dude on the train, strong, manly, the kind you can lean on. He wrote my phone number on his arm."

"And this hero's name?"

"Sonny."

Mirabelle smiles.

"What's funny?"

"Your utter devotion to these guys, which you should know bores me."

"Why?"

"I don't like boys. They're childish. I don't like men. They're crude. They lack a poetic side."

"Sonny's a poet, of sorts."

"What kind?" Mirabelle's eyes flash interest.

"He's a professional rapper."

"Oh, a jingle writer."

"By the way, swans are vicious." A sudden downpour outside darkens the room, and she reaches up to switch on the floor lamp.

"No, Rosie, leave it off."

"Why?"

"In my journal I'm writing about dawn and evening and the way the light between changes. Get it?"

"Not really, but does it matter?"

"Not a whit." Mirabelle swings her body off the bed to stand at the window.

"What's the problem?" she asks.

"Nothing."

"Come on, it's something."

"You're smart and sensitive but you get all gooey around guys. I guess it annoys me."

"But why?"

"The way you waste time on this crap."

"Mirabelle, this isn't a waste. Now is the time we're supposed to be making and breaking relationships. Exploring. It's normal." She likes boys, older ones, though she can't argue that they aren't often ridiculous. But she doesn't believe all men are crude. Her father may be a wimp, but he's not crude, nor is Stu.

Mirabelle shrugs and perches at the edge of the bed. "Can I interest you in an excellent film that I'd love to see again, just so you can enjoy it, too?"

"That's sweet," she says, though it's not what she wants to do. But if she's going to move in, Mirabelle needs to want to have her here.

16.

The TV is tuned to one of Dory's weekend morning talk shows. It doesn't stop her from prattling on about how stubborn Lena can be, which isn't what he wants to hear right now. On the screen, well-coiffed ladies sit around a table, sharing things that Don't Matter. Several million people watch the show to hear stories sadder than their own. Or does the fantasy of TV Land give them hope? His fantasy gives him hope. It's what he holds on to in this holy-roller country called America, where guys like him are processed out of Dullsville into routine, and where only the fantasies of the rich are realized.

Okay, Lena's reluctance to accept their offer yesterday was a disappointment. But nothing's ever over till it's over. He'll get Zack alone in a bar. A few beers and he'll describe in gory detail what happened to the daughter of a made-up friend while living in a shelter. Then he'll urge Zack to share these indisputable facts with Lena, and wake up the fear she ought to have—that to refuse the refuge of their house is nothing less than negligent.

"Stu, where are you?"

"At your side, lady."

"Lena in her robe all day . . . not like her. What else can we do?"

"Nothing," he says irritably, pissed to have his planning interrupted.

"Why so huffy?"

"I made myself available. Now it's up to them. End of story."

"Yourself available? What does that mean?"

"Don't nitpick."

Dory takes him in with that flushed expression of wanting to understand that justifies nothing in his book. "Shut off the stupid TV if you're not watching. I'm sure not."

She promptly picks up the remote and clicks the TV off, the immediate silence damning. What's the matter with him? She didn't do a thing wrong. He's treating her badly, which feels terrible. Is he really trying to make her leave him? He's so not in touch with the crap in his head to know. "Honey, we have to let them sort it out. We offered our house, let's wait and see. That's all I meant."

Ever ready to accept a half-assed apology, she nods in agreement.

When the phone rings, Dory answers. "It's Zack. He wants us over for breakfast, wants to share an idea. Are you up for going?"

"Why not?" he says, as nonchalantly as he can.

Pulling up in front of their house, he takes it in as if for the first time. It's small, almost a toy. If it didn't have a basement they could lift it, haul it elsewhere, never to be found. Dory gets out and walks quickly up the front steps in her tie-dyed sundress. Always a skinny girl, she's still all edges and points, unlike Lena . . .

"Stu?" Dory calls. Slowly he unfolds himself from the car, everything in him reluctant to hear Zack's idea. Lena opens the door in fitted jeans and a green tank top that matches her eyes, dazzling, though in her expression he finds no wish to dazzle.

She looks downright sullen, tired, maybe tearful, but that's not Lena. She didn't cry, even when her mother did the unthinkable. Maybe, alone in the bathroom, but that's more Dory. How many times has he seen her wide eyes tear up?

He nods to Lena and follows her to the kitchen, where they're all sitting around the table. French toast, syrup, jam, juice, milk, cereal, and coffee on display, quite a spread for a family that's about to be homeless. But no one seems to be eating. Isn't that odd? He glances at the freshly painted yellow walls; a few colorful prints hung here and there, shiny appliances catching the sunlight streaming through the large bay window. To have to give this up should be illegal. Should he show sympathy? "The kitchen's cozy," he hears himself say, taking a seat. Lena's eyes flicker with gratitude. That, too, is odd.

"So, Dad, what's the secret plan?" It's Rosie, of course. She'll be a handful if they move in.

"You and me, Stu, will get some of the guys from the construction site to set up a perimeter around the house and keep the uniforms out. We don't know exactly when they'll come to evict us, but waiting won't be unpleasant. We'll provide the beer, food, maybe even music." Wearing an expectant expression, Zack scans their faces. No one speaks. "The hope here, my friends, is that the cops, sheriff or whoever, will go away and not come back for a while, during which period at least one of us gets a job so we can make a handful of back payments."

"They come in the middle of the night," Casey says. "I saw it online."

"What makes you think a few friends will keep the lions at bay?" Dory asks. "These guys arrive with weapons and stuff."

"I never heard of anyone getting shot during an eviction," Zack tells her, his tone upbeat.

"A woman in Harlem did, years ago," Casey says. "I read it online."

"Well, that was then, not today, my son." Zack beams at Casey.

"Lena, say something," Dory urges.

"I don't like it," she responds.

"I'm with Lena. I mean, how long can the guys hang around? They have families. They can't afford to be arrested. It's asking a lot," Stu chimes in, wondering if he's coming down too hard on Zack's idea. Mustn't be seen as recruiting them to his house. Lena's eyes are on him. She probably can't believe he's agreeing with her. Or maybe she's trying to figure him out, which feels good.

"It's probably worth a try," Rosie muses. "Otherwise there's nothing to do but leave here. We don't want to do that, right?"

"Right, my beautiful girl," Zack says.

"Of course we could all be arrested and sent directly to a shelter. That's scary," Rosie declares, cutting up her French toast.

Stu stares at Rosie's fork reaching her mouth, realizes he's got it all wrong. Zack's plan should be encouraged because it's bound to fail. They'll have no choice then but to move in. "No harm in trying to keep the suckers out," he says, matter-of-factly, as if he'd never said otherwise.

"Mom, it's the only chance we have to stay here. We have to take it. I am not moving into a shelter. Out of the question. How can I attend school from a shelter?"

"Lena?" Dory prods.

He marvels at the way everyone waits for Lena's response. It irritates him to find himself waiting, too.

"You know what?" Lena says, getting up. "I really need some air. "

17.

The house behind her, the windshield wipers swishing hypnotically, their voices continue to bang at her brain. Yes, everyone wants to stay in the house, but how to make that happen, no one can say. Stu disagrees with Zack's idea, only to agree? Dory's clearly as skeptical as she is. And what now? She's already appealed the eviction, filled out piles of papers, and been turned down. She's visited the bank that holds their mortgage again and again, and so has Zack. She's begged for a stay. Two different managers each told her to call the central mortgage department, where she was told there was a two-month waiting list just for face-to-face appointments. The foreclosure, she pleaded, would happen too soon for that. Useless. They only have a thousand dollars left in their savings account, a few weeks before they're truly penniless. Dory will lend them a few hundred, but how long will that last? They'll have to sell the car. Old as it is, it could net them a few thousand, and anyway, who can afford gas? At her last fill-up she paid for six dollars' worth. The guy looked at her with pity.

She finds herself on the Cross Bronx Expressway, which years ago displaced too many families to count. All those settled lives, disrupted and rearranged. What remained was the juvenile detention home near her junior high school, a scarred edifice of no distinction but for the girls at the windows, arms through the bars, calling down for trinkets. Once she tossed up a lipstick, the only gift she could offer in place of freedom.

The sky is leaden, but the rain has stopped. She takes the off-ramp heading for Pelham Bay Park, Matt's favorite spot. He dubbed it the Central Park of the Bronx and often brought along his sketchpad and bottles of beer. It was there he told her not to marry Zack, but didn't say why. She chided that he was jealous. He never said anything about it again. She can almost hear his voice now telling her to prepare, change is coming. They were all so damn young. Oh, Matt.

It's nearly three when she pulls up in front of her house. Stu's car is gone. Before she calls Dory to tell her that they'll accept her generosity, she decides it's best to speak with her family.

On the couch, Rosie stares into the screen of her phone. "Did you get lost?"

"Please don't talk to me in that tone."

"We thought you went outside and would be right back. It was so rude."

"I drove around. I had to think over our options. Casey upstairs?"

"He's talking even less than usual, Mom. You should take him to a doctor."

She opens the basement door. "Zack, please come up. We have to talk." Then climbs the stairs. "Casey, I need you in the kitchen. Now."

"Talk about what?" Rosie asks suspiciously, following her into the kitchen.

"Making decisions."

"It's about time."

"Rosie, I'm saying this once. I don't want your challenging voice in my ears. We're all in trouble together and together we'll figure this out."

"Yes, ma'am."

Zack comes up, shoulders hunched. Casey slips into his seat. She waits for them to settle around the table. "It's not ideal to move in with people," she begins. "But, we're lucky that it's friends like Dory and Stu . . ."

"Mom, I am not sharing a room in someone else's house."

"Do you have another suggestion? Does anyone? Zack?"

"We'll set up the perimeter, see how much time it buys us," he says, almost robotically, as if he has lost faith in his plan.

"The perimeter won't work," she says softly.

"Dad's plan is worth a try," Rosie offers.

"And when the cops arrive, what are you going to do?"

"Mom, you're being hostile."

"I'm being realistic."

"You're supposed to take care of home and hearth and clearly you haven't done a great job," Rosie accuses.

"Damn it, Zack, say something."

He shrugs. "Can't think of anything."

"I don't like cops coming here," Casey says.

"Don't worry, you'll stay inside," Rosie responds. "Dad, you and I can work out the particulars. Mom doesn't have to participate, either."

"Mom does have to participate," she says. "I'm the one who will have to bail you out of jail and pay the fines. Understand? We're lucky that Dory and Stu have opened their house to us."

"Why did you change your mind?" Rosie wants to know.

"Because we have no other options. End of subject."

"You can't say, end of subject. It's my life. I'm moving in with a friend."

"No, you're not."

A lone pigeon flaps by the window.

"I'm old enough to . . ."

"I don't care how old you are. This family stays together." She glances at Zack, his eyes half-closed.

"I need to do what's right for me," Rosie declares.

"Fine. Go to Mirabelle's. I hope her parents are capable of buying your food, books, and clothing for school."

"You're not capable, either," Rosie pushes back her chair.

"Don't you dare leave this table." Heat rises in her face. "The move to Dory's and Stu's is only temporary. "

"You expect me to believe your words when you can't even get Dad to answer you," Rosie snaps.

Sadly, she understands. Rosie wants two functioning parents who will ferry her into her future.

"Rosie, honey, listen. I get that you feel betrayed. No one at this table likes the situation we're in, but living at Dory's will allow us to save money."

"What money?" Rosie asks.

"We will find jobs."

"Mom, I don't think it's going to work."

"What?" She'd almost forgotten Casey.

"You've been trying to find jobs for months. Why would it be different now?"

She takes in her son, so earnest, so different from Rosie it's hard to believe they both came out of her. "Casey, my love, with dad and I out there every day looking in places we didn't try before, one of us will land something. I promise you."

"Mom, you're in no position to promise anything," Rosie

111

says. "The truth is, we'll be stuck at Dory's forever. I can't share a room with Casey. I need privacy."

"I'll repeat it again. This family isn't splitting up."

"Repeat it a thousand times, I'm not listening because you're not listening to me. All you do is offer us bullshit and more bullshit and more . . ."

She slaps Rosie's cheek, hard.

"Oh my god . . . Rosie, I . . ."

"Don't fucking bother." Her daughter's out of the room before she can utter another word. Zack gets up and saunters toward the basement.

"Casey . . ."

"I'm going to my room."

Jesus. She doesn't hit her children. Ever.

She takes herself upstairs. Rosie's door is closed. Music is playing. She knocks. "Honey, I want to apologize . . ."

Rosie turns up the music. She knocks again. Nothing.

Casey's door is open. He's on the bed with his computer.

"Casey, moving into someone's house is difficult . . ."

"I'd rather stay here. They're all so mean."

"Who, Casey?"

"The bankers."

"You got that right."

The music in Rosie's room is still on high. She goes down to the basement. Zack, eyes closed, is lying face up on an old cot, the mattress too thin to call it one. None of the lamps are on. The semi-darkness fits her mood, but it's hot as hell. She switches on the old window fan and pulls the backless deck chair up to the cot.

"That was an ugly scene with Rosie," she says, hoping for a bit of consolation.

"I'd say so." He takes a deep breath.

"Are you ill?"

"I'd say so."

"Zack, talk to me."

"What do you want me to say?"

"Whatever you want."

"Doesn't matter, nothing matters."

"We matter. Rosie, Casey, me. Zack, please, pull yourself together, I need you now."

"Do you?" He opens his eyes, turns to face her. "You'll do what you will do. None of us can make a dent in that head of yours. Rosie's desperate to stay here. I'm trying to find a way to do that, but, no, you've decided Dory's house is our only option. So we move. You decide Dory's isn't where to go, we don't move. So don't come down here telling me you need me."

"Wow. I didn't realize you had such resentment toward me. How could I? You opt out of every conflict so fast, leaving only me there to deal with whatever's left. Believe me, I'd welcome you taking the load off my back."

"Would you? And what does that even mean, since you never agree with my ideas. You treat them the way you would some kid's. I'm not a kid. If I come up with an idea, it's thought through, even if you believe otherwise. But I'm finished with coming up with ideas. It's all yours, angel. Whatever you say, we'll do. I'm on board your train." Again he closes his eyes.

She gazes at him as the righteous anger suddenly abandons her. "You want to do the perimeter. Fine. Do it. Fucking do it. It's too hot down here. I'm going upstairs."

18.

Rosie climbs the steps to the train platform. A bit nervous, but what's to be afraid of? If Sonny doesn't live up to her expectations, it's a few wasted hours. If he does, which she wholly believes he will ... well ... then ... life is doing what it's supposed to do. She called him right after the fight with her mother. He was so receptive, said they should get together immediately. Tonight. Said being slapped is no fun, yet it releases her from a lot. What he meant wasn't clear to her, but Sonny's so upbeat. He tells her to grab the moment, that tomorrow is never.

The train lumbers into the station and she steps inside. It thrills her to be out on her own, especially now, when her parents are weirder than usual. If her mother thinks apologizing will buy forgiveness, she's dead wrong. It's not about the slap, it's about the duplicity. Everyone—particularly her father—believes her mother is strong, capable, someone who has things under control. Obviously, that's all crap. Her mother wants to move to Dory's because her father's become a zombie. Dory will give her mother support. Well, she's not responsible for who her mother married, is she?

A few more stops to the station where Sonny will be waiting. It took her a while to choose what to wear. Finally she decided on the short yellow sleeveless dress, with flip-flops. While getting ready, she phoned Mirabelle but hung up soon after Mirabelle said, Be careful, he could be a serial killer. There is something a little crazy about him—maybe it's those eyes—but crazy-wild, not crazy-loony. He didn't say what he had in mind for tonight. Maybe a café where they can hold hands across the table; more likely a bar, a couple of glasses of beer. Maybe a walk, but where would they go?

She steps off the train at Jackson Avenue onto a long, elevated platform with a low overhang. The station seems to be in a state of ruin: torn billboards, a broken bench. It's not quite dark yet, but she doubts the station lights work. Sonny didn't say if he'd be waiting on the platform or in the street. The scene below doesn't look encouraging. Instinct tells her it wouldn't be cool to wait alone downstairs, but up here she's alone, too.

What if he doesn't show? He said he couldn't wait to see her. She's considering calling Mirabelle when Sonny comes bounding up the stairs, in tight black jeans and a black T-shirt under a silver-gray vest. But it's his sculpted face that captivates her, so alive. His admiring expression and beckoning eyes ignite something deep inside her.

"Rosy-Posy, look at you, all that beauty in one human being is too much to take in, but I'll begin." He wraps an arm around her. "Sorry I'm late, had to do something for my mama. She isn't well."

"What's the matter?"

"No, sweet pea, no negatives, not now. We're on the town tonight, which feels just right."

"Sonny, you promised not to rhyme everything, it's distracting. I want to be able to talk normal."

"Come on, I have a car downstairs."

"A car, you never said." It's a surprise she wishes he'd mentioned.

"Baby, there's so much I never said. Let's go."

He takes her hand, tugs her gently through a few bleak, vacant streets filled with abandoned buildings, boarded-up windows, doorways hidden behind sheets of tin, and a gated, dimly lit liquor store with an open door. "Aren't they supposed to be fixing up the South Bronx?"

"They haven't gotten this far south. Hey, they always begin at the top, right?"

They reach an old white Toyota. He opens the passenger door for her. "Welcome to Tillie," he says, and bows. She smiles. Being alone with Sonny in a car isn't what she imagined, but that's what makes it an experience.

He waits for her to settle in before he slides behind the wheel, then leans over to peck her cheek. "I want to show you off, okay? There's a party, not too many people, friends, down on Southern Boulevard. Know where that is?"

She shakes her head.

"It's not too far. Is it okay with you, I mean, a party? We can leave whenever we choose. I want to dance with you. So, what do you say?"

"I can't stay out too late" is all she can think of, because a party in the South Bronx wasn't on her fantasy list, either.

"Totally understand. Get you home at a decent hour. No train, I'll drive you. Okay?"

She nods. It's thoughtful, wanting her to agree before starting off.

They drive through streets not very different from the ones they walked. There seem to be few working lights, though once in a while she notices lit-up apartment windows. So people do still live here. She trusts Sonny, she does, but would prefer to be heading somewhere more recognizable.

"A penny," he says.

"Wondering where we're actually going to end up, my family." It's a lie, or maybe another kind of truth.

"Well, tonight, beauty, no worries, just pleasure. Your pleasure is my pleasure, understand?"

She smiles at him but doesn't answer, instead taking in the taut skin of his face, his long, dark eyelashes, his thick, shiny, shoulder-length hair.

"We're here." He pulls into a parking space in front of a gas station no longer in service. They walk across old, embedded silver tracks that stripe a wide boulevard and enter the square courtyard of a six-story building. Fuchsia spray-painted graffiti lends color to the chipped gray brick. Above the entrance is a washed-out ancient mural of trolley cars riding the silver rails they've just crossed.

"Sorry, Rosy-Posy, we need to walk up five flights." He takes her hand.

A ticker tape of questions runs through her head, but she decides it's best to meet his friends first. The stairwells are dark, heavy with the smell of fried food. The railings shaky. Music thumps into the hallway of the fifth floor. Sonny raps a code onto one of the dark-green metal doors that lacks a number. It's a party, she reminds herself, who cares where it's held?

A thin woman in a black low-cut mini-dress with long, flaming red hair that doesn't look real opens the door. "Sonny, baby, so good you're here. Hi, girl, I'm Mona."

"This here beauty is Rosy-Posy. Let us pass, baby." Mona opens the door wider and they follow her into a large room with several sagging couches, a few metal folding chairs, and a makeshift bar featuring bottles of vodka and bourbon. She sees no beer or soda, just some OJ. There's a whirring floor fan in one corner, plugged into a ceiling fixture, but the four tiny windows are sealed shut. Lit candles flicker along a baseboard and a miner's lantern is on the table, none of which does much to brighten the room, and maybe that's for the best. She wonders if anyone actually lives here, or if Sonny's friends have simply borrowed a vacant space for the party. She decides not to dwell on this.

The sweet scent of weed and another more acrid smell she doesn't recognize fill the air. Three couples are slow-dancing to African drumbeats. Two of the women have royal-blue hair, the third is bald, with a flower decal on the back of her scalp. All three women seem to be in their early twenties. Their partners, dressed in jeans and polo shirts, are around Sonny's age, twenty-five. She told him she's seventeen, out of high school, and looking for a job, which may turn out to be true.

Mona drops on the couch near Sonny's friend from the train. He waves to her as if she's known him awhile. Actually, everyone waves or nods in a friendly, mellow but indifferent way. The train mate gives Sonny a joint, which he inhales twice and hands to her. She takes two hits before Sonny passes it to one of the dancing men. She's smoked dope with Mirabelle, but this stuff tastes different. It's already making her head spacey.

"What's in the joint?" she asks, as matter-of-factly as she can.

"Good, isn't it? It's fairy dust, a mixture of pure Moroccan hash with grass. It's not easy to find, believe me. Mind if I do a line?"

"Do a line?" she repeats, and feels like a jerk.

"Maybe you want to do one too?"

"No, I'm good."

He takes a baggie out of his pocket, lays a line on the bar counter, holds one nostril, and snorts it. She knows what it is, cocaine. She wasn't born yesterday.

Mona glides over and hands her what's left of the joint. She inhales deeply, tells herself she can use some relaxation after this day. The hits wipe away anxiety she didn't know she had. She refuses to worry anymore. Sonny won't let her come to harm.

He tugs her gently onto the dance floor, his liquid eyes steady on her, the African drums thumping. She finds herself gyrating slowly toward him, smiling widely.

19.

Dory takes the elevator to in the hospital's sub-basement and gives her name to the receptionist of the nuclear/ radiology department, who couldn't care less that it's taken her all these months to make an appointment. She's hopeful, though. Sometimes viruses last ridiculously long. At work, a strain of stomach flu puts some of her charges out of commission for weeks, then just when they seemed well they were suddenly back on the potty. It isn't exactly the runs that sent her here, though, but the nausea and the stabbing headaches she can just about dim with aspirin.

In the waiting room are comfy leather chairs, an oak coffee table with neatly arranged magazines, a water cooler, hot water for tea, even a coffee-urn for godsakes. The room couldn't have been pleasanter. But given her mood she would've preferred a dark space without frills.

She's told no one about this morning's MRI, doesn't want anyone praying or fretting her outcome. Some journeys must be taken alone, and this is one of them, though neither Stu nor Lena would agree. Alone provides opportunity to treat event and outcome on her terms without seeing either reflected in the eyes of others. She's susceptible, she is, to what people believe or fear, and above all doesn't want to be treated in that sweet syrupy way that brings death to mind. It's what she does at work, chooses cheery phrases for people who know this is the last place they'll ever inhabit.

A young woman with a stunned expression sits nearby, her fingers raking obsessively through her long hair. No more than twenty, with large gray eyes fastened on some vision beyond anyone's grasp. Her presence feels sad, hopeless, but Dory refuses to take it as an omen. She considers saying something to distract her, but a technician arrives and leads the woman out.

As she picks up a magazine, which is what people do in places like this to avoid speculating, the breakfast at Lena's comes to mind. The tension around the table was palpable. Of course Zack's plan is ridiculous. Even if he recruits ten men plus Stu, who's suddenly gung-ho to participate, they'll end up staring down the cops, no more, no less. They're not about to get violent; cop cars won't burn. So how exactly does Zack expect to stop the foreclosure? Questions Lena should have voiced instead of acting as if she were having an out-of-body experience. When she said as much to Stu in bed that night, he mumbled something about letting them go through the motions, then held the pillow close to his chest in his I'm-ready-to sleep, don't-bother-me position. The things wives learn about their husbands.

Before she can flip more than a few pages, her name is called. She follows the technician's white-clad back to a tiny, cave-like room, where a machine that brings to her mind pictures of an ancient iron lung sits, ready to televise slices of her brain. Above it, on an adjacent wall, is a small glass enclosure where the radiologist watches the procedure. The technician warns her that the MRI makes a lot of noise. She hands her two waxy earplugs, and a ball to squeeze if it gets too much for her.

She has no intention of squeezing that ball. When did she ever cry uncle? She stuffs the plugs in her ears, climbs in the tunnel, and, as the rattling and banging begins, like her old radiator trying to send up heat, suddenly decides she's claustrophobic.

Okay, best not to focus on the narrow space or noise, better to go over her mental checklist, the one she's added to and subtracted from since the initial episode. As of this morning she still enjoys eating and drinking. There's been no drop in her energy, no trouble sleeping, and she'd enjoy sex if Stu ever offered. She knows that her cardio and respiratory systems are good to go. So the test will most likely be negative, though she knows better than to count on it. Because MRIs, CAT scans, and the like find abnormalities that may never affect a person adversely yet once discovered are hard to ignore. Most bodies contain some congenital fuckup. This she believes. Before machines provided 3-D pictures of bodily spaces, people lived with their imperfections. So why is she here?

Her mind wanders to Stu, as it often does these days. Last night he went out for the newspaper. She assumed he'd stop at a bar for a few. But he was back in minutes, antsy, irritable, almost testy, making her wish he'd taken his usual detour. She's read about dry drunks. Is he really a drunk? His drinking has increased in the last year, yes, but the man wouldn't touch a drop during work. She knows it's been difficult at the plant, and that for him holding on to his job is proof not of success but of the avoidance of failure. Early in their marriage he confessed that he'd be devastated if he were fired from any job. He's been at the plant since he was a kid and worked his ass off.

"Don't move, ma'am," the voice echoes eerily inside the chamber. She doesn't think she's moved a muscle. Is she supposed to stop breathing? Is this a significant moment, the final take, the part of the brain where problems reside? Closing her eyes tight, her cold palms flat against the thin mat, she concentrates on her charge Miss Z., who never gives up hope.

20.

Driving home, the sun sparkling on the Hudson River, she considers the dumb questions she's been asked. Have you cleaned house before? Can you work with children around? Are you allergic to any detergent? What about dust? Will you work weekends? On and on, to which she replied yes, yes, no, no, I will. Never mind that the outer corridor of the agency was filled with women waiting to apply for the same work. And who's to say they didn't need a job as much or more than she did? Not that she'd give up a job to any of them. Running on empty makes her selfish in ways she never would've imagined.

Pulling up in front of her house, she takes out her cell phone and tries Dory for the third time. She answers.

"I've been calling you all day!"

"I forgot to turn it on." Dory sounds impatient, which makes her wonder. Have they changed their minds?

"We've decided to accept your generous offer to move in." She waits for some reaction but hears only breathing. "Do you still want us there?"

"Of course."

"You don't sound like your usual enthusiastic self."

"Lena, I'm at work. I got in late. Old people are wandering

around, trying to get my attention or take away the phone to talk to you."

"Okay, I get it. Zack wants to go ahead with the perimeter crap. So I have to let him do his thing and when it fails, which it will, we move in with you guys."

"Sounds like a plan."

"I won't keep you. Just want to say that I lost it, slapped Rosie's face last night for sassing me. I'll hang up now."

"You slapped Rosie?"

"I already feel terrible, don't make it worse."

"She probably deserved it."

"That feels worse."

"A drink after I finish work?"

"No. I've got to get Casey out of his room. I can't confiscate his computer. He'll hate me too much. I need one of my children to love me."

"Take him to buy something. It'll get him out, perk him up."

"Want to hear something funny?" she asks, seeing Zack through the window, pacing the living room.

"Only if it's less than three words."

"Arthur."

"Arthur?"

"I was fishing in my purse for coins and found Arthur's card. The detective we met months ago? He wrote his number on the other side. It gave me a weird jolt seeing it. I thought I'd call to ask if they hire civilian personnel at the precinct."

"Do not, I caution you, call the man with the white scarf."

"So you do remember?"

"Like an elephant." Dory clicks off.

She sits there a moment, revisiting Arthur. Could it really hurt to ask him a simple question about a job? He did flirt with her, the white scarf around her neck and all. Okay, that was dangerous, but she was drunk then. Now she's cold sober. Maybe she could do clerical work or work in the cafeteria? That precinct has no cafeteria, she'll bet on that piece of her memory. She's too old to join the civil service, isn't she? That's another question she might ask.

With the phone at his ear, Zack's asking someone called Jimmy to join the perimeter posse. Well, that's it, then. The hardhats are coming. Not waiting to hear more, she goes upstairs, but Casey's not in his room. Well, good, maybe he's out biking.

She knocks at Rosie's door. "Can I come in? I need to talk to you."

"No, you need me to forgive you."

"Yes, I do. I lost it, I'm sorry." She's speaking to the closed door, which feels ridiculous.

No response.

"We can have the conversation through the door, if you want."

Her daughter opens the door, her hair pulled back with a ribbon. She looks a bit ill. She did get in late. "Are you all right?"

"I'm fine. I forgive you. Okay? Now, please go. I'm trying to take a nap."

Then why is she dressed in jeans and T-shirt? "Rosie, you know I've never raised a hand . . ."

"I said I forgive you," and just as Rosie's about to close the door, she steps inside, noting that the bed's unmade and strewn with clothes.

"Where were you last night?"

"Out with Mirabelle."

"Where to?"

"Movie and late-night snack."

Her answers are too quick, but the last thing they need is another argument. "Listen, Dad's trying to round up his friends to stop the foreclosure. He's on the phone now."

"Am I supposed to do something?"

"Ask him how you can help. You wanted the perimeter to happen."

"Mom at my age, life changes at a startling pace. I already told you I'd rather move in with a friend. You guys should just go ahead to Dory's."

"Whoa, you cannot, I repeat, cannot live at Mirabelle's. If need be I'll phone her parents to make sure it doesn't happen."

"You would do that?"

Why is her daughter surprised? "I would do whatever it takes to keep you safe. Whatever."

"What do you mean safe? What's unsafe?"

"To be without your family."

"Oh, god, never mind. Please go. I have a stomachache. I need a nap before tonight."

"You're going out again?"

"This is my vacation, remember?"

Before she can ask where to and with whom, Rosie says, "To a summer beach party, lots of kids. Can I take my nap now?"

She's on the phone with Dory when she hears Rosie come down the stairs. "How's the stomach?" she calls from the kitchen. Rosie mumbles something she can't make out, then the screen door bangs shut. "I'll call you later," she says, then glances out the window at the summer dusk. The sky's still streaked with fading pink and silver from the sunset. She made the right decision not to curtain this window. Sometimes, early in the morning, while everyone's still asleep, she sneaks into the kitchen to watch winter's night sky lightening or summer's brightening. The silence, indoors and out, shifts her mood and often for the better. Someone once told her there was grace in getting away from oneself.

Her eyes flit to the scattering of foreclosure documents on the table, the ones she can never quite read to the end without zoning out. The print is small, the language inaccessible, and besides she can't bear to know much more than she already does about the odious process. One lackey after another, signing off on the foreclosure, and not one of them taking any responsibility for the outcome. They're like drone pilots she reads about in the paper who sit in some air-conditioned facility thousands of miles from the lands they're bombing. They don't have to view the damage or even hear the noise of it. Isn't that just like the banks? Maybe Zack's right. Why make it easy? Why accept their crap? Why not at least fight back? The anger inside her offers no answers, only the start of a headache, which sends her upstairs for an aspirin.

Rosie's door is ajar. She sees the note at once, taped to Rosie's pillow. Her limbs go soft. She sits on Rosie's bed. She knows before knowing. It's not just the slap. It's everything the girl expects and is entitled to that she can't count on anymore. Oh, Jesus, Mary, and . . . she reaches over, pulling the note free.

Mom, Dad, Casey,

I'm not running away. I'm simply going to live with a friend, someone you don't know, who is pretty wonderful and has made lots of room for me. I'm going to be fine. I will stay in touch. I do have my phone. You can call me. But I can't leave you the address because, Mom, you would be here in a nanosecond giving me grief, trying to get me home, and I truly don't want to deal with that. I'm not a baby. I will be in a safe situation. Just trust me, I beg you. Leaving home isn't impulsive even if it seems that way to you. I think it's for the best. Dad, I hope your perimeter works, but it probably won't. So the move to Dory's seems set. Casey, the room at Dory's is yours.

Rosie.

Fear and sadness collide inside her, along with a sliver of envy. Her daughter's getting away.

21.

Zack hikes down to the basement with Rosie's note. He's read it, and the contents leave him unsurprised. Rosie knows what she's doing and wants to be trusted. So be it. He chooses not to worry about her, though Lena wants him to be concerned about everything, as if tormenting himself would somehow help or make a difference. His mother did that, even worried about whether she'd find what she wanted at the store. She was constantly planning for disaster. It was tiring just knowing her. Lena's a bit like her but much prettier.

He puts Rosie's note in his pocket, pushes yesterday's newspaper off the cot, and lies down. Lately, he comes here a lot. The room is cozy, quiet. A cocoon is what it is. Being under the house allows him to be outside of everything, which is good. Unlike Lena, who wants to be in the center of it all, he prefers the vacant edges.

He stares at the perfectly plastered white ceiling, his work, and it still looks brand-new. What'll happen to it if his house is sold? Will the new people rip it out? Redo the paint job? Change everything? Well, none of that's going to happen because he's counting on stopping the foreclosure. Stu will participate, so will Jimmy and Jimmy's brother. He couldn't get any of the others to commit, but that's okay. The few who are coming will do the job. When the cops arrive, he wonders, will the scene become violent? The last time he was involved in a fight he was eighteen. Some worker on a construction site kept riding him—you need glasses, that beam's not straight, are you a moron? Pay attention. It was his first high-up job; what did the man expect? He was using a hand drill the guy tried to take away without saying please. It was the final insult. He let the man have it on the nose, which cost him the job. That was many moons ago, and no doubt left him with a reputation he doesn't deserve. At the union hall, which he hates going to, some of the big shots treat him like he's a novice, a peon. It's humiliating. Lena tells him to speak up, but she doesn't have to work with them on a thin beam a million miles high. In fact, what she doesn't know about his work sites would shock her. But he doesn't have a site now, and just when he needs her body to refresh him, when he needs the ecstasy of abandonment, she isn't having or giving any of it. He ends up jerking off. The lack of a little warmth is not healthy for any living thing. As a kid there was never enough heat in the apartment. His mom wore gloves to sweep the floor if she got around to it after her two jobs. His dad, who was brought up in New Hampshire, wouldn't buy a heater, told him to outgrow his baby skin. Then again, his dad was a Teamster, used to working on the docks until a hand injury put him on disability. As a teen, the few times he went to work with his dad he suffered mightily. His job might've been to tag some crates. Maybe he did it wrong or they didn't explain it right, but the men wouldn't stop harassing him. Hey Zack, didn't your father teach you anything? Didn't he show you right from left? No Wheaties this morning? And sure, they were teasing him, but he doesn't tease well.

22.

With phone in hand Rosie ambles out to the back porch. God, you'd think the heat would let up. Having packed only what fit in her black tote bag and backpack, she laments the clothing left in the closet. Her mother keeps phoning, the last message too dramatic to believe.

Sonny keeps phoning, too, but she looks forward to that. Their first date still a wonderful memory. Leaving the party, she marveled at her sense of serenity, drug-induced, maybe, but like a good dream she didn't want to wake from. Whatever was in those joints did more than lift her spirits. It dissolved the pain of indecision, left her hopeful. Let the great world go on with me in it, she remembers thinking. What's wrong with that? They made out in his car for a while. It was sweet. He didn't grope her or paw her. Gentle kisses and strokes, his warm hand inside her bra, then her nipple in his mouth, all of it so natural. But they didn't go all the way, too wasted. No matter. Sonny will take her from chaste to bliss any day now. She's open, waiting, and curious.

So many plants dangle from the porch rafters that she has to duck and weave her way to the cranberry vodka drink on the small glass table. Mirabelle insists she try it, though she prefers orange juice with her vodka, same as Sonny.

He's driven up to see her twice since she arrived here. They hung out in the guest room, smoking and fooling around, but he didn't stay the night. She can't lose her virginity with Mirabelle on the other side of the wall. Besides, they get a bit blitzed on that Moroccan stuff Sonny calls fairy dust, which lifts her into a zone of all things doable. Their plan is taking shape, though. When Mirabelle's parents return from vacation, she'll move into Sonny's pad, which he calls his den. Once upon a time it was what she wanted to do with Siri. How quickly Sonny's displaced him in her affections, but that's what moving forward is all about, of that she's sure.

She stretches out on a chaise, next to her friend on an identical chaise. The padded cushion welcomes her tight muscles and has her longing for some fairy dust to soften all things. "It tastes pretty good," she admits, holding up the cool glass. In swimsuit bra and shorts, she hopes for a breeze to relieve the heat of the sun, which visits the porch for an hour or so each afternoon. It's easier to tan here than on nearby Orchard Beach, though there a dip in the water would be possible.

"Was that your mother again?"

"She's having two heart attacks." Rosie gazes at the grassy incline that leads down to some scruffy woods behind the house.

"Call her back. It might stop her from pestering you." Barefoot in a one-piece shiny black bathing suit, Mirabelle sips at her drink.

"If I give her even a tiny signal, she'll be all over me. I can't deal with her while Sonny and I are figuring out next steps."

Mirabelle says nothing. Her silence noted.

"Don't you care about what I do next?" Rosie finally asks.

"I'm keeping my thoughts to myself for the sake of our friendship," Mirabelle says with authority.

"Oh really?" she replies sarcastically, but in truth she needs her friend's support.

"Yes, really."

"Knowing you, I'm sure you'll find a way to say what's on your mind sooner or later, so spill it now."

"Sonny's too old for you. He's handsome. I'll give you that, but his assets are less than zero. He's not the one to help you make decisions about the future."

"And you are?"

"I didn't say that. But if you stay here, you can finish school and live your normal life. Move to Sonny's hovel, no more school . . . well . . . you'll become one of those."

Mirabelle's tone of disdain pisses her off. "One of those?"

"A high school dropout with a job in some sleazy joint."

"You're such a snob. You think you're better than a waitress?"

"I didn't say I was better, but she's not as happy as I'll probably be with an education and a career."

"You sound like my mother."

"So what?"

Mirabelle's defiance ticks her off even more. "So what? My mother gets nothing out of living. Not me. I'm going to see, feel, take, give, know, love, experiment, experience, and it starts now, this minute, not after I graduate from some stupid school that teaches me nothing I can't find in a book or online." The words rush out on a breath.

"You're upset because what I said is true."

"You've got Sonny wrong. He's a loving, reliable guy who's been around the block a few times. I can lean on him. Yes, he's older, but so what? Where's it written that I have to be with some teenage asshole?" She suddenly realizes she's close to tears.

"I knew you wouldn't agree," Mirabelle says sadly.

"At the very least you as a friend should back me up."
"I will, Rosie, you're my best best, but I'm scared for you."
"I'm scared, too. But I'll make my way, you'll see."

23.

Out the living room window, fish-gray skies threaten rain. A thick humid haze hangs over everything like a curse. The men seem bored. Can she blame them? It's past five and no sign of the cops, a marshal, or sheriff all day. Zack was able to round up only two guys, plus Stu, who brought a friend. If the five of them stand arms-width apart, he believes the line will reach across the front of the house. Whatever.

Stu, barefoot, in dark jeans, white polo shirt, is stretched out on the lawn, Zack beside him. She recognizes one of the men from Zack's last site, must be Jimmy. She remembers his too tight handshake when introduced, and that eyebrows-up expression of his. What did he expect Zack's wife to be, a frowsy dame? Jimmy brought his brother, recently returned from Iraq, Zack told her. Hasn't she heard stories of vets who need to keep their guns on them? Her eyes search his skinny jeans for any bulge. And who's the guy Stu brought? He doesn't look much older than Casey, and doesn't seem to talk, but keeps drinking and smoking. Lord knows what he's smoking. These guys could just as easily mess up a place as protect it. Unless the uniforms show soon, they'll just continue drinking and getting raucous in that crazy, letting-off-steam kind of way.

Already Zack is trying to turn the wait into a party. He's

ratcheted up the music way too loud, the sounds reaching the neighbors, who must be riveted by the show. But who cares? The place, the house, it's not hers anymore, not after today. She turns away from the window.

Maybe she'll try Rosie's phone again. She's left desperate messages every day for the past week. Even promised in one they wouldn't move to Dory's. Outright lie. Whenever she reaches Mirabelle, the girl swears she doesn't know where Rosie is, clearly a lie, too.

Out back she finds Casey, staring at the hot dogs sizzling on the grill like he might miss one that's done.

"Want me to finish what's left and you go upstairs?"

"No."

"Are you worried about what might happen in the next hours?"

"I know what's going to happen." He's turning each frank with a long, pronged fork.

"What?"

"It gets darker, cooler, the cops show up, and Dad's friends curse at them. Nothing else will happen."

"What do you want to happen?"

"I want dad's friends to beat anyone who takes anything out of anywhere in the house to a pulp."

The virulence of his words stuns her. "Casey, that's not a good wish."

"People do all kinds of things to keep their houses."

"Like what?"

"No, Mom, you won't like it. Here, this batch of franks is done." He begins forking them onto a plate.

"Tell me what people do," she says, the plate in her hands, but not ready to leave Casey, who sounds too purposeful for anyone's good.

"Mom, the franks are getting cold."

"I don't care, Casey. Tell me what you're thinking."

"I don't know. Stop asking." For a moment they gaze at each other, then he begins opening another package of franks.

She carries the platter out front, her son's words heavy inside her. The men sound more gleeful by the minute. Three yellow hard hats lie on the lawn like forgotten toys.

"Thanks, angel," Zack says, as she places the platter on the outdoor card table.

"Isn't the music a bit loud?"

"The more noise the better."

"I doubt it," she says as much to herself as him.

He shrugs and gives her his no-offense-meant grin. She'd love him to struggle for his point of view, *convince* her, but he won't. It's who he is, as Dory told her so long ago, a guy who looks for the good and won't let the bad spoil what he finds. Isn't that what attracted her? That and his laid-back disposition, his don't-worry-our-love-will-see-us-through personality? She reminds herself he was also affectionate, funny, and endeared himself to her daily. Why is that so painful to remember?

"I'll be inside. Let me know if you need anything more."

"I will . . . in bed tonight," Zack whispers.

"Sounds like a threat," she quips with a forced smile.

When the first drops of rain hit the lawn, she goes back out to help Casey bring in the food, but he's gone. She takes whatever she can carry inside. The men have already relocated to her living room.

"Has anyone seen Casey?"

They look at her dumbly.

"Zack?" He shakes his head.

She goes upstairs, checks Casey's room, the bathroom, Rosie's room, even the attic, though that makes no sense. No Casey. She tugs Zack's arm. "He's gone. Where?"

"Probably Robbie's house. He doesn't like all the commotion."

"Casey tells me when and where he's going." His last words replaying in her head, she rushes out. She should've grabbed an umbrella but won't turn back.

Stu's car inches up beside her, the window rolled down. "Get in, we'll drive there." She does.

"His friend lives about a half-mile or so down this road. Let's try there. It's not like him, Stu. He's really upset. He mumbled stuff about what people do in foreclosures."

"Lena, he's a sensible kid, always has been. He's not about to change in an hour."

Stu squeezes her arm quickly, reassuringly. The sympathy nearly levels her. It's Zack who should be here, driving, searching for their son. But, somehow, she's glad it's Stu for whom action is as easy as words.

Sudden darkness falls ahead of sheets of rain. The sound of a million pebbles hitting the car. The frantic windshield wipers, unable to clear the pooling water fast enough, blurring the road ahead. Eerie streaks of lightning illuminate the sky. "There," she points, "his friend's house." A cottage-like place, dark and shuttered, but there should be people inside. She opens the passenger door.

"Are you sure you should go out in this . . ."

"I need to know if he's there." In the few seconds it takes to reach the door, she's drenched. Not seeing a bell, she bangs on the glass panel. Nothing. She peers inside. A curtain obscures her view. She runs around to the back, her wet feet sliding inside her sandals, her blouse plastered to her skin. A rust-stained porcelain sink leans against the house. If she didn't know better, she'd think no one lived here. She doesn't see any bikes around. Soaked, chilled, frightened, she dashes to the car. "I need to check if Casey took his bike."

Without a word, bless him, Stu begins driving back. Unremitting rain and deafening thunder keep them staring silently into the watery darkness. A sheriff's van followed by several cop cars are lined up in front of the house, red and blue lights flashing. At the front door, Casey, sopping wet, a plastic bag beneath his arm, jumps off his bike.

PART THREE

24.

Dory gazes out the window, her vision unusually sharp. Houses, trees, even bushes appear ridiculously bright, like the time she tried amphetamine and the colors became so vivid she had to put on sunglasses. Too bad she couldn't record the doctor's phone conversation. She's usually astute at capturing details, but today everything he said, except "benign brain tumor," floated away on the turbulent ocean filling her ears. She tried, she really did, to let his words sink in, but her mind gave way, and all she could focus on were the bags of food waiting on the kitchen counter for the welcome dinner planned for tonight. "Dory," the doctor had to say at one point to get her attention. "Do you have questions for me?" Framing even one felt beyond her. She said she'd phone him tomorrow, but she won't, will she? She's witnessed too many people who walk into hospitals on their own two feet and leave in wheelchairs, with a sack of medicines in their lap, their former selves gone. Not the route she intends to follow. Having her head shaved, being cut open then sewn together? It's like cutting into a melon and trying to close it again without losing some seeds. She feels fine. A few headaches, a bit of nausea, she'll deal. Her decision is simple. Live her life with Stu, enjoy the company of her best friend's family. Have weekend bang-up parties and sleep late the next morning. It's what Stu's been talking about and what she'll make happen.

Any minute now Lena and entourage will arrive with the rest of their stuff, the last trip of the day. Nothing like the crisis of a friend to pull you out of yourself. She walks slowly to the kitchen. A glass of wine is what she's after. But instead of pouring one she puts away the food, then heads back to the window, lingering there until scudding clouds obliterate the sun and Zack's and Stu's cars pull up in front.

25.

L ena carries in the last thing, a framed photo of Rosie and
Casey, sets it next to the bed in Dory's guest room, rearranged now to create space for her rocking chair and two small
tables with lamps. The emptiness inside her welcomes the
clutter. She left a voicemail for Rosie to let her know they're
at Dory's, then added that if she didn't hear from her soon,
she'd report her missing. That she was underage and could be
made to come home. She couldn't help herself. The moment
she wakes in the morning the painful ache of Rosie's absence
begins. It makes her more nervous about Casey, who pleaded
to move into Dory's semi-furnished basement. Fine with everyone. She tried to pry out why he'd been biking in that downpour. He wouldn't say squat, only that the rain didn't matter.
Too spooky by far, but there was no time to pursue it. They had
only hours to pack, move furniture into two rented U-Hauls,
then unpack at the storage space Stu's friend gave them. All day
Stu has been exceptionally helpful. She's grateful, squeezed his
arm as he'd squeezed hers in the car the day before, surprising
them both.

Throughout the move no one mentioned yesterday's perimeter fiasco. It was she who rushed to open the front door.
The sheriff, a husky, middle-aged man, looked warily at the

guys sprawled on the couch and chairs, slack mouths on faces stunned by drink, and decided there wasn't any opposition here. Thankfully, the hard-hat posse seemed to agree with that assessment and watched silently as she begged the sheriff to give them twenty-four hours to move their stuff. Maybe it was the desperation in her voice or her sopping clothes, or maybe it was relief at not having to lug furniture out onto the lawn in the teeming rain, but he nodded, said they had till midnight today. Then, one by one, the cars drove off.

"That's it," Zack says, breathing heavily, depositing two large suitcases of clothing near the dresser. His tank top is frayed at the hem and gray from sweat, his mop of curly hair longer than usual. He's hardly spoken all day. She feels a surge of sympathy for his disappointment.

"Zack, honey, we'll find work."

"Lena, we really will find work."

"Don't mock me."

"Your words are more important than mine, so I'm stealing them." That eerie grin.

"What's gotten into you?"

"You mean, who am I? That's the big question."

"God, no. You're depressed. Maybe you need some meds."

"Bring them on. Getting high seems like the perfect solution."

"I'm not talking high, I'm talking motivation.."

"I moved furniture. I carried baggage. Isn't that motivation enough? You want me to whistle a tune as well?"

She ignores this because it sounds too crazy. "Maybe an antidepressant would help you be more optimistic about getting work."

He stares at her, his expression suddenly serious. She braces herself.

"Lena, I like the way I'm feeling because I don't give a shit about anything. It's a pleasurable state of mind. I recommend it. And why won't you let me fuck you?"

She stares at him. "I can't believe that's what's on your mind."

"Believe it," he says cheerfully, his eyes steady on her.

"You know what, you've already fucked me plenty. It's why we're in this mess, or have you forgotten?"

He shuts the bedroom door as he leaves.

Lord, what's happening to them? They used to be in sync about so much: plans, visions, dreams that Zack insisted were doable. His optimism helped her get past the negative tapes that played in her head. His constant devotion and admiration made her trust him more than any man she ever knew. Making love was the culmination of their stirred energies.

Outside, Dory's patio, adorned with colorful chairs, awaits a happy family.

26.

She finds Dory in the kitchen and peers over her friend's shoulder. "Smells good. What is it?"

"Broccoli a la Dory with melted cheese and surprises."

"You've been quiet," she says. Actually, more than quiet. She's been missing in action. She hasn't even taken a look at the rearranged guest room.

"A lot in my head."

"Care to . . ."

"Let's focus on food, happy talk, and drink, and make it a celebration of your arrival."

"Okay. Listen, can you get antidepressants for Zack? He won't go to a doctor, I'm sure. He says he feels great, doesn't care about anything, and isn't eager to look for work."

Dory stops stirring, lowers the flame, and turns to her. "Maybe you should let him be. He needs time to adjust."

"Is that your professional opinion?"

"No, my experienced opinion." Dory spoons the steaming broccoli into a bowl, which Lena takes to the table, already set, then she returns for the platter of cinnamon- and clove-spiced ham.

Dory carries in the salad bowl as Stu and Zack come to the table, beer bottles in hand.

"Casey," Lena calls, going to the basement door. "Casey, dinner's ready." She goes down the steps. "Casey?" Gone, again?

"Zack, Casey's not here."

"Oh, right, he told me to let you know he wanted to skip dinner, bike over to his friend's for a while. I said okay."

"This is our first night here. We should be together."

"Well, the kid needs his friend."

"Hey, Lena, Dory," Stu interrupts. "What'll it be? Red or white wine?" He places a bottle of each on the table.

"White," she says, her mind still on Casey. So he went to see his friend; why not? He's double-digit, preteen. She can't treat him like a baby. Does she? Stu fills her glass and she promptly drains it. He refills it and she takes another long drink, the cold liquid sliding smoothly down her throat.

"Great," Stu says, sensing a party. "A toast to our dearest friends. We're glad you're here."

Dory begins passing platters of food. Zack takes one thin slice of ham and a few lettuce leaves, not like him at all. She's about to say so when the phone rings. Stu reaches back to pick up the cordless that rests on the teak sideboard. "Hello. What? Yes, that's right . . . They're here. What? Yes, okay, I'll put his mother on. Lena, it's the police. Casey's been arrested."

In the seconds it takes to place the phone at her ear, she freezes to cold calm. A brusque-voiced man gives his name, announces the precinct's location, and suggests she come in. "What happened to my son? Is my son all right?" She can barely get the words past her throat.

"Yeah. You'll hear what you need to know when you get here." He clicks off.

"It's the precinct near our house," she whispers hoarsely.

Zack stares at her, stunned.

"Lena, forget dinner, I'll go with you," Dory says, already up from her chair.

"No, babe," Stu says getting to his feet. "I'm dressed and you're not. I'll take Lena. She shouldn't be driving. Call you as soon as we have information. It's probably a stupid violation of some sort. Cops arrest kids for looking at them cross-eyed, right? It's how they make their points. Remember? We're not novices here."

Once more she finds herself in Stu's car, and once more the thought that it should be Zack visits her brain, but she refuses to care. Not now. The early evening sky bulges, white and heavy with humidity. The A/C, on high, blows icy air at her face. She could lower it, but really it doesn't matter. Houses, streets pass in a blur. The painted yellow centerline appears to thin with the car's momentum. Her eyes flick to the speedometer. Over seventy. She wants to go faster, wants to fly there. Her family is falling apart.

"What could Casey have done?" she murmurs.

"He could've been in the wrong bike lane, could've sassed a cop. If they're keeping him in the precinct it isn't murder or mayhem."

"What could he have done?" she hears herself whisper again.

"I don't know, Lena, but we'll find out." Stu's voice is soft, his tone gentle. She's grateful.

They pull up in front of the precinct, green light globes mounted above the doorway. It's a single-floor square box with aluminum siding and blue trim that sits on a small lawn. Several policemen stand chatting near parked cop cars. She has a flash memory of the dirty brick-fronted precinct near where she grew up, with its echo of doom. Not a helpful vision, but her overcharged brain is heading wherever it wants.

With Stu close behind, she hurries through the open front door into a cloud of heat. No air conditioning. Just two whirring floor fans beneath two small barred windows. The silence is creepy. A dismal pea-green room that even the fluorescent lights can't brighten. Three people sit quietly on a pew-like bench, their expressions placid, even disappointed, she'd say. Are they waiting to take someone home? The jail and its holding pens must be behind the long back wall with closed wooden doors at each end. No doubt where they've put her son.

A uniformed policewoman reading the *Daily News* sits behind a large metal desk. Thin, middle-aged, with a sharp jaw and slightly yellow pallor to her olive skin, she doesn't look thrilled to be interrupted. "What is it?"

Lena tells her they were summoned and gives Casey's name and age, trying to sound calm, though the icy fear in her gut is hard to ignore.

"Are you his mother?"

"Yes." She leans forward suddenly feeling unfit in her jeans and flip-flops.

The woman eyes her. "Have you been drinking?"

"We got the call during dinner," Stu interrupts, as if that makes it okay.

"Tell me what my son did," she pleads.

"Why was he out alone?" The question whips her.

"He went to visit a friend. Please, I beg you, tell me what he did."

The woman studies her, then rifles through some papers. "He was spraying black paint on a house when a neighbor called the police."

"I can explain," she begins.

"It's a crime to deface property. And where were you? Out? At dinner?" The sarcasm is unmistakable, but she knows better than to respond. One accusatory word or gesture from her and this woman will close up shop, and then god knows when she'll see Casey.

"Listen," Stu begins, and she panics because his voice is impatient and determined. "That house was where the boy lived. It was just foreclosed. He's really upset."

"It's not your property anymore. I suggest you get a lawyer."

"A lawyer?" she repeats. "He's a boy. He's never done anything illegal. We'll pay for the damage. Please let him go." She can feel her calm breaking up.

"Too late, damage done." This woman is enjoying her fucking miniscule bit of power. She fights the urge to grab her bony shoulders and squeeze. Instead she searches the room frantically, as if help lurks in some corner, then notes the computer on the desk. "I have a friend who's a Bronx detective. Can I reach him?"

"Suit yourself." The woman shrugs.

"I mean, please, can you Face Time or Skype him, at the 49th Precinct?" She searches madly through her purse for Arthur's card, praying she finds it, praying he'll be there, praying he'll remember her, unable to believe what she's praying for and unable to stop.

"Who is he?" Stu whispers.

She doesn't respond, hands the card to the woman. "Please. I'd so appreciate your help." She knows she's fawning now but she needs this woman to take pity on her.

"Stand there." The woman orders them to the side of the desk.

"Who is he?" Stu insists.

"Someone I met at work," she lies.

"Why would he help you?"

"Stu, stop with the questions. Just pray he remembers me and will put in a good word," she whispers.

In a few minutes, the policewoman turns the computer around to face her. Arthur's at his desk, his tie pulled down below an open collar, shirtsleeves rolled up, hair as shiny black as she remembers.

"Arthur, hi. It's me, Lena? It's been months, I know. Listen, my son, he's only a boy, is in a bit of a jam. Can you vouch for me so they'll let me take him home?"

"Is that your husband?"

"No, a good friend."

"Stella, what did the boy do?" Arthur asks the policewoman.

"Spray-painted a foreclosed house. It used to be his, so they say."

"Okay, set up a date for arraignment, and cut him loose."

"If you say so."

"Arthur, I can't thank you enough."

"Let me know what happens, Lena. Call me. Soon."

"I will. I will," she promises, grateful to the core, as he disappears from the screen.

"Have a seat till I arrange a court date. Then he'll be brought out."

The hands on the wall clock move ever so slowly. It's been more than two hours. Stu keeps up a steady stream of chitchat, but she can't concentrate on his words. Casey has to be hungry and thirsty. How scared he must be. A cascade of TV programs runs through her mind: prisoners roughed up, thrown against walls. If he has even one bruise . .

She must've said that aloud because Stu turns to her. "Lena, he's a kid who wouldn't resist arrest. There won't be any bruises."

An emaciated-looking young man is escorted out of the doors and leaves with the people on the bench. How long had they been waiting? She doesn't even want to know. An hour ago, hoping to prod the woman at the desk, she asked if there was any new information. The woman shook her head and then muttered, "Most kids spend a night in jail, not the worst thing."

The precinct doors remain open, but the night air isn't cool enough to affect the temperature inside. Outside, the green globes shine a narrow path through the falling darkness. She calls Rosie, leaves a message. Stu brings back two bottles of water from a vending machine.

"Thanks for keeping me company in the fun house," she says.

"Hey, remember, we always did like amusement parks."

"You and Zack did, the two of you rode that monster roller coaster. Just looking at it made me nauseous."

"Want the truth after all these years? I hated it. It was a macho thing. Because you and Dory were scared I had to be brave. But, then, I was only seventeen. I don't do that anymore."

"Don't do what?"

"Pretend to be what I'm not, keep my true feelings in my shoes."

"That's a good thing? Right?"

"A necessary development or a crazy revelation."

"That . . ?"

"Life isn't forever and where did yesterday go?"

"Revelation is good, isn't it?" Suddenly she's not sure what they're talking about.

"Don't know." He takes a long pull of the water.

27.

She has no intention of going to the precinct. Her mother's using Casey's arrest to lure her back. What the hell was Casey thinking? But she knows. Black paint on the house, a daring statement, a refusal to accept their shit quietly. Brave but stupid.

"Why don't you call her back?" Sonny asks.

"What's it to you whether I deal with my mom?"

"Nothing. I could say fuck'em and upset you, correct?"

She studies his face, which is so close she can't properly see his features except for his eyes, which he widens mockingly. She laughs. "I guess. But if I set foot in Dory's house, my mother will lock me in a room." They're lying across the full-size bed in Mirabelle's guest room, the bittersweet scent of fairy dust unmistakable.

"My Rosy-Posy, no one keeps you from me. You watch and see."

"Yeah, what would you do?" she teases, her voice a bit slurry, but so what.

"I'd charge into what's-her-name's house, break the chains, steal you back. Anyone tries to stop me, trouble would rain down hard."

"That sounds about right."

It's dark outside. She listens for Mirabelle, who will be back from the movies anytime now. Yesterday afternoon, with Mirabelle away at the beach, it happened. Not too much blood, not much pleasure either. Sonny was sweet, whispering that she was brave, beautiful, how joyous to be her man. Between kisses he kept up a stream of encouragement, almost there, almost done, tomorrow will be pure gold. She expected the first time to be a throwaway. At least the fairy dust somewhat mitigated the pain. She's still a little sore, which is okay. It reminds her of the achievement. Every woman has to get this done, the sooner the better.

"Listen, pretty, we need to put our plan into action, yes?"

"I also need to find some work."

"No problem. My friend has an uncle who owns a large bodega. He'll hire you to do something. It's how friends help each other, see?"

"That's one problem dealt with."

"And the others, honey girl?"

"I haven't quite figured them out yet."

She's never been to his Bronx apartment, near Jackson Avenue, not far from her school. At some point she'll officially quit school. Her parents will be pissed, but so what? Their job was to take care of her and Casey. She's not blaming them exactly. She knows things happen. But they were totally unprepared. If they'd planned smarter they would've rented instead of buying a house, or else stayed in the old apartment. Eventually, Dory will tire of the family crowding her space. Anyone would. Then what, a shelter?

Sonny uses his pinky to mix together the green weed and brown powder, then seals another joint in a flimsy white slip of paper. He offers it to her and she takes a long pull, the initial taste of the first joint hours before a faint memory. How many have they smoked? Doesn't matter. Time slips away, leaving her happily rooted in the moment.

"First we invite my friends up to meet my Rosy-Posy. Then we go downtown to party."

She looks at the perfect ceiling, no lines or cracks, as white as new snow.

He leans over, kisses her nose, then falls back beside her. "You watching a TV show up there," he teases.

"It's Snow White TV." She giggles.

"You're too old for that make-believe."

"What do you mean?" she asks, because she likes lying here, issuing words without caring about them.

"You have to grow up fast, my pretty. Especially where we're going to live."

"Okay," she agrees.

"Rosie, it's me." Mirabelle knocks on the door and steps inside. "Your mother called my phone, said to tell you they're leaving the precinct with Casey. I said I'd tell her if you contacted me."

Rosie shrugs. One thing about her mother, she doesn't give up.

Mirabelle, in shorts and a tank top, bounces down on the bed. "I heard Sonny leave. It's amazing that junk heap even runs. What did he do to the muffler?"

"Mirabelle, if it wasn't his car, you'd find something else to criticize, his shirt, shoes, hairstyle. Something."

"It's only ten. Do you want to go to the mall and have some pizza?"

"Yeah, perfect. I'm starving. Lately, I'm always hungry."

"Dope will do that."

"You think it's the weed?"

"How much are you smoking?"

"I don't know, a few joints in an afternoon."

"How can he afford the stuff? Does your hero work?"

"Yeah. He puts in hours in some garage and helps out his uncles who are builders."

"Exciting life."

"He has plans for his future."

"I would hope so."

"Mirabelle, please, don't make fun of my boyfriend, at least not to me."

"You'd rather I say these things to others?"

"You know what I mean. Anyway, yeah, let's eat." The fairy dust's edge is dissipating. She recognizes the symptoms—hunger, heavy limbs, sometimes a headache. Food helps.

28.

Dory flips through the pages of a magazine without stopping to read. Zack's silence is making her edgy. They're both on the couch. He's staring at the TV news, the volume so low it might as well be muted. "They've been at the precinct for hours," she says.

No response.

"Why do you think Casey painted the house black?"

"He wanted to do something that mattered," Zack whispers, as if talking to himself.

The garage door clatters open. Thank heavens. She clicks off the TV, places a new bottle of Chablis and clean glasses on the table.

Walking between Stu and Lena, Casey wears an expression of pure misery, his eyes half-closed, his lips trembling. He heads for the basement.

Lena looks weary enough to sleep on her feet.

"No you don't," Lena grabs his arm. "We need to talk."

"Tomorrow," Casey mumbles.

"Not on your life. Right now." Lena marches him to the table and sits him down, then seats herself across from him, Zack next to her.

"Listen, maybe Stu and I . . ."

"No, stay," Lena orders.

She and Stu join them at the table.

"Casey, what was in your head?" Lena demands in a stern voice.

The boy looks overwhelmed. Lena should take it down a decibel.

"I'm waiting, and I'm not going to stop waiting till you tell me what I need to know."

"If the house was painted black it would take a long time to clean off and they wouldn't be able to sell it," Casey's voice so whispery they all lean forward.

"But, then they would sell it . . . after they cleaned it. So?"

"Dad once said if there were a fire and the house was destroyed, we'd be able to collect insurance . . ."

"It's too late for that," Zack says.

Casey doesn't look at any of them.

Lena reaches across to take his hand. "So you were hoping to delay the sale in order to burn down the house?"

"I don't know. Are you going to hit me?"

"Oh god, no! Jesus Christ Almighty, Casey?" Lena's tone almost a cry.

"Let him go to bed," Zack says.

"Not yet." Lena holds onto Casey's hand. "Even if the house were to burn down, we are no longer the owners. Understand? We would not be able to collect the insurance. Understand? You would be an arsonist and go to jail for a very long time. Understand?" Lena lets go of his hand and collapses into the chair. "Casey, please look at me and tell me you get it."

"I get it. Now can I go to bed?"

"Let him go, Lena," Dory steps in.

"Just one more thing," Lena says. "Do you swear on your family that you will never do anything like this again?"

"Yes."

Casey then walks slowly to the basement stairs, gently shutting the door behind him.

Lena pours Chablis in a glass and downs it in more or less one gulp.

"I'm going to bed, too," Zack says.

"No, please, Zack, we need to deal with this together."

"But not right now," he announces, and heads for the bedroom.

"Maybe Zack's right," Dory suggests. "Let's call it a night."

"I need to decompress. You go to bed. We'll talk tomorrow."

She kisses Lena's cheek and whispers, "Truly, it's not the end of the world."

"That's such a cliché," Lena responds, which makes her smile for the first time in hours.

Stu pours his third glass of wine. He plans to sip it slowly. He'll empty the dishwasher, put away the dinner dishes, be active, though the couch is where he wants to be, where he shouldn't be, where Lena is sitting. Alone with her he wants no slippery words, though he has no idea what he even means by that. Is he drunk already?

"Need any help?" she calls.

"Hey, I'm capable. How about another drink?"

"Yes, please."

He pours wine into her glass, then sits in the chair beside her, near enough to touch. He eyes his full glass, the third, the one he deliberately left on the table, except without it he's as nervous as a teen on his first job interview.

"Rosie, now Casey. What's happening?"

He can sense her weariness, even so, her lovely arms, that neck . . . not allowed there, man, focus. The woman is appealing to him. Give her words.

"Casey's feeling the need to grow up fast. That's not criminal. And Rosie? She's like you, smart, resourceful, knows how to take care of herself the way you did. Not many could've lived the hand you were dealt and turned out so great."

"That's sweet." She says softly and smiles.

Should he smile back? Can he touch her arm?

"Listen, I know I'm offering you advice from a secure seat since both Dory and I are working. But Lena, you, me, Dory, Zack, people like us, we make our lives day by fucking day, with nothing ever secure, not even the houses we live in. Radio, TV, they drone on about the potential loss of the safety net. There never was one, not for people like us, not in times like these. But you're someone who's taken charge of her life, and nothing will stop you from continuing to do so." He didn't expect to say any of this. Thing is, it's true.

"Tell me, what do you think is going on with Zack? He's never been this detached."

"In what way?" he asks. He knows he's just buying time. Does he say Zack is going through a bad moment that will end, which is what he believes? Or does he say, Zack's lost it, never seen him this messed up. Could he live with himself saying that?

"He's so unreachable," she continues.

"I don't know, Lena. Losing a house can upend the best of us." What a chicken shit he is!

"Should I leave him be or keep pestering him? I'm at a loss."

He wants to smooth the frown line on her forehead, remove the mist of misery from her eyes. Just thinking about it stirs

161

him. "It's probably wise not to push Zack for a bit." It's the best he can do for now. He didn't expect conversations with her to be so tricky, not after all these years. "One more glass?"

"Why the hell not."

He's so relieved that he practically sprints to the table, picks up his drink. Brings back the bottle, and pours more wine into her glass.

"Thanks. This will help me relax. Mind if I take it with me to the bedroom?"

"Of course not." Don't leave, he thinks, as he watches her disappear into the hallway. Then he drains his own glass and pours another.

29.

Zack stands at the bedroom window, staring at his own re-flection. It's too dark to see anything else out there. Did he say good night to everyone? He did in his head. Lately, he finds himself saying things first in his head to check how they'll sound to others. Then he forgets to repeat them aloud. It's as if speaking them silently is enough, and he loses inter-est in going further. Not having to deal with responses feels good, even refreshing. Some things he's forbidden himself to say out loud: I will never do construction work again. No more repetitive pounding, no more drilling noises echoing through the hard hat until he wants to scream. He can't climb another fucking beam without wanting to jump off. He's scared. Terrified. And Lena won't hold him in her arms to make him feel better.

He lies down on the bed, still dressed. Why undress only to dress again in the morning? One routine expectation af-ter another controls his life and saps his strength. He's so tired of the same words repeated so many times—bathe, eat, crap, find work, do this, do that—and to what end? Nothing changes, nothing at all. Casey tried to do something about the way things work even if it was only with paint. His son didn't want to make it easy for them—whoever the fuck they are—to take away what belongs to his family. He closes his eyes and waits for the blackness.

Zack's asleep when she enters. She sits in the rocking chair, the darkness a shawl around her, and sips at the wine. As her eyes adjust, she notes that he's still dressed. Maybe Stu's right, leave him be. But what if he doesn't look for work? What then? Lord knows. Stu's words were sweet. He's been unaccountably considerate and not at all his usual combative self with her. Why's that, she wonders? His reassurance that she would get through the turmoil brought to mind the words of one of her teachers. After her mother jumped out the window, everyone—family, friends, neighbors, and strangers—expressed sympathy for her loss, but in their eyes she also saw awe, because such an act inspires awe. Only her high school teacher, Ms. O'Farrell, skipped the sympathy and said words that really mattered. She was young enough, Ms. O'Farrell told her, to get over the tragedy. It was her duty now to mother herself and to create the person she wanted to be, that it could be done, and Lena could do it. She didn't hold her hand or place an arm around her shoulders. Her tone was stern, commanding, and without noticeable compassion. And it sounded like truth.

30.

Sonny unlocks the three-latch door and leaves her inside while he goes down to park the car. The place is so tiny! It must once have been someone's walk-in closet. She faces an old couch with wide wooden arms and short stubby legs, a lopsided black director's chair, a crushed brown vinyl beanbag seat, and two small windows overlooking an alley. Along one wall, what passes for a kitchen—a two-burner stove next to a small metal sink. Where does he eat? There's no table. She won't check out the bedroom till he returns.

Sonny's friend's uncle has agreed to hire her. Cashier, stock person, he didn't say what, and pay her in cash. It's not exactly the job of her future, but it's a start. She'll save some money, then look for better. She'll apply for her GED, maybe even enroll in some college courses. For now, though, she needs more clothes. No doubt her mother packed them and took them to Dory's. The question is how to get them? Sonny would gladly retrieve her stuff, but that's not possible, and he wouldn't understand her family. He's an only son, close to his mom, who lives alone and manages some Ukrainian bakery near where he grew up. He won't talk about his father except to say that he met him a few times too many.

It feels weird being alone in his digs. Under other circumstances she'd call Mirabelle, but her friend's formal good-bye rankles her. No hugs, no kisses, no see-you-soons, not even a wave, though she did stand out front till the car sped away. She can envision Mirabelle's disdain on entering Sonny's apartment. Well, the snobby side of that girl needs to be combated. She'll phone her tomorrow. Tonight, though, it's not about Mirabelle. It's about her and Sonny, alone together. They've talked about making love in their own bed, night or day, free to do whatever they want, and what that might be she can't wait to find out.

Where the hell is he? How long does it take to locate a parking space? Did he forget she's alone up here with a triple-latched door?

She checks out what seems to be a fridge, a half-size cooler of sorts, and finds three cans of Bud in it. She doesn't want a beer. She's hungry. Maybe he went to the supermarket. That thought momentarily stems the fingers of anxiety creeping up her spine. But she didn't see anything open nearby. She hates waiting. He'd better not be one of those inconsiderate jerk-offs. She won't stand for it. Even as she thinks this, she knows it isn't true, which in a way is more alarming. Because, really, if something did happen to him, what would she do? Who would she call? Would it be safe to stay here alone overnight? No one would want to rob this place. What in heaven's name would they steal?

She hears footsteps before the rat-tat-a-tat on the door. She unlatches the locks, releases the chain, and stands there, arms akimbo. "What the hell took you so long?"

"My fairy dust guy wasn't where he usually is. I had to go uptown. We don't want to be without, do we?"

"Sonny, you left me alone in a strange place. What would I have done if something had happened to you?"

"Nothing did, nothing would, nothing could, pretty girl. This is my town, so unscrew that frown. Please? So baby, baby, here's my pad, does it satisfy, gratify, or make you sad?"

"Sonny, you promised . . ."

He shrugs.

"I can't say it's gorgeous, but I do like being alone with you."

"Girl is honest." He takes her hand, leads her to the bedroom, where there's a twin-sized mattress on the floor. Posters of rappers paper the walls. The one small window is covered with a red cloth.

31.

On coffee break in the small staff office, she stares at the desktop computer. This morning she felt herself slur words a few times, not like a drunk might, but more like she just couldn't hold the letters together. Some of them kept slipping back down her throat. *Can a benign brain tumor cause slurring?* she asks Google. Yes, it tells her, via way too many medical sites, it can, it does, and it will, though most of the sites indicate when it comes the slurring is usually continuous, which in her case it's not. That's a good sign, yes? Bodies are notoriously random in their assaults. One day a person wakes with an aching hip, the next day it's not even a memory. Okay, the headaches persist, but aspirin works.

For a moment, she considers phoning Stu to tell him about the MRI, her headaches, the slurring, but would it make a difference? She'd still have the same symptoms, and he doesn't do well with illness. She's lonely for him, that's all. She used to phone him during breaks and whisper seductive words about the night before, then listen to him chuckle softly. Now there aren't many nights before. It isn't as if they never have sex, but it feels dutiful on his part. Well, he's going through his thing, too, isn't he? Work, money, worry, more worry. Why add to it?

On the positive side, lately he's arriving home directly from work without getting lost in a bar. Could be he's developed a heightened sense of responsibility . . . man of the house should be present. Or maybe he enjoys being part of an extended family.

She checks her watch. It's nearly eleven. And hurries down the hallway to Mr. Todd's room. He turns off the TV and they proceed to the cafeteria for coffee. She brings two cups to an empty table and sits across from him. "Were you watching anything interesting?"

"Daytime programming is for morons."

"No argument from me. Would you prefer reading a book?"

"I can't." He looks at her as if she ought to know why.

She does, but asks anyway. "How come?"

"Cataracts, and before you say it, no, I haven't changed my mind. I don't want them removed."

"It's a very routine procedure, you know."

"There's no such thing."

His words chill her. Would she have a cataract removed? She believes she would. A cataract isn't a tumor. "It's not a big deal. It's outpatient, no hospital."

"I'm eighty-six. Everything's a big deal." His hands shoo away her words.

"There are audio books."

"I have a hearing aid in each ear. I take them out and I won't hear a word."

"There are solutions in this world, Mr. Todd."

"I'm all ears, ha." He stirs sugar into his coffee.

"There are ear . . ." but she can't find the word she wants and feels nauseous. She takes a deep breath. "Anyway, we can try to order the device."

"Who buys them?"

"I can find out if Medicaid will pay."

"A waste of time. The comfort of old people means nothing in this society. Done with us when we stop working, stop paying taxes. Simple as that. But rich or poor, every living body gets old. I take my satisfaction from that."

"Mr. Todd, you're bright, perceptive, but awfully bitter."

"And you're young and hopeful, that's the way it is."

"Well, I'm going to order you ear . . ." Again she can't find the word.

"We'll see."

"Can I leave you here and tend to others?"

"Won't be the first time."

Phones . . . earphones, she remembers on her way out.

32.

She can smell his aftershave, a citrusy mixture—lemon and lime. His strong hands grasp the steering wheel. When he phoned the other day, it surprised her. How did he get her number? Of course, he's a detective. He moved some barrels and bricks, he told her: the kid, her son, is off the illegal track, out of the system. No record. No arraignment. But this can only be done once. He did it for the kid, yes, but for her, too. Lunch, perhaps? He never said she owed him, but she does. She glances at his profile. The Roman nose, wide cheeks, square chin. She's never seen a real square chin except in cartoons. His maleness is all in his face, she decides. His short, somewhat squat body, not so much.

So far, the conversation's easy but uninteresting—about old Bronx neighborhoods where he used to patrol. She asks where they're going. He says it's a surprise. Streets of gray stone buildings rush by. She takes note of them as they cross the Willis Avenue Bridge out of the Bronx into Manhattan. She takes note, too, of his fingers, free of a gold band, not that that means anything. Takes note as well of no revealing objects in the car—kids' toys, wife's scarf. He's vacuumed it free of personal items. It's something she wouldn't think to do. Maybe he expects her to be as inquisitive and observant as he would be. The thing is, though she's here, she's not.

For some reason she remembers the website Rosie showed her, "virtual twins"—avatars of real singers—their real but make-believe features, their real but doll-like movements. They make a travesty of girls Rosie's age. Not that she could say so to her daughter, who saw in them not a gimmick but some kind of fun-magic. Right now, it's exactly what she feels like, a virtual woman in a virtual car with a virtual man, which doesn't feel bad. Yet even as she thinks this, reality, never far from her brain, seeps in as easily as wind through a crack. Is Arthur really taking her to a restaurant? She reminds herself that he's been a gentleman on every count. Still, what would Rosie say about her in a car with this handsome man who's interested in treating her to some promising hours? Rosie would be horrified. Of course she would. Real mothers don't act like their teenage children. Real mothers have jobs and houses and take care of their kids' needs. Rosie's voice in her head whispers, *What the fuck are you doing?* And why isn't it Zack's voice? She did tell Zack that Casey's arrest was thrown out, no record, but nothing more. And he didn't ask.

They're driving through Times Square. The din muted by the closed windows. She stares at the multitudes of people, the huge flashing billboards, sunlit sky, dizzying traffic. Suddenly, the scene isn't containable, and she feels miles from home.

She touches his arm, startling him. "Arthur, this isn't a good idea. I mean, of course we should have lunch, and of course I'm eternally grateful for what you did for Casey. But it stops after lunch, the-you-and-me part of it. I hope that's okay."

"Hey, lunch is all I asked for? Right?" He glances at her long enough to give her a warm smile. And she knows he's planning to feed and charm her into changing her mind. He has that much confidence in his handsome self.

"It was an old steakhouse way down near South Street Seaport," she tells Dory, who, thankfully, is alone at her dressing table, messing about with creams and whatever. "You know the kind. With sawdust, real sawdust, on the floor and waiters ninety years old if a day. The windows were covered with chintz curtains, really. Anyway, Arthur ordered some fancy wine . . . this is for lunch, mind you . . . and urged me to try their steak, which I couldn't imagine eating at that time of day, but I knew after coming all that way, I couldn't order a simple salad. So I had some cold shrimp dish. Delicious, I tell you. But the amazing thing was how everyone recognized and respected him, waiters and clientele alike, patting his shoulder, whispering in his ear, bringing out unasked-for desserts, and I swear I never saw a check. That's why he brought me there, you see, so I could revel in his notoriety, which I did. I said the things he seemed to want to hear, like, wow, they sure like you here."

"Goodness, Lena, take a breath. You sound like someone who never ate in a steakhouse."

"The restaurant's not the point. The point was the way he needed, wanted to impress me."

"Obviously, he did."

"No, not that way . . ."

"What way?"

"Where suddenly I would become smitten with him. Just the opposite. It was a laugh. I mean it was all so lacking in subtlety I could barely keep from grinning. It brought to mind those sweet blind dates when we were younger than Rosie, the boys all shiny and clean but mainly nervous, not knowing how to have a date, trying to impress us."

"And then there was Zack."

"What is that supposed to mean?"

173

"As I recall, after Zack I couldn't get you to go out with anyone."

"You didn't try. You met Stu around the same time and started going steady."

"Stu didn't go steady. Stu reserved me for when he wanted to see me."

"True. And that makes me sad."

"Which part... the smitten with Zack or the unrequited Dory?"

"Neither, really. Just how that youthful piece of it is gone, really gone, never to be reignited or felt in the same ways again. It's probably why Arthur struck me as so ridiculous, trying to engage me in ways that we experienced as teenagers."

"Yes. Instant passion. Deep crush. That won't happen again. True. And that is sad."

"Okay, so now it's you being sad. About Stu?" she ventures.

"Not really."

"Then what?"

"Look at these crow's feet," Dory points to the corner of her eye in the mirror.

"Oh no, that is definitely not what's making you sad."

"I was just commiserating with your sense of loss of youthful abandon."

"Well, commiserate with this. Where does Zack go when he leaves each morning? If I ask, he shrugs, and if I press him, he mutters something about needing to find a job. But I don't believe him. I think he walks around for hours. You have to get Stu to find out what's going on. I can't live like this much longer, Dory."

"I'll tell Stu to take him out for a few beers. Stu likes any idea that includes drinks."

"Dory, I can't figure out these days what the hell your acerbic remarks actually mean."

"Well, perhaps nothing wishes to be revealed. Did you call

Mirabelle?" Dory's changing the subject is about as subtle as Arthur's wishing to impress her.

"I'm going there after an interview tomorrow. I'm certain Rosie's living there. Maybe she's better off, nice house, own room . . . what would be the benefit of dragging her back here?"

"Where's the job?"

"A diner opening in midtown."

Casey stands barefoot inside Dory's doorway. "Mom? There's a suitcase on your bed. Are we moving somewhere else?"

"Oh, honey, no. I'm sure Rosie needs more clothes and I'm packing a few of her things. If she wants to stay at Mirabelle's a while longer, we'll let her. Casey, listen, I'm so sorry about everything that's been disrupted in your life."

He shrugs as if to say not his business, any of it. She's about to tell him his case has been dropped, but remembering that witch of a policewoman's admonition about a night in jail not being the worst thing, decides to wait another day.

"When you begin going to the new school, you'll find friends around here to bike with." His face, she notes, is pale from being indoors.

"I guess." His legs and arms so boyishly thin in cut-offs and an oversized shirt of Zack's.

"A few more minutes and we can drive to Orchard Beach, walk along the shore at twilight, have an ice cream cone. How does that sound?"

"Mom, I'd rather not. It's still too hot." He looks at her with Zack's blue eyes.

Children have silent expectations of parents, but what his might be she hasn't a clue. If she reaches out to enfold his slim body, it'll alarm him, of that she's certain. "Okay, later, honey."

"Bye, Casey. I love when you visit," Dory says.

As soon as Lena closes the door, Dory again peers at her face in the mirror. She sees a problem, even if Lena didn't. With her left eye, a miniscule pulling, not quite a droop, but it will be with another half millimeter. A smidgen of medical knowledge can be a dangerous thing, though she's learned a lot about bodies, caring for her charges: fingers that can't button blouses, hands that can no longer maneuver feet into socks tell their own stories, as do the medical records she reads daily. When something worrisome appears in one of her charges, a little lump, a changed gait, she knows not to ignore it. Their bodies are what they have to warn them of the impending future. But at her age the body is often a conduit for the mind's distress, which is why a tic in an eyelid can come and go with the tensions of life. Still, the short, stabbing jabs in her head, the slurring, and now the eye . . . are they the mind's distress or the tumor? Oh, Christ, Lena is the one who focuses on disaster, not her.

33.

She parks the car a few streets down the road from what was once her house. She has no desire to see it, none at all. She doesn't care or even wonder if Casey's black paint is still there. It's as if the house itself had turned on her and she's ignoring it as punishment.

Her journey to midtown was a waste of gas, the waitress job already filled. Do people get there in the middle of the night? With the bag of Rosie's clothes in tow, she trudges toward Mirabelle's. The air is thick. Listless leaves on thirsty trees hold on to the weeks of heat. Though she's walked this path before, the houses she passes seem strangely untroubled.

Mirabelle's house is a stately Victorian with a white exterior and royal-blue trim. There's no car in the driveway, but maybe it's behind the elegant wooden garage door. She notices the stone birdbath and macramé feeders on the front lawn near well-tended shrubbery. They have landscapers; they must. The grass, the bushes, all so neat and velvety, not a weed in sight. She can't see the backyard from here, but imagines it decked out with padded seats and tile-topped tables, and maybe a broken chair put outside to deal with later. She's done that herself.

She hopes Mirabelle's parents are back from vacation. She's spoken to Mirabelle's mother a few times on the phone, but never met her. Using the brass knocker on the front door, she waits for what seems like an eternity before a barefoot, fiftyish woman opens the door. She's wearing a silky, pale-blue caftan with a Mandarin collar. Her face appears worn, even ravaged, the eyes embedded in deep hollows. A drinker?

"Hi, I'm Rosie's mom. You must be . . ." and she steps in so the door can be closed. The onrush of air-conditioning a welcome relief.

Mirabelle, also barefoot, appears behind her mother in shorts and a strapless spandex top. "Hi, Lena."

"Hi, sweetie. I'd like to know if it's okay with your parents to have Rosie stay here awhile longer."

"But she's not here any more," Mirabelle's mother says.

"Please, I'm not going to make her come home. I promise. I just want to give her a kiss and her clothes, that's it."

"She's not here," the mother repeats in a whispery voice. "Mirabelle, you need to deal with this." And she promptly flees the scene.

"Mirabelle, what's going on?" Lena asks.

"Well, Rosie was here, but not anymore. I don't know where she is."

"Of course you do."

"No," this said in a soft voice.

"You two are fast friends. Rosie wouldn't leave here without telling you where she's going."

"She didn't tell me."

"Mirabelle, don't make me bring a cop to your door to get you to reveal where Rosie is. She's underage, and I can do that. So please, tell me. I will let Rosie know I threatened the information out of you," which is what she's doing.

"Rosie left a few days ago with a guy she's seeing." Mirabelle admits, reluctantly.

"A guy? She's seeing a guy?" Her insides cramp so hard she nearly keels over. "Who?"

"His name is Sonny. I don't know anything about him."

Of course she does. "Where did the two of them go?" She tries to keep an even tone but desperation gets in the way. "Rosie wouldn't leave here unless there was an apartment or whatever. Right?"

"Yes, that's true. But I don't . . ."

She's tempted to grab the girl's arms and shake her hard. "Mirabelle, you do know and you must tell me right now."

"Rosie left an address, but I don't know if it's real. I mean, I don't know if that's where they went."

"Okay. You need to get it for me. Now."

While waiting, she's takes note of the plush living room, the thick green carpeting, the off-white couch that spans a wall, the ceiling light fixture that could've come from a ballroom. Not her style, any of it, but still . . . it took time and thought and money to pull it together. Does Mirabelle's mother enjoy her home or pace back and forth in it like a trapped deer? Is that why she drinks? And why is she still dressed in a caftan at this time of day? Rosie did say the father works in the basement. Is that why mother and daughter walk around barefoot? Did Rosie have to take off her shoes as well in order to spare the father a footfall of noise? No one ever knows what really goes on in another's home.

Mirabelle returns with a small scrap of paper. Her eyes scan the address and her chest tightens. "This is in the South Bronx."

Mirabelle nods.

"Jesus, fucking, Christ," she mumbles to herself and heads back to the car.

On the highway, her mind in turmoil, she drives in the fast lane. Can't get there soon enough. Leave home, meet a guy who promises to care for her, then does god knows what else? Christ, it's such an old story.

She fleetingly thinks of phoning Dory to calm herself. Then again, the fear sucking the air out of her body can't be calmed. Rosie is feisty, smart, and sure of herself, right? But who is Sonny? Maybe an artist who found the cheapest place he could, in which to practice his trade? Except she doesn't believe it. Even if it were so, Rosie's too young. She isn't leaving her daughter there. No way.

Exiting the highway, she drives through streets filled with open lots and boarded-up stores but not a parking spot anywhere. Isn't the South Bronx being rehabilitated? From what she sees there's no big change from years ago. Under the shadow of the elevated tracks, she drives past open bodegas, liquor stores, a mini-mart, a beauty salon, even a children's clothing store. People are out shopping, milling around. Finally, she maneuvers the car into a tight spot in front of a ninety-nine-cent everything store. Leaving Rosie's bag of clothing in the car, she strides toward the address on the scrap of paper.

The narrow brick-and-wood-fronted walk-up is wedged like an afterthought between two apartment buildings that have seen better days. In the dim vestibule on a scratched brass plate, she makes out the bell for 4G and presses it. Nothing. She presses another bell. A thin, tinny, blip of sound and she enters quickly to begin the trek up to the fourth floor. Muffled voices, probably from TVs, accompany her, as do the pungent odors of garlic, fried food, and pine-scented detergent, which repel her with their familiarity.

Four dark metal apartment doors face her. She can barely make out the "G" on one of them and rings the bell. It doesn't work. She knocks. Waits. Knocks again. Presses her ear to the door. Nothing. She wills them to be home and knocks a third time, far more insistently with the side of her fist. She doesn't care who it disturbs. Finally, the door opens on a chain and eyes peer out at her.

"Hello, I'm Rosie's mother, I . . ."

The door closes. The decisive sound of the chain being unlocked, the click of one, two, three locks, and the door opens. The power of mothers, she thinks. This must be Sonny. Tall, skinny, blond, large eyes, small nose, an ear stud. Handsome in his way, she supposes. Is this Rosie's taste? But he's much too old for her daughter and doesn't seem the least bit embarrassed in his gym shorts and naked chest. "Can I come in?" Her voice restrained, gentle, inquiring. She mustn't threaten, or he could close the door on her.

Her eyes slide across a dimly lit room of shabby furniture. "Can I talk to Rosie?" still in a gentle tone.

"Yeah, the thing is . . . Do you want me to wake her?" He seems genuinely puzzled.

"She's sleeping? It's almost two in the afternoon?"

"Yeah, well, we didn't get back till this morning and . . ."

Already, this is too much information for her. "Yes, please, wake her."

"I'm Sonny," he says guilelessly.

"Please call me Lena."

They look at each other. Clearly, he's not sure about waking Rosie.

"Would it be all right if *I* woke her?" she asks.

"No. I mean . . . that'd be too scary . . . I mean, shocking."

"Of course, you're right. Please ask my daughter to come out to the living room. Thanks so much."

181

"Yeah. Okay."

"I'll wait right here."

He disappears through a doorway and she can hear him saying "Rosy-Posy, get up, get up, your mother's here in the living room. You better get up." Then silence. Then whispering. If someone doesn't come out soon she's going in. She looks at the couch and decides to remain standing. The room is beyond hot, though a floor fan churns the humid air. Only then does she realize the windows don't open. God help them.

She hears a rustling, a door creaking. A closet? Is her daughter naked in there? Oh lord . . . she begins to pace the length of the wall. Sonny returns. "She'll be out in a minute. I have water. Do you want a glass?"

She feels some pity for his discomfort. "No, but if you have a cold beer . . ." Beer might put him more at ease, her as well. She doesn't need another nervous person in the room.

"Shit. Sorry. We finished them yesterday."

"No problem." She was young once, too, right? Wrong. She's not Rosie's age anymore. She's her mother. Big difference.

Rosie saunters out of the bedroom, barefoot, in shorts and a halter top, her hair tangled from sleep, her eyes a bit puffy. "Hi, Mom. What's up?" Rosie's make-believe calmness doesn't fool her one bit. She knows her daughter, and Rosie isn't ready for her mother's appearance, that's for sure.

Rushing over to embrace her daughter won't work. "Honey, it's so good to see you. Everything's fine."

"Fine? You're working. Dad's working?"

"Well, no . . ." She won't be put on the defensive by a fifteen-year-old. "But I'm here to take you back to Dory's. School is starting. I'm sure Sonny will understand you need to be with your family."

"Mom, listen, I'm not going to Dory's. I'm not going back to school. I have a job, so I no longer need to be a burden to you and dad."

"Burden? Don't be ridiculous. You're too young to be on your own, too young to make these kinds of decisions without family input."

"Mom, please, I don't want to fight with you. This is my life, not yours. I can do with it what I want. So, please, just go. Now that you met Sonny, the two of us can visit now and then."

Sonny has plopped onto a beanbag chair as far from the scene as he can get. "Sonny," she says, "You can't live with my daughter. She's underage."

"Mom, don't pull that shit. My life doesn't belong to you or to Sonny. It belongs to me. So forget about involving Sonny in this family spat."

"This isn't a family spat. And you do belong to me. And you are underage. And if Sonny continues to cohabit with you, I will press charges, and he will go to jail. Is that what you want?" She tries to keep her tone even, but the truth of what she says blows back at her heavily. Rosie's sleepy face redefines itself in anger, her lips stretch tight and her eyes squint.

"You do that, Mom, and we're finished. I will never talk to you again. I promise. I swear."

One knife, two knives, how many of these can the heart survive? "Look, I don't want to cause trouble for Sonny, but how old does he think you are?"

"My relationship with him is none of your business." Rosie goes to stand next to Sonny.

"You're wrong. You are my business and don't ever forget that."

"Sonny, say something," Rosie orders. And Lena hears her own voice imploring Zack.

"Listen, um . . . Lena . . . I'll take good care of Rosie. You don't need to worry. She'll be fine."

"Fine doesn't include quitting high school."

"High school?" For a moment he looks stunned, then he gets a hold on himself. "It has nothing to do with life. It's a place to hang out until you're ready to go for it. Rosie's ready to go for it. So am I."

A place to hang out? She takes a deep breath. "What do you do for a living? How do you support yourself?"

"At the moment, I don't get paid for my gigs but . . ."

"Gigs?"

"Mom, you wouldn't understand. He's building a resume, a reputation as a rapper/poet. He's already made one album. And tonight . . ."

"How do you pay the rent?" she insists. Actually, how this Sonny lives doesn't interest her. What interests her is having Rosie recognize the instability of the situation.

"My uncle owns a gas station. I work there and also at another of his places. I plan to take the exam to become a cop . . . maybe, but . . ."

"Rosie needs to live with her family. You two can find ways to see each other, to date like other young people."

Rosie stares at her. In her daughter's face she sees the old wiliness, how to tackle mother. "But we've already established a monogamous relationship. I know you know what that means. And going backward to dating would constitute a divorce of sorts, which neither of us would agree too, see?"

She's had enough of this back-and-forth crap. "Rosie, you're coming with me. I don't want to discuss this anymore."

"What, pull me out of here by my hair, shackle me, take me to Dory's, tie me to the bed, lock windows and doors, send me

184

to a juvenile detention center? There's no way you can force me to go with you or to stay at Dory's. Just what are you thinking?" Rosie glares at her, not a drop of give in her expression.

Can she really force this child to do anything? How?

"If you refuse to come home . . ."

"Home? What home? You lost our home."

Her throat tightens. "I mean Dory's. If you refuse to go there with me, I will, I promise, go to court, get a restraining order on Sonny . . ."

"Mom, he hasn't treated me badly, what are you talking about?"

"I will press charges against him for cohabiting with a minor."

"You are being gross, you know that? For a mother who claims she wants to see me happy, you are truly doing your best to be a bitch."

But she detects uncertainty in Rosie's eyes and decides the legal path is the one to pursue. "The two of you can talk it over today. I'll return tomorrow to pick you up. If you disappear or refuse to leave with me, I will go to court the next day and press charges. Sonny, I hope you're listening?" Her tone stern, even hostile. How else to make them understand that this isn't a negotiation?

"I hear you, and I don't like what you're saying. I'm not doing anything illegal," Sonny says.

"You most certainly are. Rosie isn't sixteen yet and even then she's not legal for another year. So think about that."

"Mom, I'll just run away again, and this time you won't find me. I mean it. You know I'm as good as my word." Her hate-filled voice is too much to bear for even another minute.

"And I, too, am as good as my word. So talk it over." She walks out, her body trembling, her heart pumping as hard as the slam of the door behind her. She slowly descends the steps. Zack needs to come with her tomorrow. He's the father, dammit. Even as she thinks this she doesn't completely trust what he might do or say, and wonders, oddly, if she ought to bring Stu instead?

"I told you she could be a bitch. She gloms onto an idea and you can't move her. Either I find somewhere else to stay tomorrow where she can't find me or . . ."

"Hey, pretty girl. Don't get all perturbed. Let's smoke some fairy dust, helps to figure out problems. Is it true, you're not even sixteen?"

"So what? I'm older than my years, always have been."

"Just thinking . . . legally, she has a point."

"She's not going to any court. It's the last place she'd appear. She hates all that crap."

He looks at her without conviction.

"Listen, Sonny, if you're all worried, I'll just leave. Just tell her I took off. I'm not staying where I'm not wanted . . ."

"Baby, I want you . . ."

"That's not good enough. I want you to want me in a bigger, deeper way than any threat my mother tosses out."

"I want you in a big, deep way." He grabs her arm, pulls her close. "As deep as I can get," he teases.

"Be serious."

"Always. Listen, I don't want to hear about this now. To-night's my big gig and I need to feel all positive. Okay?"

"Okay," she says.

34.

Sonny's quiet, his eyes fixed on the road. Unusual. He's a rapper, a chatterer, a talker. He's nervous. She gets that. Some agent is supposed to be at the gig in Queens, watching him in particular. Something big, Rosie, is what he keeps saying. He looks outstanding in his cobalt-blue shirt, open at the neck, sleeves rolled up, revealing sun-bronzed skin.

"Why so quiet?"

"Conserving energy, keeping it bottled inside so it'll explode on stage like TNT. You've never seen me that way. The stuff I've done so far has been bullshit small."

"I thought maybe you were worried about my mother's threats."

"Baby, no woman like that is going to put me up against the wall. What's the matter with you?"

"I don't know, just thinking out loud." But it wasn't his attitude this afternoon. Feeling unexpectedly alone, she reaches over to squeeze his thin, muscled thigh, encased in tight black jeans. He gives her a too-quick smile.

They pull off the Long Island Expressway, drive past Jamaica Hospital, then turn onto an avenue of shops and bars and people traffic, where he parks the car.

He points to a restaurant; on its façade is painted a lopsided log cabin. "The room behind that bar is where it all happens."

She follows him through a crowded, noisy pub into an over-air-conditioned back room filled with young people. The wrap-around wallpaper features fake porthole windows. Ashy pink fluorescents cast a misty light. A four-piece band on a small platform sits across the room from another four-piece band. No one seems to mind the jumble of music; the sounds are evidently there to inhale, not decipher. After a few tokes of whatever, people hear what they need. She, too, could benefit from some fairy dust, and Sonny's the keeper of the stuff.

Already, girls are orbiting around him, touching his arms, shirt, belt, for godsakes. It's revolting. He's chattering away, enjoying the attention.

"Sonny," she calls, trying to break into the circle around him, wanting to establish that he's hers. He doesn't even answer though she's sure he notices her small struggle.

Again, she calls his name, this time loudly. He looks at her blankly, then waggles a few non-beckoning fingers. She could be anyone. Is this happening? Did her mother spook him with that restraint-order crap? She is underage, but if you love someone the way he constantly says he loves her, then you should be protective. Has she read him wrong? Is he just a wimp? Siri wouldn't confront his aunt and uncle; her father won't confront her mother. Now, Sonny's behaving like a scared little boy. Does she want to be with someone like that? She does. She wants his body close. She wants his admiring words. They have fun together. She needs to be more tolerant, more patient. It is, after all, *his* night. Once they get home, everything will be the way it was.

She stares at the groupies circling him. One girl has hold of his hand, another's slung an arm over his shoulder. And Sonny? He's yakking away, as happy as a pampered lap dog.

She knows it now. She needs him to give her some sign of recognition. She shoulders her way into the circle, and touches him. "Sonny?"

He looks at her for two seconds, no more. "Later," he says dismissively.

Disbelief chokes off speech, though her brain shouts, fuck you.

She leaves before the tears begin to spill. How could he ditch her this way? The Rosie he can't be away from for a minute, the Rosie whose body he wants to paint, whose breasts he wants to live between? They made love twice today, long and delicious, every inch of her alive to his touch. How could he forget? A bitter sadness fills her throat.

One little threat and suddenly he's indifferent? Dismissive? She hopes her mother does go to court and drags his bony ass to jail.

What now? No way in hell will she appear at Dory's door in the middle of the night, poor waif, and face her mother's victorious silence or her father's indifference. Not a chance. Mirabelle's the only path left. Except it's already well past midnight. Even phoning now will create a ruckus. Basically, she needs to kill a few hours till it gets light, and then call and ask if she can come back.

Outside, the heat feels swampy against her air-cooled skin. People are still cruising the streets. She walks down the avenue, turns a corner, and promptly spots Jamaica Hospital atop a slight incline, below which are a parking lot and an emergency room entrance.

She'll sit there for a few hours. If anyone asks, she'll claim a bad stomachache. You wait hours at a city emergency room if what you have isn't life-threatening. Of course a thermometer to measure emotional distress would get her a room with a bed.

She walks up a ramp, passing a garage housing ambulances, and two automatic doors open into an air-conditioned lobby. The guard asks if he can help. She's ready. "I have this awful stomachache . . ." He points at the long hallway, tells her to check in at the first desk she comes to, then go through the next doors to the emergency room.

She registers at the desk, provides Sonny's name and address. No one questions the gender of names anymore. The woman looks her over with an expression that reads: another druggie. Why correct her?

A second door glides open, and she's in a crowded ER. A cacophony of voices hits her like so much static, so do the odors, medicinal and otherwise, that fill the room. Seventy or eighty seated bodies absorb the cool air. Her eyes slide past faces filled with fear, pain, sadness, and something more she can't quite identify. She tries to ignore the bloody clothing and block out the low moans, though it's difficult. Gray metal folding chairs are lined up in too many rows to count. She finds an empty seat in the middle of the last row and prays the ancient man half-asleep beside her won't expire. On her other side is a young man with a two- or three-year-old on his lap. Now and then he croons, "You're my little man." The boy doesn't respond, just rests his head against the man's chest. "Is that your little brother?" she asks, wanting to push Sonny from her mind.

"My son, Jamal. My little man here is sick. Waiting three hours now and nothing. This system sucks royally. Why you here?" He aims beautiful, dark but tired eyes in her direction, and she wishes she had some glamorous ailment to share.

"Stomachache," she says. Heartache, she thinks.

"Yeah, they can be bad, I know." His voice close to a whisper, as if raising it might disturb Jamal.

"Your boy has your eyes," she tells him.

"Like a big old moose." He's clearly teasing Jamal. "I'm Roland."

"I'm Rosie."

"Glad to meet you. Wish it was at a party instead."

She smiles. "Me, too, but I just came from one, and it sucked bad." He's younger than Sonny, she decides, but sounds older. "Do you think Jamal would sit on my lap, give you a break? Bathroom. Coffee, whatever?"

"You are one nice lady. I don't think so. I need to hold him. He's scared, real scared, but he's my boy, and he'll be all right real soon. Right, son?" Jamal just looks at her with his big eyes.

"What do you think is wrong?"

"He stopped eating yesterday and wouldn't play, either. I don't know. He went to his grandmother's and she called to say something was off. So we came here. Where else?"

She could think of a few better places, but says nothing. Without insurance or money they're at the mercy of the city.

"Hey, Jamal," she says softly. "You will be out playing soon."

"I told him the same, but, you know, he's a wise one, knows he needs the man in the white coat to tell him he'll be okay. Then you watch him perk up."

"Is that true, Jamal?" she asks.

Jamal nods once.

"So, Rosie, what happened at this party?"

"My boyfriend ditched me."

"Did you fight?"

"I wish."

"Maybe he was having an out-of-body moment?"

"You mean drugs?"

"You said it, not me."

She smiles. "No. It's complicated."

"Well, what isn't? Thing is . . . party shit like that, I mean it feels bad, but actually it's just disappointment, which is kind of like a tropical downpour. Comes down hard, then before you know it the weather changes."

"Roland, that is a wise thing to say. Thank you." Truth is, though, she isn't ready to think about the night because, disappointment or not, once her anger subsides, the misery will set in. That's a given. "Can I ask you a question?"

Roland shrugs. "I don't mind."

"Jamal's mom?"

Roland puts his finger to his lips and she gets the message. Something about the loving way Roland takes charge makes her sad about herself.

A nurse with stethoscope around her neck appears up front, disappears into the examining rooms, then reappears.

"Why don't I go find out why no one is calling your name? Maybe there's a glitch. What's the last name?"

"Yeah. Shakur. You try. I did an hour ago. Fat, ugly hag said, wait your turn."

She makes it into the aisle but the nurse is moving away fast. "Excuse me, excuse me . . ."

The nurse turns to look at her.

"The Shakur family has been waiting for hours. Why aren't they being called? Can you make sure their name is on whatever list you have?"

"Honey, we have lots of people to treat, some bleeding, some dying. Their turn will come. No one gets lost." And she's gone.

Before returning, she checks her phone. It's ten past two. No missed calls, no calls at all. Not that she was expecting any. Not really.

She takes her seat beside Roland just as his name is called.

"Thanks, Rosie," he says, though she had nothing to do with it.

"Good luck," she tells him.

"You, too."

She watches him stride down the aisle with Jamal in his arms and wonders if this night will change Jamal's life. Or hers?

35.

The bed bounces and Rosie opens her eyes. Mirabelle, khaki shorts over her bathing suit, is perched there.

"The day is passing. Move your carcass off the bed."

"God, Mirabelle, you're heartless. I was up all night. I went through hell. Some pity here, please." But it's more than pity she wants. Its reassurance that the awful sadness—unlike anything she's ever felt before—is temporary.

"I want to feel sorry but I can't." Her friend's face is aglow.

"Why's that?"

"Because I'm glad. He was bad for you."

"And you were able to assess that by what . . . meeting him briefly as he came and went from here?"

"I told you he wasn't as reliable as you thought." Mirabelle's righteous tone annoys her.

"I'm curious. I truly am. How did you come to that conclusion?"

"Are you being sarcastic?"

"Serious." She wants someone to turn off the light, except it's the sun streaming into the uncluttered space, so unlike the ER.

"He was unstable. It was apparent in his ways and means." Her friend looks at her as if to say, how could you not know?

Sonny's dumped her. She hates her mother. Her friend is

glad for her misery. She's not discussing this. Not one word more. "You're right, drop it."

"This afternoon my mom called your mother to ask permission for you to stay here, so you needn't hide."

"What did my mother say?"

"She said fine, what else? Come on, let's go to the beach."

"That is the last thing I want to do. How could he ditch me like that? The man was all over me for weeks."

"Callow youth. Look, he used you. Face it, men do that. Better to learn now."

"But I miss him."

"You'll live."

"How do you know, you've never been loved like that."

"That's not a friendly thing to say." Mirabelle strides toward the door.

"Wait, silly. I just want you to appreciate the state I'm in."

"I appreciate it. Do you want to go to the beach or not?"

"I need a shower first."

"I'll be out in back."

The hot, needlelike spray helps to soothe the limbs but not the hollowness inside. She'll have to suffer, won't she? She's seen the films, read the novels; love lost hurts. She wants something in exchange for the pain. Sonny adored making love to her. He'll regret losing that, won't he? She hates herself for not being out-of-her-mind angry. Except she is, she's pissed beyond words. So why does she still want him to call her? If he called right now, she'd hang up, she would, but it would give her satisfaction to know that he was pining. Oh, she's pathetic.

She wraps herself in a large, comfy towel. Whatever clothing she had with her is still at Sonny's. Someone will have to get it, but not yet, not for a while.

36.

Stu, on his ten-minute break, stands outside the plant, which takes up an entire street. In the smoggy distance the Whitestone Bridge is barely visible. Despite the white sheet of sky, the sun's rays bake the concrete. There's nowhere to lean that wouldn't burn skin. Nearby, two fire hydrants, stray grass vying for air through broken pavement, cigarette butts, empty soda cans, and candy wrappers. The guys outside having a smoke are quiet. Must be the heat. Those at the plant the longest still don't open up with him the way they used to. He let down his team. He's off their trust list, wouldn't be the one they'd tell first about a mutiny. He doesn't blame them.

His phone vibrates. It's Zack. A text. He says a little prayer before reading that Zack can't meet him. Thank you Buddha, God, and Allah, he whispers silently. He does not want to be with, talk to, or hear about Zack. He does not want to help Zack. He only sent the invite to meet because Dory asked him to do it for Lena. And for Lena, any mountain would be scaled. But she doesn't ask for mountains to be climbed. She doesn't even ask him how he's feeling. Isn't that a message? Except, except... she's become gentler with him, even a little dependent, he'd say, which is what he wants. He needs her to need him, even if their needs are different. She needs him to explore Zack's head. He texts the man, but he can't make the man comply, can he? Lena needs cash. He finds someone in the plant to buy her car. He and she will drive their vehicles here on Saturday. The man will meet them. Take her car. They'll return in his, alone together, and who knows what that might mean? The thrill of possibility renders him back into the funnel of high school excitement. He's never been a smoker but suddenly wants a cigarette, something to drag on deeply, because the influx of unexpected energy has nowhere to go.

Break over, a line of guys begins to trail back in. Christ and truly, he hates having to go inside right now. The plant gobbles up time along with fantasy. Hates, as well, having to cover his face like the man in the iron mask, hates what he's supposed to do and what he's not supposed to do, because they're no different. But what he hates most is not being allowed the confidence of knowing that the job is his for as long as he wants it.

Before he enters, he needs to calm down, think aside—that is, aside from Lena—and settle into the dead mindset in which he does his work. To lose concentration is to lose an eye or burn his partner. None of that has ever happened, not to him, but he's seen it happen.

He bends his head beneath the too-low beam of the narrow doorway, some short person's bad idea of revenge. How many times has he wounded his forehead? But not today, today he's alert, activated by the need to get through to the last bell and go home, where it's all a different story now. And Saturday always comes.

37.

Leaning over the railing, watching the East River's slow-moving current, Zack thinks: What is a man without a place he can call home? He never used to have such thoughts. Now they're nonstop. Buying a house meant something. His grandparents rented; his parents rented; his uncles and aunts rented. *He* bought a house. Evidence of arriving somewhere, no matter the size of the lot. Owning it gave purpose to the miserable hours on the job. Coming home to Lena's loving arms erased the need to think further. Both are gone; so is his value as a provider, a lover and a father, all of it stolen from him by a bank.

Lena packed up the house so quickly, ready to move on, undeniably future-oriented. It's not what he needed. He wanted her to hesitate, to share in the defeat of it. Instead, she bitched about why he didn't tell her sooner. He couldn't. True, he kept silent to protect her, but that was only a part of it. Mostly he couldn't bear to acknowledge the loss. After twenty years of marriage, why couldn't she get that? She still doesn't understand. And for the first time ever he's fucking angry with her. Maybe even outraged, except he isn't sure what that's supposed to feel like. He is sure that he can no longer accept her cold distance. All he ever wanted for both of them was to land somewhere safe. Now he knows there's no such thing. She needs to hear all of this and more, even if it means she eyes him with pity, or worse, wonders why he can't suck it up and go on like other men do. Well, he can't, and that's too fucking bad for him, but also for her. And if anyone cares to ask, he's pissed, furious. Yet he feels righteous, determined, invincible, and weird.

He leans further over the railing and takes a few deep breaths. No, he telegraphs to anyone watching, he's not jumping. Why should he? They owe him, and he wants to retrieve what's his. Besides, he can swim and the plunge isn't that far. No, he's not about committing hari-kari or whatever it's called. He's already slid down the long rope and reached absolute bottom, and he's not going to take this shit anymore. Wherever that leads him, so be it.

He heads downtown, intent on reaching the tip of Manhattan, where the Hudson and East River meet. No idea why, except it's what he wants to do. And he's determined to do what he wants without defending his actions to anyone, including himself.

At the South Street Seaport he considers the few moored boats and one lazy tug. What would it be like to own a houseboat? Would it feel the same as owning a house? He doesn't believe so. Boats represent luxury, what one does with extra money; the peel on the peach one can afford to throw away.

He doubles back through narrow streets, where shop windows offer sweaters and shirts resting in flakes of gold paper. He passes a bank. It's a storefront with a few ATMs inside and not a teller in sight. The door's unlocked. He walks in, eyes on one of two machines. "Please insert your card." He chuckles. He stares at the screen. If he bangs it hard, the way they did the phones in the old neighborhood, will it release cash? He bats it lightly, nothing; slaps it harder, not even a rattle.

A man enters and goes to the machine next to his. The guy inserts his card, thumbs the screen a few times, and money slides out. He's transfixed by the transaction. The guy feels him watching. "Anything wrong?"

Zack shakes his head. "Just taking in some extra A/C." The man nods curtly, clearly wanting out. Let him go. He has nothing to do with Zack's life, nothing at all. Yet he follows him out. The guy's BMW is parked right in front, a woman inside keeping the A/C going. The guy probably has a boat. He stands there till they pull away, then continues walking.

Stuck like a fat finger between two shops is a run-down bar with a dead window sign advertising Schlitz Beer. Does anyone drink that anymore? In his pocket are fourteen singles plus some coins. A bottle of Bud shouldn't cost more than three dollars tops, if that.

He pushes open the wooden door. The place is dark, damp, narrow as a train car and not much longer. Two stepping-up to-old-age men sit at one end of the bar. At the other is a woman whose age is indecipherable in the darkness. There aren't any tables, and he slips onto a stool closer to the woman than to the men. The bartender, hitting on seventy he'd say, waits quietly but expectantly.

"I'll have a bottle of Bud." Which is delivered promptly. He places four singles on the table and even gets back some coins. There isn't much scenery to take in, but the woman is eyeing him. He tries a smile, and she moves a few stools over to sit next to him. Shit, now he has to buy her a drink, too? But her mouth is aiming for his ear and he listens intently. "Ten dollars standing up in the storage room." As soon as the offer is made he feels his prick waking. Then she smiles and he's relieved to see all her teeth, but what if she has some sexual disease or worse, AIDS? He's about to shake his head when she presses a little square packet into his palm, a condom, and suddenly he's hard as a rock.

He drains the beer in three long swallows and follows her into an even darker back room, where the mingled smells of whiskey, beer, and dampness make breathing a chore. He can just make out whiskey cartons and empty beer cases piled floor to ceiling, and wonders where is this get-together going to take place. But she has it all figured out. First, she extends her hand for the money, which he places in her palm, and it disappears so quickly he can't say where. Gently, she tugs him into a narrow space between two columns of boxes and leans against the wall. He gets a whiff of some heavily scented perfume that reminds him of maple syrup. She waits for his fumbling hand to unwrap and roll the condom up over his penis, then lifts her skirt and wraps her arms around him. She's not into foreplay or make-believe talk, thank god. He's inside her in a nanosecond, and after one, two, three, maybe four grunts—she doesn't make a sound—it's finished. She moves away quickly and disappears. He isn't sure what to do with the condom and finally drops it behind some boxes.

When he re-enters the bar, she's in the same spot as when he first entered. He feels the men's eyes on him, forfeits the coins, and hightails out. A few deep breathes of fresh air and he begins to walk uptown. Who would believe it, but he's never been with a prostitute. Not ever. A first and last, he promises himself. Still, something glows inside, a feeling he can't quite put a name to, though it might have a tinge of revenge to it. But no regret. In fact, he's proud of himself. He needed the release. He met the need. Pat on the back is what he decides.

He heads for Chelsea Piers. The walk will take him past the docks. He can remember when no one lived around there, just water, old piers, and dry-docked boats. Now, tall buildings as slim as giant three-ply Kleenex boxes dot the landscape. Posh restaurants offer glass-filled glimpses of nirvana.

He turns east on one of the side streets, passes a meat market with open doors, and peers inside what looks like a warehouse. Two big trucks are unloading huge sides of beef. His eye is caught by a stained cardboard sign taped on the outer door: "Help Wanted."

38.

In the car Stu hands her a two-thousand-dollar check. Lena gives him a wide smile. His mind, a camera, freezes the light in her eyes. Her gratitude is his reward, be content with that. Except her naked arm, round and soft, her faint scent, almond—or is it vanilla?—is torturously close. A drive-by fantasy enters his head: he's nuzzling the secret space behind her ear. Isn't that where perfume's dabbed, or is that just in the movies? He could ask her. No, he can't. Lena isn't the romance-soap-opera type, whatever that is. Well, he knows what that is. His mother watched them daily. It was her hour of living with other people's misery.

"My friend is real happy with your car. He couldn't wait to drive it away."

"Sort of sad, though, as cars go. We've had it for years. Of course, I'm one hundred percent thankful to you for setting up the deal. I keep touching the check to make sure it's there. I guess that's sad, too."

"Lena, you're a trooper, making the best of all this crap."

"You think?" her voice softer than usual. What's that about?

"Listen. We should celebrate, have a beer, a glass of wine, toast to the check being a harbinger of better and bigger to come. What do you say?" A brief halt to his breathing while he waits. The right answer will send him over the moon. The wrong one will be what he expected in the first place. The next few silent seconds . . .

"Absolutely, Stu. Why the hell not? Where?"

"Let me consider the universe for a moment." But it's his rising excitement he considers. When he glances at her, she smiles. At his words? At him? It doesn't matter. He'll take either or both. He'll take whatever he can. Oh, sweet Jesus, the prospect of Lena and him at a bar together, alone, raises a bagful of thoughts. Primary among them is the need for him not to drink too much, to stay in control of what he says. He's known her long enough to understand that a wrong word on his part will turn her off. If he remembers the past correctly she tends to be unforgiving. Right now, though, she's willing to spend time with him. That means he has to listen real closely, show how interested he is in her turn of mind. God, how ridiculous he's being. He's embarrassing himself to himself.

They're coming up to Fordham Road. "There's a corner pub near Kingsbridge, across from the old VA Hospital and by a tiny park. I think you'll like it."

"Why?"

"You would complicate my life by asking."

She says nothing.

"It's wood-paneled and has those fancy stained-glass windows, like in a church."

"Religious figures?"

"If you drink enough."

She laughs. "I see. Okay."

She's staring out the window and he wonders if there's anything in her mind that would match his thoughts. He decides not. He also decides not to complicate or fuck up the possibilities by saying another word till they arrive, at least five minutes.

The universe is with him, a parking space right in front. Then again, not many people in bars at two in the afternoon. He opens the door for her. She looks inside. He watches her every move.

"If you don't like it, we can find another . . ."

"Actually, I'm quite taken. It has atmosphere. How do you know about this place?"

"A story not worth telling." He touches her elbow to guide her into the rear where, at this hour, the few tables are vacant. The only other human in the place is the bartender, who doesn't rush to take orders. That's good, too. "What'll you have?" he asks her.

"I'm toying with the idea of a glass of Merlot, but it's awfully early, don't you think?'

"Not when it's a celebration."

At the circular bar, he orders the wine and a Sam Adams, though bourbon straight up would be a gift. He sees her eyeing the windows, the swan-like turn of her neck. Her bare-shouldered sundress moves when she does; cool and colorful, it demands a beach house where gentle breezes would wind the fabric around her legs.

"So tell me the story of this place," she says taking the wine from him.

"First the toast."

"Of course. You make it."

"To old friendship and the strength of a shared past." When did he become so poetic?

"That's beautiful, Stu."

She appreciates the finer things. He knew it.

"So . . . the story, please."

"What story?" he pretends.

"Is it lurid?"

"No. It's sad, I think."

"Good."

"Why good?"

"I hate shallow anecdotes."

Christ, does he have to come up with some deep shit? Just tell the truth, as his second grade teacher said every day of that year, or it least it felt that way.

"This is the place I come to after work when I'm feeling empty, which can be more often than not. It's never too crowded, though there are always people at the bar willing to spin their tales. After an hour or two of listening to improbable events, which a few drinks will make essential to share, my life seems fine. I'm ready to face the future—or the lack of it."

"Stu, that is sad. What do you mean lack of future?"

"The sameness, Lena, the same crappy job that can disappear any time, the same route back and forth, the same fucking worries about the same problems that never seem to be solved." Oh shit, is he whining? "Can we talk about something else?"

She looks at him for a moment. "I saw Rosie yesterday. She was living with an older guy, a rapper of some sort. I threatened to go to court and slap him with cohabiting with a minor and said I'd be back to take her home."

"She's one determined girl, isn't she?"

"Don't say 'like her mother,' because I was never that stupid."

"That's just it, you couldn't afford to be. You had to take care of so much so young . . ." He sees the shine leave her eyes.

"What can I do to help?"

"That's sweet, Stu." She touches the back of his hand, pats it actually, and he resists the urge to take hers and fold it beneath his. "Zack should be asking me that. Zack should be worrying about his children. Zack has become some kind of phantom. Who is he? Where is he? What is he fucking doing all day long? I'm so angry I could haul *him* before a judge."

To agree with her is clearly stupid, to disagree no less so. "I asked him to meet, but he said he couldn't." He glances into the middle distance, fearing she'll see in his expression how glad he was for Zack's lack of response. "Why don't I go with you to pick up Rosie?"

"You would, wouldn't you? But she's back at Mirabelle's."

And in the wonderment of her tone he hears what he's been waiting for. He can't be sure, of course, but it feels like Lena's finally taking him in. Actually doing it. It's all he wants. He finds her hand, squeezes it, does not let go. "Yes, I would've." He has no idea what his face reveals, but hers seems surprised though not offended. She isn't pulling her hand away. Yet. Unfortunately his heart is pumping so fast that he's surely headed for a stroke. Wouldn't that be ironic? Tragic, he decides, looking at her.

"Stu? What's going on?" Her hand retracts, her tone soft, questioning, maybe confused, and who could blame her?

"I can't even begin, Lena."

"Begin what?"

"I don't want to upset you."

She shrugs, and he has no idea whether that's a go or a no.

"Something I've been living with," he says.

"What?"

Is she being polite? Does she really want to know? Does it

matter? He drains the beer, looks around quickly, as if someone might stop him. "The need to be close to you."

"Stu . . . I . . ."

"I know, I shouldn't share stuff like this . . ."

"What are you saying . . . since when?" He's bewildering her, but he can't stop now.

"Since you were seventeen."

"Stu, come on."

"It's true. You loved Zack and I loved you and Zack was my friend."

"And Dory?"

"That's just it, I love Dory. A wonderful person, more than great, and I can't imagine hurting her in any way. But lately I've been thinking I married her to stay close to you. I know, don't say it." This is the first time he's thought this. He's not even sure it's true. Is he going to regret this?

"Stu, I don't . . . I mean, after all these years . . ." Her eyes steady on him, her face serious as hell.

"My feelings for you . . . well, I buried them . . ."

"Stop."

"I don't mean to shock you."

"Shock . . . ? Your words are . . . I don't know . . . indigestible." She looks past him. "These last months have been awful. You and Dory offering us your house has been pure survival. And survival takes up all the space in my head. I don't know where to put your words. I don't even know what they mean."

"They mean I want to be with you somehow, somewhere."

"Stu, there's Dory . . ." her tone close to a cry.

"I know." So this is how it ends. Fuckfuckfuck. But he can't give up. He'll never have another chance like this. "Do you feel anything toward me?"

"What is it you want me to feel . . ."

"Tell me how to please you." He's going for broke here.

"Stu, we should go."

"Is that what you want?"

"I think so."

"Let's have another round."

"Why?"

"It's too weird ending the afternoon this way. I mean . . . there's probably more we need to say to be easy with each other again." He sounds like an idiot.

He watches her consider.

"Okay, one more round. Where's the ladies' room?"

Locking the bathroom door, she leans against the wall to take a breath. How to react to an old friend hitting on her and sending a shiver of excitement into her dull plod? How to read the unexpected, scary, pleasant buzz it gives her? It's not just the wine. Stu's an appealing man; any woman would cop to that. She has to admit, if only ever to herself, that his attentions are flattering. The last time a guy overtly flirted with her was at a gas station a year ago, and what was that about? Telling her of all the beautiful women who came into the place, she was the one he wouldn't forget. The guy meant nothing to her, yet his words lifted her spirits, which nearly shamed her. Is that what's happening now, the woman in her being noted? But this is Stu, not some stranger offering bullshit compliments, an old friend she always found attractive, maybe more than attractive. Damn his sincerity, it's disturbing, disarming. Lord above, has she gone bonkers? Why is she even pondering this? Dory's her dearest friend. Forget the drink. Go home. She stares at her face in the mirror. It offers no guidance, none whatsoever.

The second round is already on the table.

"Have I scared you appropriately?" He doesn't sound glib, but vulnerable.

"You have. I'm too fragile for this." She means it to be a joke.

"You're not fragile."

His tone too serious to ignore. "Stu, we need to rein ourselves in here." His second bottle of beer remains untouched. "Aren't you drinking?" she asks, then gulps down the wine.

"I want to remember everything I say and everything you say."

"I'm not used to you being so intense."

"You want funny and light?"

"Yeah, I think so."

"Can't do it, Lena. It's taken too long to gather the courage to say any of this to you. If I turn you off in some way, which I'm too conceited to believe, tell me that, and I'll back off."

"Oh, Christ, Stu, I have no idea how to respond." Her eyes are on the back-lit window, Mary beneath a halo.

"I want to be with you."

"Well, you're with me right now," is all she can think to say. But his persistence feeds scarily into the dark, unexplored place where her old unfulfilled wish for adventure resides. Once she stole a lipstick, not because she needed it, but to see if she could. She downs the rest of the wine, knows she'll have another. Merlot in the afternoon on an empty stomach, no good can come of it.

39.

It's nearly five when they pull into the small motel parking lot. More drinks, more talk, plus a few too many confessions gobble up the afternoon. A real marathon of words came out of her. It's as if she's been shut down for ages. Clearly she shared too much, but he shared, too. More than she had known before. His attachment to his mother and her wish for him to lead a life different from the one he's now living. When she died, he said, he wasn't prepared for the future emptiness or the surprise finality of it. Something, she admitted, she didn't feel about her mother's death. He knew about her mother's death, but not why she married so young. Too much, she thinks, she told him too much, but it felt like release.

The motel is new, he tells her, part of trying to make the Bronx matter. They laugh. She likes that he can make her laugh, likes that he isn't too corny or silly, likes the way he takes charge, leaves her in the car to register, then walks her to the room, his arm tight around her waist as if he fears her disappearance. If only her brain would quiet down, but it's on full throttle, warning her not to be here, even though she's already here.

The room is small and functional: bed, dresser, small TV, padded chair, and a bathroom. A window overlooks small, cloned houses that advance up the street to the Whitestone Bridge, of which only the highest arches can be glimpsed.

He snaps the blinds shut, the light in the room dims. Her brain records each action he takes a second after it happens, then continues to caution her to leave. She likes the way he leads her to the bed, his fingers circling her wrist. Likes the way he gently lays her down, carefully, then slowly, eyes steady on her, hand on her back, raises her some to remove her dress, then back down to peel off her panties and leans over to softly kiss her belly. She likes the precise way he undresses himself, not with excitement but deliberately, eyes steady on her, wearing an expression of pleasure or is that happiness? He's proud of his body, his erect penis, that's clear, and she's proud of it, too, noting how much he wants to be with her. How is it possible to take him in this way while her brain continues to warn her to go home? It's a dissonance she's never experienced. It makes her feel both crazy and lazy. She needs her brain to shut down, to stop its yammering. She likes how he remains beside her and not immediately on top of her, the way he takes her hand to his mouth, nibbles each finger, then his lips gently roam her body, a butterfly lick, here, then there, places he needs to explore. Slow, everything slow. Her skin next to his warmth feels cool, silky, sensuous. But her brain won't stop sending messages. Once she was trapped in an elevator; the alarm didn't ring; the squawk box was static. Her eyes located a panel that led onto the roof of the car, just as the elevator began moving again. There's always an exit, she tells herself, and searches the pale-blue ceiling, a poor representation of the sky.

She notes his body on hers, the muscled weight of his chest, the wiry hair and surprisingly pliant belly. His mouth on hers tastes of beer and chocolate and spearmint. She notes the way he holds still for a beat as if he, too, can hear the litany in her head and is giving her time to quiet. Her brain orders her to push him off. So she makes the deal, the only one possible: let it happen and accept that she'll be forever tainted, and at that moment her body rises to invite him in and her brain finally goes silent. He murmurs words she doesn't try to understand. His grateful moans mingle with the deep, satisfying, indecipherable sounds coming from her. His hunger feeds hers and how long later, she can't say, her body shudders so violently she fears to let go, her arms tight around his back. After a minute or two, his breath brushing her cheek, the acrid scent of beer still there, her heartbeat thrumming against his chest, her arms relax, and he slides off, but remains close at her side. He lifts her hand, kisses her palm, but thankfully says nothing. For a while they lie side by side. She listens to the deafening silence in her head, stares at a framed photo of horses unfettered by saddles in a field of wildflowers and wonders if they've been set free or put out to pasture.

"This didn't happen," she whispers, then scoops up her clothes and heads for the bathroom.

She turns on the shower but stands near the sink. The room steams up. And she admits it this once, if only ever to herself, the day was glorious, not just the loving but the previous hours together. He'll never know this because she'll never tell him. The memory is hers and hers alone and so is the guilt. She steps into the shower. The hot water runs down her back. Her brain in severe judgment remains frighteningly quiet.

He listens to the staccato beat of the shower. Her last words repeat in his head: this didn't happen. Her tone held no anger.

It denied no minute of their pleasure. It was intimate, a secret between lovers understood without further explanation. Is he reading too much into her voice? No. He won't go down the Stu path from elation to doubt and then misery. This did happen and the taste, smell, and feel of her are tattooed on his body forever. He wants to be able to call it all to mind in the middle of the night, on his way to work, before the first sip of bourbon. It's his, all his. Someone once told him that most people live their entire lives without knowing true passion. He's no longer one of them.

The noise of an overhead jet shakes free a memory. As a kid he was obsessed with flying. He'd go out to the airport just to watch the big birds come and go, longing to be inside one. It didn't matter where it was headed. Then his mom won some raffle for a weekend in Florida and instead of taking his father, she took him. Finally, he was in a plane. He savored every minute of it. He looked out the window, walked the aisle. It was terrific. After the trip, the obsession dissipated, but never the memory. It's how he feels now. The fantasy of Lena satisfied, but not his feelings for her. Anything more is up for grabs, including his future.

40.

After another MRI, which the doctor insisted on, she finds herself in the waiting room of the Brain and Nervous System Health Center of the hospital. She phoned for the appointment because she needs a prescription for the nausea, which has become hard to ignore. If truth be told, at least to herself, the whoosh in her ear has gotten louder, too. Yesterday's momentary vertigo at work could be a fluke, but medicine for nausea will help, that much she knows.

Padded chairs along a mirrored wall face a kidney-shaped reception desk, behind which two women talk to each other in low tones, between typing into computers and answering constantly ringing phones. She envies them the normalcy of their day with its routine needs and problems. To be at work and not sitting here would be a gift.

She filled out a million-page questionnaire, mostly checking "no," except in the little section, so disturbing, that homed in on everything happening to her, and to which she found herself checking each box "yes."

Her eyes are drawn to the TV-like monitor on one wall featuring a 3-D cartoon of a rotating brain. As a kid she always found cartoons frightening. Things happened in them without rhyme or reason.

With four prescriptions in her purse, she walks slowly through the hospital lobby, out the gliding door, into the parking lot, and beeps open the car. Sliding behind the steering wheel, she takes off her sunglasses and stares out the window. She can neither accept nor reject the facts. A strange limbo indeed. This time her mind locked in each word from the doctor's mouth. A tall, imposing man, he named the tumor. It's an acoustic neuroma on the eighth cranial nerve, which connects the inner ear with the brain and has two parts. One part transmits sound, the other sends balance messages to the brain. Depending on the size of the tumor, it can press on nearby cranial nerves that control the muscles of facial expression and sensation. Deficits will continue to increase as it grows, which it will, nobody knows by how much or how quickly. When large enough, the tumor will press on the brain stem and be fatal. In the months between both MRI tests, he said, the tumor had grown quite a bit, large enough to make surgery difficult. If she considers going that route, however, which is the one he'd recommend, there's no guarantee the entire mass can be excised without causing unpleasant side effects. Radiation is a possibility, but it would have unpleasant side effects, too, and they're likely to persist. His voice, neither cold nor warm, was firm and clear. Only when he was pointing at the MRI film, explaining the origin of each deficit already there or likely to develop, did her mind shut down, and even if she looked as if she were listening she wasn't, though he kept talking. Her charges may be years older than she is, but she's watched many of them get that glazed look that goes with the what's-the-use-of-hearing more? They already know their comfort zone has been breached, never to return. So why bother pondering more details? It's how she sees it now. To operate, to radiate or not, it all seems irrelevant. Either way, her life will change drastically and not for the better.

The SUV in front of her pulls out to reveal the white brick hospital building, where patients wait to heal or die, spending endless hours wondering when the next blood will be drawn, the next meal will arrive, and who if anyone will visit tonight. She's not ready for any of that. She's also not ready for the future the doctor laid out. But what would ready feel like? No answer. She feels distant from herself, as if space has grown around her that can't be bridged. Maybe she's in shock. Maybe not. Maybe it's how she copes, or maybe she hasn't absorbed the news. Or like an earthquake, maybe it's a tectonic shift, lifting her out of her life to an altitude high enough from which to view it. Or maybe deep down—and this is the strangest thought of all—she doesn't care.

Stu's car is in the garage when she pulls in. They must be back from the sale of Lena's car. There's no point in keeping the tumor a secret any longer. She'll cook dinner, and then after dessert tell everyone. Hearing the news in the company of friends will give Stu time to process it. Telling him alone in bed would overwhelm him, send him to the nearest bar, though either way he'll probably end up there. He can't handle unfixable problems.

Zack's in the kitchen, her striped apron around his waist, every pot in the house simmering with something, the table already set.

"This is unexpected," she says.

"I like to cook. I raided your freezer, defrosted the small turkey. It's in the oven, along with sweet potatoes. I'm heating stuffing and vegetables, too."

"Sounds like Thanksgiving."

"Yeah, sort of."

"Okay, I give up. What's going on?"

"I've decided to never work in construction again. No, actually I decided that a while back, but today I decided to announce it." He grins.

"Is that a decision to celebrate?"

"Absolutely. Concrete decisions are liberating."

"Why no more construction?" She can't help asking.

"I don't want to explain. It's how I feel. That's it. That's enough."

Maybe she ought to adopt Zack's approach. I have a tumor, I don't want to discuss it. That's it.

"Well, you seem to be . . ." she pauses, "certain."

"I got a job in the back room of one of the warehouses in the meat-packing district, counting and weighing sides of beef and keeping records of same. Seven hours a day by myself, no lifting, no carting, no heights, everything simple and done mechanically." He turns back to the stove and opens the oven door to check on the turkey.

"Well, good luck." It sounds awful, but why say so? "I'm going to wash up."

41.

In bare feet and comfortable caftan, fresh from a shower, Dory pads down the hallway not the least bit hungry, but calls Lena and Casey to dinner. Her voice sounds hoarse to her. Words move quickly through her head like those streaming across the bottom of a TV screen.

Beer and wine are on the table. She'll drink. Why not?

"Where's Mom?" Casey asks, emerging from the basement.

"Go get her. Tell her we're waiting."

Lena comes out of the bedroom and follows Casey to the table, an odd expression on her face.

"The car sold?" she asks. Her voice sounds far away, as if someone has put earmuffs on her ears.

Lena nods.

"Dig in," Zack orders, setting down the last platter.

"I didn't know you liked to cook," Lena comments, deadpan.

"How could you? When it comes to the kitchen, 'no entry' is stenciled on your forehead."

Lena purses her lips but doesn't respond.

"So, listen, my friends. I have an announcement and here it is: I'm never going back to construction work."

Lena glares at him. "Why not?"

"Because it's what I want. Do you have a problem with that?"

"This isn't the time or place."

"Yes it is. It's time you knew, and we have no other place."

Casey stares at his father. "But, Dad, what else can you do?"

"A mighty good question, son, and the answer arrived today. I got a job in the backroom of a meat market. It pays above minimum and I'll be by myself, weighing sides of beef. Anyone have a problem with *that*?" Zack looks only at Lena.

"Well, congrats," Stu says. Though he sounds less than enthusiastic.

"Lena? What do you think of my job?"

"Does it have benefits or a union?" Lena asks.

"Nothing satisfies you, my angel, nothing."

Lena seems about to leave the table.

"I, too, have an announcement," Dory hears herself say. Heads turn to her. All thoughts on how to share the information instantly fall away. "I have a brain tumor." Crap.

"For real?" Stu asks, breaking the stunned silence.

"For real," she replies quietly. Then, her gaze fixed on the platter holding the sliced-open sweet potatoes, their orange insides exposed, she fills them in matter-of-factly on what she's learned from the doctor. No one interrupts. When she looks up, Lena is crying.

"Lena, you never cry." Her friend begins to sob. It unnerves her. "Lena, please stop. I'm sorry."

"What do you have to be sorry about?" Zack shouts. "It's your life on the line. Lena's crying, big fucking deal, a normal response for a change."

Lena moves quickly down the hallway.

"Dad," Casey says. "Everything is wrong."

Stu's silence feels heavy, disapproving. He's staring into his plate as if he's about to be sick. Except, surely, he can't blame her for the illness? Of course he doesn't. He's over-whelmed. She expected that. He's undoubtedly processing, which takes time.

Zack heads down the hallway.

He finds Lena face down on the bed, no longer audibly crying. "You've upset Dory more than she already is. Do you hear me?"

No response.

He stands over her. "I'm talking to you. Turn around, damn it, and answer me," his voice unnaturally loud in his ears.

"I have nothing to say to you, maybe ever again."

She finally does turn around, her face wet with misery.

"Now listen closely. I'm sick and tired of your poor-me atti-tude, the woman wronged by her loser husband. You're not the only one in the house whose feelings matter. I've spent weeks thinking through feelings of my own. So let me enlighten you, angel. I will no longer put up with being pushed away in bed. You do that to punish me, but, my beauty, I'm not a child, and I won't be treated like one anymore. I've spent more years than not adoring you, and this is how you respond to me in a crisis? Are you listening to me?" His anger is rising with each word. "Answer me, god fucking damn it!"

She nods.

"I want you to say 'I'm listening.'"

"Get out, Zack."

"Not on your life. I'm staying here, and we're getting this wagon back on the road." He likes his combative tone.

"I'm not sleeping with a man who I find . . ." she hesitates.

"Say it, you've always wanted to. Say it for fuck's sake."

"Irresponsible."

He ignores her response. "Does fucking me make you nauseous?"

"Why are you being so vulgar?"

"Vulgar? I'll tell you what's vulgar. Having to pay a whore to hold my balls, that's vulgar." Oh damn.

She gets off the bed.

"Don't leave this room." But already his anger is cooling.

She sits in the rocking chair and stares at him. He knows that expression. She's deciding exactly what to say, because that's her, precise.

"I'm waiting." He hovers. He won't back off now, no matter what.

"You have been zero available to me and the children as a husband and a father since the foreclosure. Understand? I blame you for Rosie leaving. She didn't want to be part of a family without a father. While you lay there in the basement waiting for the world to come to your aid, Rosie was gallivanting around with some older guy in the South fucking Bronx, and you never even asked 'where is my daughter?' What kind of father . . ."

"Stop, just stop, Lena. Rosie's not a baby. In fact, she's too wise for her age. She was begging for trust and you were smothering all her impulses. She hated that."

"Her absence is an open sore for which I hold you responsible. Responsible, understand? I should be able to enjoy watching her first date, the prom, whatever."

"Who do you think we are, the fucking Brady Bunch?"

"I can't talk more about Rosie. It's too painful."

"Well, at least we're talking."

"Oh. You mean you and the whore didn't talk?"

"It was a desperate five-minute fuck. I never saw her before or want to again. What did you expect me to do, jerk off?"

"Why not?"

"Well, I did that, too, but you know after awhile it felt stupid, depressing, while you lay there all comfy in your beauty sleep like I was nothing, just air you could easily ignore. Is that how you feel? Because with all you've said, I still have no clue what it is you want from me."

"To search for a job the way I did. Every night sitting at the computer, lining up places to go in the morning, rain or shine. But, no, you bedded down in our basement deciding it was more important to figure out how you felt about things. And now, what? You roam the streets doing the same? Well, lucky you, avoiding the mess."

"I did try for weeks to find work in construction, but I was glad I couldn't. No, not glad, relieved. I hate the work and the weather. There were times I felt like jumping off one of those high beams. But I didn't. I stayed because it brought in the bread for all of you. Did that ever cross your mind? Did you even have an inkling of *my* misery?" He wants to continue shouting, but a weird choking sound, close to a cry, clogs his throat.

"I'm not into guessing, Zack. Like I wasn't into guessing that you hadn't paid the mortgage. How could you keep that from me all those months? How could you put us all in jeopardy?"

"Okay, I made the wrong call." His tone now sounds petulant, even to him, which is disappointing. He wants to retrieve the anger, the righteous feelings that somehow seem to have floated out of reach.

"Wrong call? Is that how you define it? Wrong call? Neglecting responsibility is the wrong call? For shit's sake, Zack, how could you simply believe everything would somehow, god knows how, take care of itself? How stupid is that?."

Her accusatory tone nearly undoes him, but he can't stop now. "Listen, I agree. I did wrong. I get it. I do. But you never tried to forgive me. You stayed angry and distant."

"Distant? Never tried . . . Jesus! How many times did I ask you to consider taking meds for depression? How many times did I encourage you to believe in yourself and to believe you'd find work?"

"You're not blameless. You stopped sleeping with me."

"Do you think I'm some kind of robot? Do you think I want to make love with someone who looks at me as if I'm about to hand him another problem, someone who resents that I haven't fallen apart like he did? What kind of man wants to make love with a woman he resents? What kind of man is that?"

He wants to say that she has it all wrong, all of it. He doesn't resent her. He's never stopped loving her. Instead he hears himself say, "I was overlooked, neglected, made to feel beside the point."

"Well, you know what, Zack? I'm sorry you felt neglected. But so did I. Except it didn't stop me from keeping on keeping on."

"Mom?" Casey opens the door a bit.

"Yes, honey, come in," she says.

"Mom, are you okay? I heard Dad shouting." Casey's concern rips at her insides. She can't lose him the way she has Rosie. He needs to be kept out of the disarray.

"Of course, honey."

"Casey, I love your mother. No one can or will ever love her as much as I do. I would never, ever hurt her. Okay?" He slings an arm around Casey's shoulder. "We're just straightening out some crooked thoughts. When we're done, everything will be fine. Right, Lena?"

"Yes."

Casey searches her face. The boy knows her, knows, too, that everything is far from fine.

"I left Rosie a message, told her Mom was crying and Dory was dying and you sounded odd," Casey says, still looking directly at his mother.

"That's fine, Casey. Rosie needs to know. She loves Dory. Can I give you a hug?" She extends her arms.

"Maybe later. See you." He leaves the door ajar.

"Baby, I meant every word I said to Casey," Zack tells her. "Every word."

She says nothing.

"I will be a more responsible husband and father, but you need to take responsibility for some of what went wrong between us. Losing that house may have meant even more to me than to you, but you never considered that. After all our years of marriage it should've occurred to you that I couldn't face telling you because I was devastated. We have to fix this. I love you." His tone rings strong, hopeful, different than usual. He can hear it, feel it. And from her expression, he thinks she can too.

"Zack, right now . . . I'm numb."

"I'm patient. I won't lose you. I won't lose us." He'd love to lift her out of the chair, press her against him, but it's not the moment. "I'm going out for a while."

She watches him slip from the room. Zack's tone, his attitude, especially his anger, was different, less adoring but more assertive. Is it possible he's on a new path? He's messed up royally, but he's right. She did, too. Does that make them even? He did hand her a tiny gift. Those five minutes with his whore wiped out a fraction of her own shame. She believes him that the whore meant nothing. She can't say the same about Stu.

Truth is supposed to clear the air, and he's a forgiving sort of guy, but he'd never get past the truth about her afternoon with Stu. The thing is . . . Stu happened . . . but he can't be the reason for whatever decision she makes about her marriage. Perhaps people with lots of money can act rashly, but in her life, choices are determined by circumstance. And circumstance demands that Dory have all of Stu's attention even if, god forbid, it means her family moves into a shelter.

She wanders over to the window, her limbs as stiff as if she'd been lifting heavy boxes. Under the night sky, she barely makes out the patio, but knows it well. The flowers Dory planted along its edges, arranged by color, pink next to purple next to yellow, something musical in their array. She doesn't know the names, never asked, but when they bought this house Dory phoned to say she'd been to a garden shop for the first time ever. In addition to bulbs and seeds, she bought a birdhouse and bird feed, which struck them both as funny. Who from the Bronx ever bought stuff like that? Dory said—and she remembers it well—that even if the landscape beyond the yard was gray and boring, her satisfaction changed the view.

42.

Zack walks quickly toward the bus stop, the last moments with Lena energizing. He has a mission and missions can't wait. It's still so goddamn hot out. He doesn't do well in such weather. Delicate boy. No, he's not, he's determined. Lena will see that. She has to. What he said to her, and more importantly how he said it was all positive, every last thing, though unusual behavior on his part, but isn't that the point—to scramble the picture, create a new design? What's wrong with that?

A woman waiting at the bus stop glances at his feet. Damn, he's still wearing slippers. So what? This is New York. Anyone can wear anything. There are no rules except for nudity, though right now every piece of his clothing seems to weigh a ton. He wonders what time it is, but doesn't want to ask her. If he hears how late it is, he'll be forced to abort until tomorrow, and he can't. He must do this now, for Lena.

The bus shelter has a backless bench with three partitions. The woman's encased in one of them. She's in her sixties, he'd say, wearing a blue dress that reaches her swollen ankles. What's she doing out alone so late? Maybe she works for one of the upscale houses and is on her way home, the bus her daily mode of transportation. On her lap a tote bag made of soft, flowered material, big enough to hide a baby. The woman glances at him again. Has he been staring at her bag? Is she worried that he wants to rob her? He looks away, but he feels too antsy to be sitting like this. It's as if he's channeling Stu, who often declares himself too antsy for his life. Poor Stu. How's he going to survive Dory's illness? If it were Lena with a brain tumor, he'd moan, cry, drink, take drugs, go into the grave with her, none of which he'll share with Stu. He isn't exactly sure what he can offer that would be helpful, except to reassure him that however he's felt about his marriage—and the negatives have been commonplace these past months—it's possible to turn a page, take a leap, rectify. It's just what he's doing in his relationship with Lena. He's already promised himself to focus, pay attention, take responsibility for whatever, so help him god.

He looks down the road. No bus. Damn, damn. If he continues to pace in these slippers, the woman will think he's mental, and the slippers make him shuffle. Everyone knows people who shuffle are a bit off. So he sits, leaving the seat between them free. He's glad not to be alone, glad not to concentrate on what he'll say or do, because he has zero to no idea, only that he's got to succeed.

"These buses take a long time to come?"

She eyes him hesitantly, clearly something about him seems best left alone. She nods. Smart woman. Acknowledge his presence, don't insult him, but don't engage either. He gets it and focuses on the pockmarked road.

The bus drops him off near their old house. He walks over to inspect it. To his satisfaction, broad zigzag black lines still decorate the front of the house like so many bolts of lightning.

The rooms are empty. These mortgage banks, fucking incompetents! They throw out his family and the house remains vacant, no payments coming in, nothing, and what exactly have they gained? Stupid assholes. His family should move back in. Who would know? Not the bank. They're not about to follow up on foreclosure unless they have a buyer. Who's going to buy a place on a road with three empty houses? It'll be months, maybe years, before they resell it, by which time it will need rehab work. He sincerely doubts anyone from the world of finance or real estate checks up here or takes care of the space. He'd bet that the bank doesn't even have these houses on its radar screen. They should retake the house. It's theirs. Lena won't agree, though he sure as shit thinks it's a great idea. The neighbors would cheer one less empty house on the road. They could set an example for other foreclosed families. Who knows? Maybe they could start a movement? Squatters. How illegal is that?

He continues his journey, his brain wrapped around the house with the cool black design.

The tawny porch globe illuminates the lawn and front door. Do they expect visitors at this time of night? He walks around back to check out the rest of this imposing house. No welcoming rays of light from there, and—who knows? —a watchdog could be waiting to bite into flesh.

Inside, no doubt everyone's asleep. Sorry, folks . . . he rings the bell. To his dismay, it makes a tinkly sound no louder than a spoon-tap against a glass. He uses the wooden doorknocker next, thud, thud, thud, watching the windows for a light to come on inside. Again, he uses the knocker. Then peers through the glass side panel of the door. Somewhere inside, a light does finally come on. He hopes it's not the man of the house. He knows nothing about the parents. A father should know, he can hear Lena say.

Mirabelle opens the door. Her eyes widen. "Rosie's dad!"

"That's me. I need to talk to Rosie," he says in his friendliest voice. But adds, "Right now."

"Did something happen to someone?"

"Please wake my daughter, tell her to come down. Right now."

"But what happened?"

"Mirabelle, I'm not about to say anything to you that I haven't said first to my daughter. So, please, let me in and go get Rosie. We'll keep our voices down and not wake your parents." Because that's the last the last thing he wants.

He takes a seat on a thick, velvety couch that grabs at the fabric of his pants and makes movement nearly impossible. His eyes fasten on a huge chandelier. Is it for light or show, he wonders?

Rosie appears at the top of the staircase, barefoot, in pajama bottoms and shirt. "Mirabelle, I'll fill you in later," he hears her say. She slowly descends. "What's up?" Her tone casual, careful.

"Get your stuff. Your place is with your family and it's where you're going now." He's taking a chance. Ordering this girl to do anything usually backfires. Then again, he's rarely been the one to issue demands.

"What? Are you on crack or something?"

"I'll ignore that. I'm your father, and you need to pay attention to what I'm saying."

"My father? You didn't even blink when I left. Or you couldn't because you were one of the disappeared." God, she sounds like her mother. He stands. He needs to be upright with Rosie.

"I don't care what you think or what you say . . ." he begins.

"Well, that's encouraging . . ."

"Shut up, Rosie, and listen real closely. I'm not leaving here without you. If you don't come home with me, I'll wake Mirabelle's parents and insist they throw you out. If you want that kind of scene, I'm up for it."

"I don't think so." Her tone remains calm, which is troubling. If she sassed him it would be more like her.

He takes a few steps toward her.

She puts up her hand. "Don't come any closer. Who are you? Why are you really here? You never cared that I was gone. You didn't phone once or leave a message. Mom's a pain in the ass but she never stops trying to reach me. Why should I care about anything you say, father or no?" her voice suddenly shaky.

The words stab at his gut. "I love you, Rosie. Don't you know that?"

"I don't understand that kind of love. I can't trust someone who fades out during trouble, who allows Mom to step all over him."

"This isn't about my relationship with your mother. Get your things and come home with me." He's really messed up with this girl.

"What? You're going to strongarm me, drag me screaming through the streets to a bus? Mom already used that threat and you can see just how well it worked."

"I hope it doesn't come to that, but you're going home with me." He stares at her hard. He wants her to understand that he means what he says.

"Dory's house is not home."

"Do you think any of us enjoy living as guests? Do you realize we did it for you and Casey? If we didn't have kids, we'd be free to get in a car, and who knows travel somewhere, find work elsewhere."

"Good idea. Go for it."

She turns, ready to walk back up the steps. In one stride he's behind her, his hand on her shoulder, holding her back.

"Let go of me."

He hears the shock in her voice, and he can't blame her. "Not until you hear me out. Come sit down and let me talk." He backs off, drops onto the couch again. "Please, Rosie, give me a chance here." He's pleading now. He can hear it and so can she. After a fast second of thought she sits on the edge of a cushy chair. Fine, he doesn't need her beside him though he'd like to hold her hand.

"Look, I'm not ready to forget everything," she announces, in her I'm-being-reasonable tone. "I'm mad at Mom. She fucked up my relationship with a guy I cared about. She doesn't understand me. I can't live in the same space as her."

"That's ridiculous. She got you out of a bad situation and you're too young and stupid to realize it. She risked you hating her in order to save you. You can't imagine what that feels like because you're not a parent."

Even as he says this, the truth of it hits him. "And your mother is right. If we don't stay together as a family, we won't be able to move forward. I've gotten a job. It means we won't have to stay at Dory's forever. Casey needs his sister. It's not good for him to be the only light in the house. And, damn, I miss you so bad I can hardly talk about it. I've changed. I intend to seek out and take major responsibility . . . for whatever. Fickle father has disappeared. We'll put up a partition in the basement, you'll have privacy and . . ."

"Just stop. I'm not going back with you." Her determined chin rises combatively.

"Don't you care that Dory's going to die?" It's a low blow, but he's desperate.

"Aren't we all?" She won't look at him.

"I can't believe you said that."

"Believe what you want. I am going to live my life the way I see fit, and neither you nor mom is going to determine how I do that."

"Rosie, that's our role as parents, to guide, care for, be there . . ."

"Spare me that song. I don't want your guidance, your care, or your presence."

"You can't mean that."

"Well . . . I do."

Rosie looks past him and mimes a yawn, her palm lightly hitting her lips. Suddenly his head begins to pound, his eyes mist, and he's filled with helpless fury. "How can you be so hard-hearted? I guess we did fuck up with you, our daughter who seems about as sensitive as the wooden floor we stand on. If you distrust us that much, well then, go your own way, make your own life, good luck to you. Best wishes, and don't bother letting us know about you." His voice is low, intense.

She stares at him.

His fury spent as quickly as it rose, he's stunned by his words. He knows he doesn't mean them, can't believe he said them. Lena would've been more careful. Shit. What's the matter with him? He glances at her stony, unreadable face. If he tries to undo the damage now, she won't hear him. They'll continue to argue. It could get worse. He knows her well enough to predict that.

With effort he hoists himself off the couch and heads for the door at a snail's pace, praying with each step like he's never prayed before that she'll say something, anything, to stop him. He doesn't dare turn to look at her. He might grab her or start weeping, and hasn't he done enough damage for one day? He closes the door gently behind him.

Dory's house is padded with sleep when he returns. A night-light in the kitchen casts an eerie green glow. The table is free of the dinner dishes he set out only hours ago. He considers a bottle of beer, but decides he's too tired to drink it. Even too tired to think about what a mess he's made of the situation. He drags himself into the bedroom. Moonlight leaks through the blinds. He undresses, trying not to make a sound. The A/C is going full blast. He thinks to lower it, but climbs into bed instead. Lena's faint floral scent reaches him. She's asleep, her back to him. Lena may not respond well to his visit with Rosie. In the morning he'll tell her anyway, the good, bad, and the ugly. No more avoidance.

Eyeing the dark hair falling easily over her perfectly rounded shoulders, he hesitantly, almost shyly, slips an arm around the satiny skin he's missed so much that he could cry. He waits for her to inch away as she's been doing lately. But she turns to bury her face in his shoulder. And he wonders if he's fallen directly into REM sleep because, surely, he must be dreaming.

235

43.

"Rosie," Mirabelle calls softly, padding down the stairs. "What happened? Is someone hurt?"

"He came to take me home, the highwayman without a horse."

"Why are you talking this way?"

"What way?"

"You're never poetic."

"Never?" But she is feeling weird, and can't explain her state of mind even to herself.

"Did something happen? Can you answer that simple question?"

"Everything is the same." Which can't be true. Her father charged in with an attitude bordering on aggression. Unless he's having a breakdown, why the sudden transformation? No one goes from laid-back to caveman in one leap. It doesn't work that way.

"He expected you to walk out with him in the middle of the night?"

She sighs. "I think so. Please, Mirabelle, go up to bed. I need to think. We'll talk in the morning, I promise."

"If you're sure. I am your best friend and I'm here for you, whatever."

"I know, and I appreciate it. Now go." She hears Mirabelle's step on the staircase, then sits back in the overly large chair and hugs her knees. Why should anything he says matter now? One day he wakes up and decides it's time to get his daughter home? Well, tough shit, it isn't that easy. He messed up her future. They both did. Her mom stalking her. It makes her furious. She still thinks about Sonny, though not every minute the way she expected to. Being loved, though, she misses that. Nevertheless, her mother rejected him without knowing him. That's sinful. If he'd lived in a palace her mother would've felt differently about him. Gross.

Why in all the world are her parents trying so hard to get her back? They can barely take care of themselves, let alone her. It wasn't just anger that propelled her out the door, it was insight. They should celebrate her self-sufficiency. Instead her father mocks her, calls her stupid. That, at least, is one thing she isn't. She gets it. He's trying to impress her mother with his post-midnight visit. She won't be used, not for his or anyone's purpose.

Not that she wants to live here forever. Mirabelle's parents spook her. They talk softly, walk softly. She finds herself whispering most of the time. They go to bed so early. Two years ago, when Mirabelle's mother invited her to spend Christmas with them at a ski lodge upstate, she was ultra-excited. How beautiful it would be, how romantic, and she'd never been to a lodge. Her mother didn't want her to go, but she insisted. All three days away she was lonely for the noisy holiday goings-on at her own house, filled with people acting silly and crazy after a few drinks. When she returned, her parents, even Casey, were so happy to see her. Her mother declared she could never, ever, not in a million years, be away for Christmas again. Dory said the holiday hadn't been the same without her.

Of course she's upset about Dory. She loves Dory, but the way her father used it. So manipulative. It wasn't going to melt her into complying. Stu must be freaking out. She imagines everyone sitting around the table discussing Dory's illness, offering advice about next steps to take. It's what they do when crisis strikes, and her voice was missing at the table. Maybe that was what prompted her father to come get her. But if so, why didn't he say that?

She stares at the chandelier. It is a magnificent room, but so what?

She wanders into the darkened kitchen, where the well-stocked fridge's buttery light reveals an unopened bottle of vodka. She stares at it, unscrews the cap and takes a long drink.

44.

In bed with Dory for hours and still wide awake. He understands now. Sleep will never come. He takes his clothes to the bathroom, dresses quietly, tiptoes out to the garage, gets in the car, and prays the clatter of the opening door wakes no one.

He's not sure where to go or what to do or how to get through what's left of the night. He turns the key in the ignition. The A/C comes on and so does the radio, which he promptly switches off because music of any kind seems inappropriate.

He heads south, driving slowly under a moonlit, charcoal sky. Clouds as wispy as smoke ride along with him. Except for a few trucks, the expressway is free of traffic, unusual, like everything else in his life right now. Is it bourbon he needs or a place to sit with no voice other than his own nattering in his head? He takes an exit, makes a few familiar turns, and arrives at the bus-shaped diner, open 24/7. He parks beside the only other car in the lot and hikes up three dirty rubber-matted steps. The lighting inside is dull, but at least it's air-conditioned.

Before he can settle in a booth near the window, the waiter is out from behind the counter with pad and pencil. Thick and powerful, the guy reminds him of his father, not necessarily the best of memories. "Coffee, black, please." The waiter looks disappointed. What did he expect, meat and potatoes at this time of night?

If his mom were alive, he'd be sitting at her place instead of a diner. A boy who didn't give up his thoughts too easily, he could always talk to her. She listened and as far as he could tell never judged him, no matter what he said. His mom made sense to him, even if she always repeated the same few mantras during stressful times: every body has a story and each person's problem is the worst in the world. Married to his father, who returned from Vietnam addicted to alcohol, she hated that war with a fierceness that couldn't be breached. No one was allowed to mention it in her presence. She blamed it for the ruination of her husband. When his father died, he felt relief. His mother's burden had been lifted. She was finally liberated. Eighteen months later, she died of a heart attack. Dory dubbed it a broken heart, but he couldn't see it, until now, when a sliver of the truth of it cuts into his thick brain.

At bars, at work, people share stories of impossible situations, but he's not good at venting. Even if he were, what would he say? I just learned that my wife's going to die a slow, horrible death, and this afternoon I made love to her best friend? Who would he say it to? He doesn't exactly have a line of friends waiting to sort out his problems. Once upon a time he could bank on Zack for anti-anxiety words of comfort. But he's fucked that possibility forever. He can't even look the guy in the face now without the neon light of Lena flashing in his head. The hours with her were beyond amazing. He planned to conjure them up at least once a day forever. Yet it's no longer what he wants to hold onto. Dory's illness has altered something deep inside, something he didn't know was there. He can feel it, but has no idea what it is.

He stares out the Bronx-grimed window at the two- and three-level attached brick houses beyond the parking lot. He and Dory considered buying such a place when they were looking, but decided that being a Siamese twin to a neighbor didn't appeal to them. They're in sync about such decisions, where to live, what car to buy, what's for dinner, who to visit, who to cross off their list. His drinking upsets her, it's true, but did she ever throw a tantrum or act out one of the TV sitcoms, "Don't you dare go out tonight, or else"? No. She's not like that. What makes him happy is fine with her. She's his best friend, a repository of more than half his life, the person he could talk to about anything if he chose to, anything at all, except Lena. But what does that matter now? So why has he been skipping over her virtues and only tallying up the shit-stuff of late? Which is what, exactly? That she loves him too much to bear? That her tender ways make him feel guilty? Or is it that her body no longer sends his prick into instant upright? Is sex the only glue that counts? He really can't say, except Dory is a piece of him, like his liver or his kidney. Is that love, he really can't say either, except that he never even stopped to think about any of it before. He feels lost, panicked, and not because he's going to have to play nursemaid to a sick wife either. It's something so much deeper and bigger, and it's clawing at his insides.

He gazes at the waiter, idly thumbing through the pages of a newspaper. By the quick turn of the pages it's clear the guy is just looking at pictures or headlines, probably killing time till his shift is over and he can go home to be easy again. A hot streak of envy courses through his body. With Dory gone, how will he ever feel easy again? Even when he thought about leaving the marriage he imagined her there where he could find her, a body active with life, a woman he could always come back to, who loves him in that way.

He glances at the cold coffee, drops a five on the counter, and heads out into the sudden fog of heat, which sends goose bumps up his arms. The night sky is receding, offering up a pencil-thin red line of light beyond the farthest houses, and it's the loneliest sight he ever saw.

Leaving the car in the driveway to avoid the noise of the garage door closing, he tiptoes through the house to the bedroom. Undressing quickly, his clothes scattered on the floor, he slips in beside Dory, who is or isn't asleep. He can't say for sure. He sidles up to her naked back till his knees fit inside hers, till his chin rests in the smooth, soap-scented neck space below her ear, and whispers, "Dory, help me."

45.

Cocooned in a blanket at a comfort level that will dissipate the moment she moves, it takes a while before the rhythmic thudding penetrates her brain. Her eyes open on the clock: 6:45. She nudges Zack. Empty space. He must be in the bathroom. The thudding continues. Someone's banging on the door, and no one's responding. Damn. She slips on a robe and shuffles through the hallway. Zack appears and follows her. Coming up from the basement, Casey beats them both to the door.

"Ask who it is," she calls.

"Who is it," Casey says with little gusto.

"Who's there?" she shouts.

"Rosie."

Stunned, she watches Casey unlock the door and pull it open. Her daughter in sundress and flip-flops, wearing a backpack and carrying a small bag, offers her presence wordlessly, then announces to no one in particular, "I came because Dory's sick. I'll put my things in with yours, Casey, okay?"

Rosie walks past them. Casey follows her. She makes a move to follow them to the basement, but Zack puts a restraining hand on her shoulder. "I was going to tell you this morning," he whispers.

"Tell me what?"

"I went to see Rosie late last night, told her she had to come home. She told me to get lost, said I wasn't a good father, and that nothing I said mattered. For some reason, she changed her mind. Are you mad that I went to see her without telling you?"

"No. It worked." Still somewhat stunned, she wonders what to do next.

"Lena, she isn't the same kid who left our house. She's lived with a man. Who knows what other experiences she's had? She's not going to toe the line easily."

"I just wish I knew what she might need from me."

"Give it time." He strokes her hair. "Last night . . . making love . . . I didn't expect . . . well . . . it made me so happy."

She smiles. What can she say? She did it for him? It was comforting to feel him take her in so easily. But Stu was present as well, not a shadow on the wall but a physical weight inside her.

"I need to finish dressing. I can't be late for work." He grins and heads back to the bedroom.

Almost instantly, she starts for the basement. Zack's probably right. It's too soon. It could be the world's stupidest move. Still, she's the girl's mother. She has to try.

She pushes open the basement door. "Rosie, Casey, is it okay to come down?" She descends the few steps without waiting for a reply.

Rosie's on the futon sofa, remote in hand, surfing channels. Casey, on the floor, propped up against the sofa, is watching something on his laptop. Her eyes sweep the room, two floor lamps, red director's chair, red-and-black striped rug, two windows, and a small A/C unit. Decent enough. A white curtain across a ceiling rod hides the washing machine and dryer.

"You both look comfy," she begins.

No response. This is all on her.

"What are you watching?"

"Mom, I'm going upstairs to get some breakfast," Casey says. She feels a wave of empathy for him, avoiding what's to come. If only, she thinks, and takes a seat on the chair facing Rosie, whose eyes remain on the screen. "So you heard about Dory?"

"You mean when Casey phoned? Or when Dad made his middle of the night visit to Mirabelle's? I'm sure he was afraid to wait for morning because by then Dory could be dead. Really, how dumb is it to barge into someone else's house at that time of night? What's going on with him? He was all confess-y."

"Confess-y?"

"Yeah, wanted to let me know that he's no longer the father I knew. He's a new man and some other stuff, the kind of stuff you tell your shrink not your daughter."

"He was trying to let you know that things are changing."

"Are they? How?"

"Well, he has a job," it's the first thing that comes to mind.

"Great, my father finally got a job, which most fathers already have. What does that have to do with me?"

"We're not going to be at Dory's much longer."

"Oh? Just a year or two or three?"

She tries to locate the hard sarcasm in her daughter's face, but it's as lovely and unblemished as ever. "Can't you just talk to me?"

Rosie mutes the TV. "You should've thought of that before stalking me. I cared about Sonny. You scared him away. You didn't let me have my experience. You made me unhappy. My own mother! I still miss him. Though I'm furious at him as well for being such a wimp. He should've stood up to you or ignored you instead of buckling. Now you expect me to slide into an easy relationship with you?"

Of course she's right, this oh-so-smart girl of hers. How can anything be easy with all that's happened? "He wasn't good for you," and even she can hear how lame it sounds.

"I'm not in the mood to rehash it, especially with you."

Remembering the little girl who loved telling her stories about every possible thing, at times boring her to sleepiness. "Tell me about your time away, where you were, what you did . . ."

"You mean how did I spend my summer, or what did I think of Mirabelle's parents?"

She doesn't reply to her daughter's taunts.

"I drank whiskey and vodka. I smoked fairy dust, that's drugs. Each time I did, it felt so good I wanted more and had more. Nothing mattered but the moment and the moment was happy. You should try them. And then with Sonny there were all the times of day when he would begin to undress me. He would . . ."

Leave now, she thinks.

"Poor Mom. Cat got your tongue?" Rosie's eyes blaze at her.

"You're here. You're safe. I'm grateful, relieved and I wanted to reach out to you."

"Reach out to me? What does that mean? I'm not across the ocean."

She turns away before Rosie can see her distress. There's so much she wants to say to this girl, that the future is hers, that whatever's happened will be superseded by the things, good and bad, still to occur, that she's sad about the time they've lost and wants to make up for it. Yet she can't bring herself to say any of it, too afraid her words won't matter one bit. "Rosie, just know I love you," is what she settles for as she leaves the room.

Her mother's bare feet and slim ankles disappear up the stairs. The basement door shuts. What did her mother expect, a grand reunion? And if she's so delirious about having her back, why not admire her spunk and determination? Nothing, she fears, will change. She powers off the TV.

Why *is* she here? Yes, Dory? But no, Dory, too. So what is it? Mirabelle couldn't understand why she would leave her guest room only to be a guest in someone else's house. A point well taken. She gazes at her phone on the sofa and has a quick chat with herself. Go ahead. Call him! Why the hell not? Because he won't want to talk to her? Of course he will. He's not an asshole. And if he picks up, what'll she say? It'll come to her. She dials the number. He does pick up. His voice sounds so the same.

"Hi, it's me, Rosie. Are you surprised?"

46.

Without knocking, she enters Dory's bedroom and lies down next to her friend, whose pale red hair, loosened from its usual ponytail, softens her slim face. "Are you available?"

"Why?"

"We haven't talked one on one since you told us about the diagnosis. I'm sorry I reacted so childishly, but I was stunned. I still am."

"Me, too, except... I don't know... I'm weirdly not freaking out. I keep thinking tomorrow or the day after I'll have some kind of hysterical breakdown. Or maybe not, which is even weirder, don't you think?"

"I will do everything for you."

"No you won't. I'm the caregiver, remember? It's my job. It's what I do, what I've done for more than half my life. I can care for myself."

"You're just in denial."

Dory sits up. "Maybe I am and maybe I'm not. But I'm explaining, plainly, it's who I am."

"That's your message? Don't deal with the illness? Pretend it's another day in the happy life of Dory?"

"You sound pissed."

"I am. You're always there for me. I want to be there for you."

"I have to get ready for work. So you can leave my room or watch me get dressed. Up to you."

"I'll go, but I'm not done with this conversation."

Dory swings her legs off the bed. "How about meeting at that dirty little bar near my work, tonight at five? Just the two of us? A few drinks before dinner? It could open up some secret spaces."

The last rays of evening sun light her way through a neighborhood of half-standing buildings and gutted shops. The few functioning stores look less than inviting. Finding Dory's dirty little bar for which she has neither a name nor an address is proving more difficult than she expected.

She doesn't want Dory to pick up the tab, so it's one drink for her. She's parceling out money from the car fund for train and bus fare and essentials like replacing Casey's rotting sneakers. She's actually darning his ratty socks, and hasn't bought him new underwear in she doesn't want to think how long. Once upon a time, people could apply for welfare, but where to go now? She even takes off her black "interview" dress as soon as she gets home, to save it from having to be cleaned. She's been job-hunting all afternoon.

The first two possibilities were already filled by the time she arrived. The last was for a bookkeeper at a shabby midtown hotel called Wonderland, the kind of place that sells rooms by the hour. The guy who interviewed her was pretty seedy himself, though quite polite. He told her he used to do the books on his own, but the IRS pointed out it was a bad idea and suggested he hire a part-time bookkeeper. He was offering three four-hour days at eleven dollars an hour, no benefits. She assured him she could do the work. He showed her a tiny room, called it the "office," though except for a desk and a window, it could have been a prison cell. He still had a few applicants to see, but promised that as soon as he made a decision, he'd phone her either way.

Finally she recognizes the frayed beer posters in the window and pushes the door open. He's there, the same bartender whose name escapes her, though she remembers Arthur well enough. Decent man. Came through for her. Three young women occupy the rearmost table, their heads bizarrely close together, whispering as if the world were a secret. They look no older than Rosie, who left the house before she did and went god knows where.

She sits at the same table, and out the window spots Dory slowly cross the street.

"Hey, where's your drink?" Dory asks, coming in.

"Waiting for you."

Dory orders two scotches, neat, and places them on the table. Then seats herself carefully as if her body might miss the chair. "To us, of course," Dory raises her glass.

"Indeed." She takes a tiny sip. "What's his name?" She indicates the bartender with her chin.

"Mikel?"

"Yes, that's it. I was really drunk that night, can't do that again."

"Why not? It's good for the spirits."

"You're so peppy!" With her face thinning, Dory's penetrating cat eyes look larger than ever.

"Am I supposed to be hunched over in agony?"

"Of course not, but I can't stop thinking about the tumor."

"You and Stu can console each other."

A shiver of fear runs through her.

"He's truly freaked out." Dory reaches across the narrow

space and sets the empty glass on the bar. "Another, please."

Stu must not become the subject of their conversation. "Is it okay for you to drink?"

"You hear the one about the dying guy who begs for more morphine? The doc won't comply, worried he'll become an addict. Here's the thing, Lena. I refuse to dwell on what's to come when there's nothing I can do about it."

"Have you explored surgery or other options, or are you just running with the first crap they hand you?"

"The doctor was crystal clear," Dory now sounds annoyed. "It's there, a tumor large enough and too close to the brain stem to guarantee successful treatment. That message is not going to change, issued by a second mouth. With or without surgery, the comforts of my life will no longer be mine, so why go through the mess and pain of invasive treatment for that chance in a million, that so-called miracle that ends up in Ripley's? I can't see it. What I do see is the way some of my charges suffer after they become ill, particularly the ones whose families want to keep them alive no matter what. Bedridden, overly drugged, weeks of nightmare hallucinations, food tubes, mouth sores, loss of vision, diapers, and worse. There isn't much of them left to die. Who does that serve?"

"But you're such a fighter, that's always been you."

"What difference does it make, what I do, Lena? Nothing will change the outcome. My gait's already slowing and my balance is tricky at times. I'm having some trouble hearing my charges, especially the ones who speak low, and I'm nauseous a lot. Food doesn't taste that good anymore, but I make myself eat, even if it's only ice cream, which, thank the lord, tastes the same."

Dory's words overwhelm her. How had she missed all these signs? Worse, she can't think of a reply that will mean anything.

"I want to remain who I am and enjoy what I can as long as I can, even while I'm losing ever more of myself. In other words, being treated like an invalid before I am one is exactly what I don't want."

"I hear you."

"Then why are you badgering me?"

"Because I'm scared . . . I can't bear the thought of you not being able."

"Let's not suffer the pain that isn't here yet. Okay?"

"You were always ridiculously brave no matter how dire the moment. It made me envious. It still does."

"You're forever worried about next steps. What's the point?"

"Being prepared, I guess."

"There's no such thing, Lena, unless you mean having enough food for guests." Then Dory adds, out of nowhere, "Stu's brave, too. We're a brave pair. Remember when he punched that guy in the bar who slapped a woman?"

She nods, but doesn't say it was Matt who punched the guy.

"Heroic, actually."

A garbage truck rolls noisily past the window, stopping nowhere she can see.

"Remember City Island, that guy's boat? How Stu managed to wrangle us an hour for free? He's so good at sweet-talking people into doing what he wants, what they might not otherwise do."

What is Dory telling her?

"And you, my friend, have been acting weird. Why?"

"It's Rosie," she says quickly.

"You need to give the girl time."

"She won't talk to me. She's lost all respect for me."

"Believe me on this, it won't go on forever."

"And why is my son glued to a computer like nothing else in the world exists? Is it shyness? Preadolescent something? Or have I failed him, too?" Her eyes well up and she blinks a few times. And Dory catches it. She always does. It frightens her what else Dory might see.

"Is there something more troubling you?"

"Zack, too." It's true, but also another way of justifying whatever strangeness Dory's noted. "After you announced the diagnosis, he came into the room and angrily accused me of many faults, chief among them that I refused to sleep with him. Then he told me he had paid a whore for a five-minute fuck and blamed me for that, too." Dear lord, she's rolling out her woes to gain Dory's sympathy when it's her forgiveness she needs.

"You must have exploded." Dory says, strangely unconcerned.

"He begged me for mercy, explained his torment, vowed his love, admiration, devotion, and so on. Somehow it touched me." She can't seem to stop blabbering. "He promises to take more responsibility for whatever. Do I believe him? Maybe. Can he do it? I have no idea."

"You're wearing the interview dress. Any luck?" Thank god Dory's changing the subject.

"A little side street hotel called Wonderland with water-stained ceilings and a musty smell. I can't help but think it's come to this, any job for a buck. What's the difference between me and the women sidling through hallways with their johns?"

"The hotel doesn't sound appealing."

"I can't bear even one more day of job hunting. So, dear god, let it be Wonderland. If it is, there'll be two of us with salaries and we can look for a place of our own. With Rosie back, we need to make a home again."

"Stu will miss you."

"Why? I mean, it surprises me."

"He enjoys the extended family."

"Won't you miss me?"

"Oh, I'll see you a bunch, wherever you are."

"Of course you will. You must," her tone too needy by far.

Dory studies her but says nothing.

Suddenly, the usual ease between them feels endangered.

She stares out at the half-darkness and can hear her mother intone, "Too tight, too tight."

As they enter the house, her phone rings. It's Wonderland. She listens, thanks the manager for letting her know. Clicks off.

"Bummer," Dory says, seeing her expression.

"What does it matter?" She laughs. It's more of a bark, actually. Sitting cross-legged on the couch, Casey glances up at her, then back at his laptop.

"I'll prepare dinner," Dory announces.

She walks down the hallway, just as Dory asks Casey where Rosie is, but she misses his answer. To blot out the world she ratchets up the bedroom A/C to high and switches on the fan as well, then slips out of her shoes, and, still dressed, climbs into bed.

She pulls the duvet up to her ears while the last hour replays in her head. Does Dory know something? Who would tell her? They were careful, but is anything fail-safe? Guilt is making her paranoid. She knows it. The sooner she finds a way to move out the better it will be for Dory and for her, but how to do that when getting a job feels as impossible as winning the lottery?

"Mom?" Casey tiptoes to the bedside. "I can bring in a tray of food. Do you want that?"

"Honey, no, please just let me be."

"Will you be okay tomorrow?"

"Absolutely. Go eat with everyone." Her sweet boy obeys and gently shuts the door.

She pulls the pillow close to her chest, wanting the kind of sleep that's deep and dreamless. Her mind refuses to comply. Wonderland was about as low as she could go, and they didn't want her either. What if they cancel her food stamps because Zack's working? She's scared, furious, and everyone's to blame, including her, and there's nothing she can do about it.

She remembers her father on payday, placing the envelope on the kitchen table. Neither she nor her mother was allowed to ask how much was inside, only to see it as proof that he was on the job. There were weeks and months when nothing was placed on the table, and they weren't allowed to mention that either. Did it drive her mother crazy, not knowing from one week to the next how, or if, they could pay for necessities? Will that happen to her, too? She closes her eyes; cloud-like gray and white shapes begin to float past her lids with no promise of sleep.

She's still awake when Zack comes in but keeps her eyes shut while he undresses. He switches off the fan, lowers the A/C, and gets into bed. A short time later he's snoring lightly. Before he can reach for her in his sleep, she slips out of bed and leaves the room. A glass of something strong may help quiet her mind.

The house is silent, but a pool of dim lamplight reveals Stu in the club chair with a bottle of wine. He lifts it toward her.

"I need something stronger," she whispers, and gets the Johnnie Walker from the side bar, fills a glass, then turns to face him. "Couldn't sleep."

"Me, too." His face is in shadow. Only the white T-shirt interrupts the darkness.

"Stu . . ."

"I know." They're each whispering, urgently, gently.

"We'll always be friends and I don't regret . . ."

"Me neither," he says. "Lena, I'm sorry. I'm . . ."

"No, please, don't say sorry, that makes it worse. Let's file it away, leave it as a good memory."

"In Casablanca, they always had Paris. We'll always have Motel Cozy Nook."

She smiles. "Okay. But, still, it wasn't good. What I mean is it was good but it wasn't . . ." she can't find the right words.

"I know what you mean. I'm in the same place . . . confused, worried, sad, actually terrified about Dory . . . it's all so. . ."

"Me, too, but Stu, we have to be with each other as if nothing. . ."

"Of course."

"The thing is . . . it's not smart for me to be living here much longer."

"Where will you go?"

He didn't say stay, she notes. "I'm not sure. But I want Dory to have all of you all the time."

"She does, she will. I'm going to take her on vacation in a month or so, someplace special. Don't say anything. I want to surprise her. I'll take care of the whole deal. Just the two of us elsewhere feels right."

"It does." And there it is, the bond between him and Dory, the one that's always been there. Of course it has. "I'll take this with me," she lifts the scotch bottle and tiptoes back to the bedroom.

He watches her disappear down the hallway. Replays her step-ping out of the dark, still lovely to behold even in shadow. She seemed calm but sad. Of course she is. Dory's her best friend, his too. It's a shame they can no longer be relaxed with each other. It's strange, when he thinks about it, that each of them is an only child, which makes their bond sibling-like, which makes what happened between him and Lena either inevitable or incest. Just add it to his list of fuck-ups. For some reason, maybe because he's drunk, he remembers the animal game the four of them used to play after a few tokes. Who would be what animal in an-other incarnation? Zack was either a Collie or a St. Bernard. He, too, was a dog; no, maybe a tiger. Lena, they all agreed, was a lion, and Dory he dubbed a hummingbird, her movements so quick and sharp that she could move through space without disturbing matter. Yet for weeks now, he's caught her steadying herself us-ing the walls or any furniture handy. He's noted how she's begun to perch on the edge of the bed for a minute before standing. He could've asked why. Was he so without curiosity? Or was he afraid to know? Yes to both, damn him. He gets it now, of course, her balance, the dizziness. But all this time he could've offered something, a hand, a word of concern, anything, and he didn't. He's doomed to live with these regrets forever. And why shouldn't he? He deserves no peace of mind given the time he squandered trying to figure a way out, not back into his marriage. Stupid. Stupid. Does it always take some tragedy to make sense of what could have been or even of what was?

And now another thought rises to plague him. Is it sinful to let her die loving him so much it hurts her to leave him? Wouldn't it be helpful to break through her illusions? Of course, she'll hate him. But he's earned the hatred, pursuing his desires at her expense. First, he'd tell her about his oh-so-brief tryst with Lena, then admit how wrong he'd been not to work on the marriage. That he's a fool and a bastard not to have seen what was right in front of his face, that it took learning about her illness to make him realize how crucial she is to his life. Will he sound like those sniveling middle-aged men who mess up, then get down on their knees to ask their wives' forgiveness? The thing is, he doesn't want her forgiveness. That would kill him. Maybe he should just shoot himself.

He drinks the last of the wine straight from the bottle. Then hoists himself out of the chair, tosses the empty bottle in the trash, places the glass in the sink.

In the bedroom he undresses, slides in behind Dory, and wraps his arm around her waist. When she inches closer, her body so warm and alive, his need for her is sudden, urgent, nearly violent.

47.

The kitchen is bright with morning sunlight. Rosie sips her juice. What an amazing day yesterday. Siri was somehow taller, his hair longer, darker, thicker. The shadow of a mustache grew beneath his nose. His skin seemed more coppery, his eyes as large and luminous as ever. They hugged shyly, then took a subway down to the restored Ground Zero, and walked around holding hands. Being there, they agreed, was both sad and beautiful. Later, behind a church near the river he kissed her long and lovingly, then held her hand again.

More talkative than she remembers, he told her there'd been a girlfriend for a few weeks. But it was Rosie he missed, Rosie he wanted the whole time. Did she understand? She nodded, praying he wasn't still a virgin. She didn't tell him about Sonny, though she shared Dory's situation plus that of her family, including her mother's lack of trust in her. He agreed that it was difficult to live in an unsupportive environment. His sympathy and understanding were just the medicine she needed.

What she didn't need to hear about was his plan to join the Marines as the quickest way to become a citizen. It's the quickest way to become a dead citizen, she responded. Even if he isn't killed, he sure as shit could come back wounded or brain-damaged. Hasn't he been watching the news? And what if the Marines are sent to fight in Pakistan? What then? Could he do that? Aren't they his people, his family of sorts?

He's not thickheaded, he pointed out, but how else can he get a decent job, apply for college scholarships, all those sorts of things? Okay, he has a point, but she's not about to sit at home worrying about him for endless months. If he wants her devotion, which seemed evident, he'd better become a citizen the slow way like other immigrants.

Her eyes flit to the time. She's due to meet Mirabelle at eleven. It's nearly ten. Strange, her mother, an early riser, is still in bed. No one wanted to wake her. But they should have. The night before when she wasn't at dinner, her dad told them that their house remains empty, unwatched. He saw it, even went back twice to make sure. It's off the bank's radar. He's certain of that. They should move back in. He swears no one will throw them out for a good long while, enough time to make some money, and—who knows—maybe buy it back. Though how could he be sure of that? Her dad doesn't think things through like her mother does. Still, he spoke with a kind of passion that she's never heard from him before. Stu offered to loan them his generator and promised to figure out how to get the water turned on. Dory mostly listened. Casey was really into the move. He asked if the paint was still on the house. Yes, and dad loved it. Wouldn't erase it for anything.

It's a thoroughly great idea, she'd say, and in fact did say, especially since it will give her back her room. Until her mother weighs in, though, it won't be real, which sucks. Someone should tell her about the discussion.

She goes down the hall and knocks on the bedroom door. No response. She pushes it open and peeks inside. Her mother's in bed, the blinds drawn. The rocking chair in the corner looks eerie, as if someone invisible were watching.

"Mom?"

Nothing.

"Mom? Wake up. There's news to share."

Nothing.

She opens the blinds. Isn't that the first thing they do at a crime scene? Daylight streams in, lighting up the adjacent wall like a movie screen. Her mother's head the only part of her visible, half her face buried in the pillow. She tugs the duvet down to her mother's shoulders and sees her dress. Her interview dress! Why didn't her father deal with that? "Mom, what's going on?"

Her mother's eyes remain closed. She's sleeping like a dead person or—she's dead. "This is ridiculous," she says, then shakes her mother's shoulder. Is her mother in a coma? The thought scares her. People do die in their sleep. She leans closer to see if she's breathing and smells the whiskey. She's drunk. After sleeping so many hours? She shakes her mother's shoulder harder. "Mom, enough. Get up or I'm calling 911."

She waits. Once again she bends close to see if her mother's breathing. It's hard to tell in the dress. She's watched enough TV to know what to do next and begins searching her mother's neck for a pulse. Her mother groans. God, something did happen to her mother. A stroke, a heart attack? She *was* acting weird last night, going straight to bed.

"Mom? Mom?" she whispers again, surprised by the depth of her concern and desperation. She wants her mother intact. Fearful, she reaches for her mother's cell phone on the night table to call her father, but can't find his work number and dials Dory instead. It goes to voice mail. "Dory, something's wrong with mom. I don't know what to do. Call me or come home right away. Please."

Her mother groans again.

"Mom, it's me, Rosie. I'm here. Please say something, anything. What's wrong, Mom? What's wrong?"

"Okay," her mother croaks. "I'm okay."

Unexpectedly relief floods through her. "Mom why are you wearing your interview dress? Sit up. I'll help you." She grabs her mother's shoulder from behind and pushes her toward a sitting position.

Lena shakes her off. "Rosie, let go. I'm awake."

Her mother looks awful, her face puffy and pale. "Shit, Mom, you scared me! You don't do that to your kid."

"Why are you trying to wake me?"

"Well, it's late. And I wanted to tell you about our dinner conversation last night. Very exciting news." She perches on the side of the bed.

"What?" her mother asks woozily.

"Our old house is still empty. Dad thinks we should move back in. Why not? He's certain it's off the bank's radar. Stu's going to give us his generator for lighting. We could bring back our furniture. Dad says it'll be a long time before they kick us out, if ever, and by then you'll have a job, too, and we'll have money again. He's right, I'm sure. It's a great idea. Don't you agree?" She's speaking fast and wonders if her mother's taking any of it in because her face has a strange expression on it. It's as if she's hearing something entirely different from what Rosie's saying. "Mom, What's the matter with you? "

"Who knows what's possible," her mother mumbles.

"Casey and I can each have our rooms back. How about that?"

"Nice," her mother says vaguely.

"Mom, stop acting this way," Rosie says sternly, alarmed yet again. "Are you sick? Does something hurt? Are you still drunk? You can tell me." Her mother's eyes are red-rimmed. Was she crying?

"I need more sleep."

"Okay." She's glad to obey. She tiptoes out, praying Dory gets there fast.

As soon as the door closes, she falls back on the pillow. She needs sleep or a ton of black coffee or both. Rosie's concern reached through her stupor and she didn't want to ruin the moment by arguing with her, but what's Zack thinking? The house belongs to the bank. Getting the children riled up? Has he forgotten what happened to his last idea? Has he forgotten the humiliation of the scramble to get out? Her phone rings.

"Dory?"

"Rosie called. She sounded scared, said something was wrong with you. What's the matter?"

"I had way too much scotch, didn't fall asleep till dawn. I'm still in bed, half-dead."

"You should be relieved not to get the Wonderland job."

"Relieved? I can't go through even one more interview, one more rejection. My cheeks hurt from smiling at faces that couldn't give a crap about me."

"Are you awake now?"

"Sort of."

"Lena, I wasn't going to share this with you because I don't know if it's going to come to pass, but I have an idea. Well, I've asked to meet with my board of managers, the people who run the nursing home. I plan to tell them about my illness, and

263

that sooner rather than later I'll have to leave the job. At that meeting I'm going to propose that I train someone to take my place as a caretaker. Someone who will follow me day in and day out to learn everything, someone they won't have to pay much until she's ready to do the job on her own. That someone will be you."

"You need to leave the job? Oh my god, when?"

"The deficits are kicking in. Soon I won't be able do much of what I do without holding on to something. Imagine taking an old frail woman to the bathroom and losing my balance, down will come two. By then, of course, my hearing might be gone so I won't hear her scream. Well, aren't you thrilled with my idea? Why aren't you grabbing at it like the brass ring on a merry-go-round?"

"Dory, I can't be excited that you have to leave."

"I'm not asking you to be happy about that piece of it, but what about the job piece?"

"They may not agree to this."

"That's true, but this place hates change. I've seen it over the years. If I can make my leaving into a smooth transition, they might sigh with relief. But you're right, we have to wait. You haven't said you would take the position."

"I would, I would, I would. I'm just afraid to get my hopes up."

"Okay. Don't get them up. See you later."

For a moment she stares at the dead phone, amazed that such a tiny machine could deliver such a huge message. She doesn't want to be excited. It's Dory who can't do the work much longer . . . Yet she can't suppress the hope now flowing through her.

48.

On his break, Zack sits on a milk crate outside the meat-packing place, a can of Coke in hand. Across from him, the metal doors of a vacant plant, next to an old building that now houses galleries. His brain is filled with thoughts of moving back into the house.

He visited twice more, cased the area a few times to watch which cars were passing by. Nothing. Didn't even see a cop car, but he can't count on that remaining true. The two nearby houses have been vacant god knows how long, right? The families could've moved back in a year ago. Who would've cared? Who would've even known? This foreclosure shit couldn't be more disorganized. No one understands the mortgage companies. No one even knows who's in charge, who to go to for help. Didn't he read something in the papers about families taking over vacant houses, people refusing to submit to this crap anymore? It's definitely a good time to move back in. He can feel it. His children were all for it. Rosie wants her privacy. He gets it. And Casey, the most enthusiastic of all, wants to return to his old school, his one good friend, his usual bike paths.

He knows he's a ridiculous optimist, but damn, someone has to dream. How many times has Stu said he envies him for expecting the best? Stu, being Stu, walks around and around the bush and by the time he finally picks the flower, it's wilted.

There'll be rough patches. He expects that. Still, together, he and Lena can smooth the way. It'll be a struggle to convince her, he can count on that. Well, he'll struggle, he will. The move back is doable, a chance to be at ease as one only can be in one's home. Dory and Stu are angel-sent, and he'll remember their generosity forever. Still, and it's really a teeny unfair quibble he'd never give voice to, he has to watch the TV programs that they like, which is only right.

He checks the time, a few more minutes. The guys here don't bother much with each other, mainly truckers in and out. Fine with him. Meat that doesn't make it onto the freezer trucks gets distributed among the few workers. Fine with him, too. He flashes on the scene in that old Charlie Chaplin movie where the conveyer belt gets faster and faster. It's not that bad here, and as long as the meat keeps dropping onto his marble slab he's working.

Zack unlocks the front door, goes straight to the kitchen, opens the fridge, pulls a bottle of Beck's from the carton, pops open the cap, lets the bitter cold liquid run down his dry throat. It's so quiet. "Hello," he shouts, "anyone home?"

Lena comes out of their room in those loose silky black slacks he loves. "I'll have one of those."

Good start, he thinks, and takes out another beer, opens it, hands it to her.

"Where is everyone?"

"Got me. I slept late. Rosie was gone when I looked for her. I've been busy rewriting my resume."

"Oh yeah, how come?"

"There are things I thought would make me more desirable."

"Hey, you are quite desirable."

"Gave you that one, didn't I?"

She seems relaxed. The moment is with him.

"So, Rosie told me about the discussion last night," she says. "You must've been kidding, right?"

"Wrong. Dead serious."

"How?"

"Lena, shut it for a moment and listen." He takes her hand, tugs her into the living room, where they sit facing each other.

"I know what you said. Rosie filled me in. Just because you want to do this doesn't make it feasible. The bank will call the police. What, then, Zack? The kids all revved up with expectation? I just need a salary to add to yours and we'll find a cheap apartment somewhere. So it won't be the best neighborhood. So we'll survive it, but it'll be ours. No one will take it away as long as we pay the rent."

She looks directly at him for what, he wonders, approval, agreement? Not possible. "I hear you and I understand you but you do not see my point."

"Zack, I'm not an idiot. We all loved the house. We all felt comfortable there, but it's gone. Let it rest in peace. Please!"

He watches her down the beer, not sure how to proceed. "You're being stubborn, Lena. Truly. People are doing this. It's not just us or me. I read the other day that somewhere . . . I think Arizona . . . five families moved back into empty houses and . . ."

"Those are squatters. I don't want to be a squatter. I want to be a tenant or an owner. Can't you get that?"

"I've scoured the area. No real estate cars or patrol cars, nothing. No one watching. Think about those empty houses on the road. How fucking long have they been vacant? Those people could've moved in a few weeks after being dispossessed, and who would've done what? The banks are totally disorganized around these foreclosures."

"Zack, all kinds of real estate signs are on the lawns."

"How do you know that?"

"They were up before we left."

"I don't believe it, I don't," he says more to himself. "So what? There are no signs on our lawn. I'm telling you, the house is off their radar."

"I get that you think this can work. Maybe it could for a week or two. But mark my words, we'll be thrown out soon after. It's on their radar, in their computers, and someplace, someone is watching."

"Just allow yourself to consider the possibility. . . . Please? Consider, that's all I ask." Except that's not true. He's going to make this happen. He knows he's right, but he needs to give her some time and space because he knows her, too.

"Okay, I can do that. Let's start dinner. Where's Casey? "

49.

"Zack and I will clean up after dinner, " Lena says, taking a seat. "Are you guys enjoying the meat surprise Zack brought home?"

"Pork chops, center cut," Zack informs them.

"Dad, we've been eating too much meat. It isn't healthy," Rosie chides.

"Where's your brother?" Lena asks.

"He took his bike and left around breakfast time."

"It's nearly seven and getting dark out." Lena says.

"Well, you took away his phone after he painted the house. Not a smart punishment," Rosie says.

"I took it away because we're cutting back on anything extra. I would've taken yours, too, if you were here."

"He's just riding around. My brother's weird. He enjoys looking at scenery and stuff. You know that."

She doesn't know that. What she's sure of is that no matter where he wanders, the boy comes home for dinner. The one time he didn't he was in jail.

"I wonder if we should drive around . . ."

"Let's have dinner first," Dory says. "If he doesn't get here by dessert, we'll drive through the area."

She pokes at the food on her plate, tries cutting the meat

into slivers, and catches Rosie watching her.

Zack, putting down his fork says, "So, guys, I spoke to Lena about moving back into the old house."

"Zack, please. I just want to finish up here and find Casey." If she had her own car, she could take off and damn the food.

"I filled Mom in," Rosie says, eyeing her.

"It's getting late. I'm going to walk around the neighborhood. . . . Maybe he's stuck somewhere." She tries to keep the anxiety from her voice.

"Mom, I'll go with you."

"Great. Come on."

"Should I come, too?" Zack offers.

"No, help with the washing up."

"If he calls while you're out, I'll text you, and if you can't find him, I'll drive you around," Dory says.

"No, I will. You rest," Stu says.

She flashes back to the foreclosure night, Stu driving her in that downpour to find Casey. Only now does she recognize the unspoken electricity between them. No way will she ride alone with him again. Before she can figure out how to turn down his offer, Rosie's at the open door, waiting.

The early evening sky is filled with clouds as transparent as smoke. They should've taken sweaters. Her daughter's in cut-off jeans, a green sleeveless blouse, her blue-painted toenails splayed in flip-flops. "Aren't you chilly?"

"No."

They pass houses alight with evening chores. No one is out on lawns.

"Mom, this is futile. We have no idea where to go."

"Let's walk to the bike path, it's not far. We'll follow it for a while."

"Nothing happened to him. If he were in jail or a hospital, someone would've called us."

Her daughter's words make sense. Still, given a mother's fear for her children's safety, sense doesn't matter.

In a newly paved area, the bike path runs alongside and above the highway. Rush hour's about over. There's not much traffic, except for the rumble of trucks.

A blue evening haze descends and the first stars begin appearing. She can't remember the last time she and Rosie were out alone together. Once, when she was much younger than her daughter, her mother was well enough to walk her to school. It may have been the only time. Her mother, wearing lipstick and a dress, held her hand the entire way and several times mumbled, "Grab it where you can." It puzzled her at the time, but her mother said so many strange things. In the end she just ignored it. Now, she wonders if her mother was trying to say something about the value of certain moments over others. She strokes the back of Rosie's head, the wavy hair soft. And thinks to share that memory, except it wouldn't mean a thing to her daughter. How strange it all is . . . someday, her daughter will recall memories of her. What will they be?

"Rosie, you think I don't trust you, but I do."

"It sure hasn't felt that way."

"At your age so many mistakes can happen . . ."

"That's how I'll learn, by experience."

"Where I grew up, adolescent girls regularly got pregnant, went on the hard stuff . . . you get the picture."

"The picture is your picture. I didn't grow up that way. It's not going to happen to me."

She finds her daughter's words strangely uplifting. "You're right. Are we friends, now?" she asks softly.

"Absolutely not. You're my mother, not Mirabelle."

She laughs. "Thank god for that. Are you looking forward to school?"

"Yes and no."

"No?"

"Someone I care about graduated last year."

"Who's that?"

"No one you know. By the way, I plan to get a tattoo."

This is a test. She's not going to fail. "Well . . . where?"

"Really? You always said it was a form of mutilation. What changed?"

Of course it's mutilation, she doesn't say. "Where?"

"Um . . . back of my shoulder."

"What of?"

"Not sure yet. Mirabelle has a swan below her belly button. But that's not my thing."

"Think I'm too old to get one, too?" she asks playfully.

"What?"

"I'd get a rose, for Rosie, maybe on my thigh."

"Ugh, no mom, you *are* too old for that, and the thigh is very sensitive."

"You're probably right."

She glances at the highway. Why would Casey go down here? He'd have to climb the railing, and what would he do with his bike? Anyway, it's getting too dark to make out anything but the headlights of cars.

"Mom, the stretch ahead is empty. Let's turn back."

"We'll borrow Dory's car and drive around. No need to uproot either of them."

"Sonny gave me driving lessons . . ."

She doesn't respond.

50.

"Just us two," Dory notes, more to herself.

"Another glass of wine? We'll finish up the kitchen later," Stu says.

"Why not?" She follows him into the den with fresh glasses, the couch there worn to comfort. He carries in a newly opened bottle of French white. He's been doing that lately, buying expensive wine whose names she can't pronounce. Does he fear the cheaper stuff might somehow worsen her state?

"What's all this fancy wine about?"

"The best for the best." Barefoot in sweats and T-shirt, he looks ready for bed.

"Don't butter me, Stu. It makes me feel something's wrong with me."

"Something is wrong," he says quietly.

"Well . . . yes . . . but treating me with kid gloves is insulting."

"How?" He sounds almost curious.

"If you'd been diagnosed with something serious and suddenly I open doors for you, lay blankets across your lap, prop pillows behind you, how would that make you feel?"

"Like a prince."

"Oh for shit's sake, you know what I'm saying. It's infantilizing. At work, visitors treat all old people like they're demented."

"I want to make things easy for you."

She takes in his earnest expression. And for a moment looks past him into the darkness outside the window. "What does that even mean? You can't alter the situation."

He slips an arm around her shoulders. "You don't know how to accept help, do you?"

It's true. Self-sufficiency was her father's credo. He would cite the grocery store sign: *God helps those who help themselves. All others pay cash.* Is it that her father didn't trust anyone, or that he believed help wasn't available? "If I could I would."

He squeezes her shoulder, then tops off his wine glass. "Yes, you would, I know it," he says somberly.

"The night you said 'Dory, help me?' I was awake. I heard you. I understood you meant you didn't know what to do for me. I get that you love me. At times I get that better than you do."

"Baby, you astonish me . . . you're right, I love you. I can't imagine life without you, that's exactly what I wanted to tell you. Thing is, I can't communicate that way. It's too soapy and . . . I don't know . . . it's weird but when I do say stuff like that it leaves me feeling empty, like I've given something away." He gazes at her. "So what happens now? Am I supposed to ignore the situation?"

"Just be yourself, the guy I love, inconsiderate soul that you are." She takes him in the way she used to long ago, the eyes that tell no tales except she can read them; the face, a little thicker now but still handsome; the lines sharp, the generous lips. Her man.

"Yup, that makes it easy. Drink up," he says.

"Your answer to everything."

"It does help."

"I hope Casey's all right. I've been concerned about him. He's too quiet for his age. Of course, still waters . . ."

"I'm quiet. What about my still waters?"

"You don't have them."

"Is that bad? What does it mean anyway?"

"Everything deep kept below the surface."

"Oh, definitely, that's me, Dory. What's the matter with you?" His words hit them both.

"Good, Stu, it's what I want, just be your inconsiderate self. It really is helpful, I swear."

He says nothing, but offers her his loopy smile.

"Stu, would you be happier now if we had had a child?"

"A strange question."

"I know."

"Would you?"

"Not at the moment. But during our first ten years together, the thought arrived quite often."

"You didn't talk much about it."

"Neither did you," she says.

"It just didn't happen, so I accepted the fact."

"We could've adopted."

"Where are you going with this, Dory? I mean, talk about water under . . ."

"I have no idea. Lately, thoughts arrive in my head and insist on being spoken. I'm beginning to feel like a puppet through which someone other than me is talking. Okay, that sounds crazy and I'm not. Please remember that."

"Dory, you are the least crazy person in the universe."

She decides not to share her recent unbidden conversations with relative strangers, in which she reveals her illness without being asked and without caring about their responses. It seems to be a way to hear the diagnosis out loud, maybe to own it.

"Has this been happening at work, too?" he asks, unusually concerned. Another surprise. For months, he's been indifferent.

Now his fear is changing him, but he won't say so and neither will she.

"Yes, there, too. Work . . ." she begins, sounding so wistful she finds it unnerving. "I'm not going to be able to be a caretaker much longer. Losing my balance, hearing, whatever, it puts my charges in jeopardy." She makes a mental note. Must alert Mr. Todd about leaving. His mind is as sharp as a steak knife. He needs to be given details. "Maybe something good can come of it, though. I'm asking the board if Lena can take my place. I'll teach her everything. I hope they'll agree. You realize leaving the job will be the end of two salaries."

"Dory, you are not to worry about money."

"I'm not." Some earthly things she's already letting go of. "I'll clean up the dinner stuff."

"No, you go to bed. I'll do it."

"See you're at it again."

"So fuck me," he says jovially.

"Maybe I will. I'll be in bed," she gives him her glass and passes her hand seductively across his lap.

Dory leaving work, that's big. He wasn't expecting it so soon. But he can sense her downward spiral. How carefully she steps out of her clothing, the new pill bottles in the bathroom. Her twists and turns in bed. Her fitfulness reaches into his sleep and wakes him. If Lena gets the job, she'll be out of here shortly. That will be for the best. How could he have considered for even a second telling Dory about Lena and him? What was he thinking? He wasn't. It was the wine and the guilt, plain and simple. Thank the gods, who have rarely been good to him, that he sobered up. Most nights, though, sober is the last thing he wants to be, because, sober, his thoughts are all about losing Dory. Whatever in him has shifted, and something has, it's left him with a growing need for closeness, weird considering how recently that felt like suffocation. Even after they make love now he wants to stay inside her, suck her life into his. It's ghoulish and scary.

He pours the rest of the wine into the glass. Well, he's done something nice for her. He called a travel agency, and Jane or someone was eager to be of help. What the hell was her name, can't remember now. What did he do with the brochures? Doesn't matter. Jane or someone was ever so happy to plan ten days in Italy, starting with Rome. Only the dates remain open. At the plant the human resource assholes are making him wait for approval. They act like they're doing him a favor, when he hasn't taken vacation in more than two years. Not that anyone ever notified him of that.

He can hear the TV in the bedroom, the volume louder now than in the past, which he doesn't believe Dory realizes. Whatever she's watching, he'll watch, too. Then again, he's pretty sure they're not going to be interested in what's on.

51.

"Zack, this isn't our car, and if anything happens . . ." Her eyes flit to the speedometer, passing seventy.

"Lena, I know how to drive."

"You're going too fast. It's dark out. I can't see a thing, Casey or his bike. Zack, do you hear what I'm saying?" He stares ahead. It's pissing her off.

"Mom, chill. Dory will call us if Casey gets home, which he might."

"I'm scared," she says suddenly. "Casey isn't you, Rosie, he's a homebody unless he's in trouble. Why doesn't anyone share my fear?"

"Because you never let in any light," Rosie shoots back.

"What does that mean?"

"You go straight for the worst outcome. Why?" Her daughter sounds almost curious.

"I don't know." But of course she does. Growing up in a home where there's not one extra dollar, where a cold without health care becomes pneumonia, a faucet leak becomes a flood, a late-night phone call is never a wrong number, and an absent child spells disaster. But she won't say any of it. They've tried, she and Zack both, to keep the bleakness of their pasts away from the children. Zack's been better at it than she has, hopeful against all odds. She glances at him, his eyes on the road, mouth clamped shut.

He takes the ramp onto the expressway and joins a caravan of trucks rumbling through the Bronx night. The shadow of a semi dwarfs them before moving past. Then it hits her. "You're driving to our old house?"

"Lena, I'm almost certain Casey is near that house." Zack speaks cautiously.

"So he's sitting outside a dark house on a dark road, waiting for us? Are you both having the same delusion? "

"I think he's camped out, maybe on the back deck," Zack says quietly.

You think, she wants to shout, but Rosie's presence inhibits her. "When did you and dad decide on this plan?"

"You were gabbing with Dory when Dad and I went ahead to the garage. It made sense that Casey would go to the house."

Nothing makes sense to her. She stares past her anger at the darkening sky, no longer sure what she's looking for.

The car turns onto the familiar road with its bus stop. The glow from the single street lamp dimming as they move past it. Salmon-colored light escapes from partially shuttered blinds in the occupied houses.

As they exit the car, she looks around quickly. No Casey, no bike. "There's no sign of him," she says. Her disappointment though is greater than she'll admit. Somewhere in the last half hour she'd begun to believe Zack knew what he was doing.

She can just make out the defaced façade. Otherwise the house looks remarkably the same. She's worked so hard to put the place out of her mind. Being here feels almost unlawful.

Stepping closer, she thinks she sees . . . no, she's being drawn into their delusion. "Oh my god!"

"What is it?" Zack asks.

"The door's ajar," she whispers. "It's been broken into. Someone's inside, maybe a homeless person." But she knows. Of course it's Casey. She knows that instantly. He's jimmied the door open, trespassed, maybe even defaced the walls inside. Casey, who Arthur warned her would not get a break the second time around.

In silence they enter into the darkness of the vestibule. It takes just a few seconds to make out Casey hunched against the living room wall, beside him the bike, down flat like a sick animal.

"Casey, where's your flashlight?" Rosie asks.

He produces it from a bag attached to the bike handle. Rosie uses it to open a circle of amber light. It catches Casey's alarmed face.

Lena drops down beside him, folds his hand between hers. "Honey, are you okay?"

"Yeah," his voice a purr in the dark.

"Did you fall off the bike? Is it broken? Is that why it's lying beside you?"

"Mom, stop. Give him a chance to say something."

"I'm not hurt," he says quietly.

"When did you come here?" Zack asks.

"This morning. It was light. I could see everything inside. No one saw me."

"How do you know?" Rosie asks, sounding intrigued.

"Was the door unlocked when you got here?" She sends up a quick prayer, make him say yes.

He looks at her, blinking unnaturally, "No."

"How did you get in?" Zack asks.

Who cares, she thinks, it's how to get him out without anyone seeing them that matters now. "Probably a homeless person came in last week to sleep, left the door open . . . who's to say?" she implores.

"Mom, he just said the door was locked. Are you losing it?"

"Don't you see," she hisses. "This is breaking and entering. It isn't our property. He could go to jail. We have to get out of here now, close the door, leave. No headlights until the car is free of the road." She takes a deep breath and stands up, ready to pull Casey upright.

"Mom, you're scaring him, that's number one . . ."

"I intend to."

"And, two, he didn't deface anything. He just sat here. Big deal."

"Zack, help me out."

"Rosie's not all wrong. We could always say the door was open and then it's just a squatter thing."

"A squatter thing!"

Casey, who hasn't said a word, looks up at her. In his flashlight-yellow face she sees her little boy, the toddler who took in each of her words as gospel and made her feel all-knowing; her son who's sat here for hours, alone and miserable. Was that the only way he knew to reach her? Oh, lord. And waits for the grief to find her. "What is it, honey? I'm here. I'm listening."

"Mom. I'm not leaving." His voice is soft, low, pleading.

"This isn't our house, Casey, not anymore." Her tone is equally soft. Oh, Jesus, can a young boy have a breakdown? Is that what's happening? She's always thought of him as so grounded, even if he does spend hours on that machine. She takes another deep breath. "Honey, give me your hand, please, let's go. Let's call it a night. Please. You haven't eaten. You need light, nourishment, a shower. We can talk about this later.

Please give me your hand." She leans over, tries to dislodge his hand from his lap, but he resists.

"Mom," Casey says softly. "We all have to move back here. It's our only chance to be the way we were before."

The depth of sadness in his voice cracks her heart. "Why do you say that, Casey?"

"We're not the only family that's lost a home. I saw hundreds of others online and hardly any of them stay together. It's our only chance."

Her legs threaten to fold beneath her. She slides down the wall next to him and now he allows her to take his hand.

"Mom, this is our house. They stole it from us," Rosie says evenly. "We paid that mortgage for years, we fixed it up, we lived here. Casey's right. We need to take back what's ours. It's the only way to go on together."

Her head is a swirl of thoughts and she can't seem to grab onto any of them. In Zack's half-shadowed face, confusion. He wants to agree with the children, but not oppose her. His confusion, she's surprised to note, touches her.

"Dory's sick. How long do you think we can stay there? How long, mom?" Rosie shines the flashlight in her face.

She can't see her daughter's expression but knows it's as fierce as her voice. "Not long," she murmurs, sensing defeat and sensing as well that if they don't move back in, her children will blame her forever. And, maybe they'll be right. "Okay," she says, "we'll try it. But if they throw us out again, we agree right now to move back to Dory's until I can find a cheap rental. That means both of you, understood?"

"Got it," her daughter says. "Tomorrow we can begin to pack up clothes and whatever. Come on, Casey, we'll put the bike in the car."

"Be quiet about it," she warns, knowing that it doesn't matter any more, knowing as well that the move back will be an act of futility.

It's after midnight when they pull into the garage. Casey and Rosie go downstairs. She and Zack tiptoe to the bedroom. "We shouldn't do it," she whispers, as soon as the door closes.

"What? Go back on our word?" He shakes his head in disbelief and begins undressing. Then adds, "You've said over and over that we need to keep the family together. That's where Casey heard it, not online, and he decided the only place to make that happen was the house. Now we have a chance to do that and you won't take it." His tone, more than despairing, shames her.

"Okay," she says softly, "we'll do it," and waits for a word from him. But he climbs into bed and turns away from her.

With sleep a distant promise, she tiptoes out of the room. A nightlight in the kitchen casts lengthy shadows. To her surprise, Dory sits at the table with an empty water glass and a bottle of pills. Her lips are pursed as if she'd sucked on a lemon, which looks almost comic.

"What's wrong?" She asks.

"Just swallowed pills for the nausea. Thought I took them before bed but obviously I hadn't. I heard you all come in."

"Casey broke into our old house and didn't want to leave."

"So that's where he was."

"He said if we didn't move back in the family would split apart, that we had to do it. He sounded desperate. He sat there all day, alone. What a horror. And he did it to send me a message. Am I so hard to reach? Don't answer that. So we all now go squat for a brief time before the sheriff or whoever kicks us out again. What a waste." Her eyes flit to the wall calendar, still in December of the previous year, as if everything had stopped there. "Zack promised to be more responsible. How responsible is it to bring a family into a squat only to be evicted again, how fucking responsible is that?"

"Maybe Stu can talk to him."

"It's too late. He's a dreamer who expects miracles."

The refrigerator motor clicks on with a gentle hum in the otherwise silent house. Outside, too, a stillness, so unlike where they grew up: the police sirens, fire engines, car mufflers, and thin walls through which babies cried, parents fought, women screamed, men accused. She'll have to return to all of that, because where else to find a cheap rental? "In the projects," she says, "all the nights of noise. Do you remember?"

"I do."

"And the smells."

"I do."

"Would you rather not chat?"

Dory shrugs. "Too many thoughts to express. They seem to need my concentration. It's as if there's a little bubble following me, writing out questions, insisting on answers. Sometimes even when I close my eyes at night, it hovers over my head, waiting. When I respond, the words inside the bubble disappear as smoothly as erasing a blackboard. Eerie, no?"

"Not really, considering all that's on your mind."

"My memories come in scenes now, almost like paintings or drawings, except the people in them don't speak. Try as I might I can't get a word out of them. I should go to bed, I'm starting to sound weird," Dory murmurs, her face pale in the dim light.

"I was wondering. Would it help to join one of those support groups?"

"Where people cheer themselves along on the way to death? What in heaven's name for?" Dory replies with great disdain. And the absurdity of the suggestion hits them both. It feels good to laugh some.

"I don't know . . . I thought maybe it would be easier to talk to strangers than to the people who love you."

"Forget it and anything like it."

"I will. I have. The nausea . . . is it better?"

"It takes a while."

"Can I do anything?"

Dory shakes her head. "This journey is mine alone.. No one else can experience it. Not you, not Stu, no one. I plan to follow it as I wish."

She slides her hand over Dory's cool fingers grateful to the core for her friendship. "I can't imagine not having you beside me."

"Don't imagine it yet, okay?"

"Don't be annoyed with me, please. You mean more to me than I can find words for."

"Sounds like love."

"It is. I talk to you about things I can't say to anyone else."

"Women do that for each other."

"What, if anything, have I done for you?"

"Deep, constant relationship from way back. I count on it. A woman who always appreciates me just as I am."

"You're right about that."

"Good," Dory murmurs, almost to herself.

"I've made terrible mistakes," she's shocked to hear herself say.

"You'll outlive them." Dory's face gives nothing away.

What awful bag of demons is she unzipping? Penitent, she

looks into the shine of the deep-brown mahogany tabletop and wonders what to say next, but Dory isn't waiting for a reply. She's gazing past Lena, with a serene expression and a distant look in her eyes. Must be the pills.

52.

Praying not to wake anyone in the still sleeping house, she moves stealthily, a fugitive escaping before Lena can ask where she's going so early. She tiptoes past her orderly kitchen, her well-furnished dining area, her comfortable den. It's how she takes in each room now. Fully. She slips into the garage, gets in the car, and heads for the bridge.

Though she had another fitful night, she isn't tired at all. Then again, sleep has become a joke. Her head buzzes with jumbled thoughts, plus a stew of memories creep out of the folds to fill the sleepless hours with images of life lived and owned. Often there's the beach, the four of them cavorting, drinking, and slathering sun lotion on each other's backs. Lena didn't actually enjoy the beach, complained about too much sun, sand in her hair. She and Zack, the water lovers, swimming, jumping waves. How boring it must've been for Lena and Stu to sit there, watching them, for god knows how long. Weird to see now what she couldn't see then.

The sleeplessness is more than reflection or review. It's a reckoning of sorts, a time to consider what there wasn't time to know before. And lately in the half-light of morning a feeling of utter disconnect visits her, as if she's unlatching herself from life, as if everything solid has evaporated, leaving her untethered, unable to find ground. Though it's often accompanied by the nausea, she can't help wondering if it's a taste of death, or preparation for it?

Some of her charges speak of death as around the corner, a given. She's not that accepting, and not that old, either. Still, her equanimity in the face of it puzzles her. Maybe in another life she was a Buddhist. More likely she's simply not as brave as Lena thinks, not even as brave as some of her charges. Miss Z, who has accommodated to that ultimate insult to her mobility, a wheelchair. Mr. Todd, who's having difficulty swallowing but eats his mushy food without too much complaint. She won't do as well. She'll resent losing pieces of herself. She already does. If eventually she has to be wheeled around, the dependency will be awful for her, more than awful, impossible.

As she reaches the Triborough Bridge, it rises to greet her with its view of Manhattan skyscrapers. The World Trade Center towers are gone, of course, but in their place another gigantic structure. How stupid is that? Cramming even more workers into a building to prove what? The thinking of these people eludes her, thank god. She rolls down her window. The humidity has lifted, the bright-blue sky is cloudless.

Montauk is still a few hours away, but she doesn't want to stop until she arrives at the point, the tip end of Long Island. She hasn't been there since her honeymoon, twenty-one years ago. They stayed at a hotel perched on craggy cliffs high above the ocean. Below was a long strip of beach, people stretched out on blankets, a scatter of seagulls along the water's edge. It all looked tiny, a diorama in a shoebox. At night, the sea whooshed and cried through the wide-open hotel windows. The noise

bothered Stu but not her. She adored the sound, the cool closeness of the rocks and water, so companionable, so reassuring
in their constancy. Though she knows the houses and narrow
sandy streets will have changed over the years, the cliffs and
ocean will still be there.

If the hotel is gone then the car path to the cliff edge may
be gone, too. She and Stu walked that path every morning.
Less than a half mile. At the steep, rocky edge, where the cool
wind always blew, they'd sit and talk, newlyweds that they were.
Funny, when she thinks of it now, they never hankered to travel
anywhere exotic. Of course, travel takes lots of money, but it
wasn't just that. They wanted to save and buy a house one day.
They were nesters, both of them, just as happy at a nearby
beach, or later on their own patio, where, after work, they
would sit drinking, laughing, telling tales. Why does it seem so
long ago? She's being sentimental, which is totally against her
belief system.

The hotel is there and open for business. It appears smaller
somehow and a bit frayed, scuffed by wind and salt water, but
not a smudge of grime on the pristine windows. She drives
around to the rear, finds the path, and the car rolls over the rut-
ted dirt to its end. She gets out and sits on the flattest patch she
can find. It's pleasantly windy. The waves crash against the jag-
ged rocks, then recede again and again, the repetition hypnotic.

She allows the wild beauty of the place to fill her. Returning
here feels like the impulse it is, but coming isn't an idle adventure. It's where she can get ahead of what's to happen.

Beyond the distant lighthouse she searches out the white
wall of the horizon and listens for foghorns. Except for the surf,

all is quiet. As the position of the sun changes so does the color of the water, from black to deep green. One area resembles a great hazel eye. Except water has no color; it simply reflects. She remembers this from the high school science class where she and Stu first hooked up. Not that he would ever commit to going steady. He would simply show up at her apartment or wait around in the hallway downstairs. She'd find him leaning against the mailboxes or sitting on a step. Some late nights he'd phone her to meet him and Matt at Tina's pizza place, or just him at the neighborhood bar, never saying what he'd been up to earlier. She didn't care. She just felt joyous to be with him. No secret that he was always drawn to Lena, but it was her he married, her he came home to, her he built a life with these past twenty years. In their first apartment together, near the projects, they had lots of parties, so many more than they've had since moving to the North Bronx. And he wasn't as restless then as he seemed later. Poor Stu, he can't do enough for her now. He sleeps curled around her, no doubt anticipating the time when she won't be there. He hasn't said as much, but he doesn't have to. He'll miss her. He'll pine. He'll cry. He'll drink, of course he will, and he should, but then he'll move on, because humans do, most of them, and he will, too, of that she's certain.

Lena will miss her, then find her way, because she'll have to. She's a mother. A mother doesn't leave her children willingly. Was it selfish not to try harder for a baby, not to go to the fertility clinic or take the adoption route? Did she forfeit not only the connection but also the chance to live on in an offspring's memory? She'll never know, only that her devotion to her work, her charges, was satisfying and illuminating. Though in no way children, they needed her physically, spiritually, in every way possible. So many stories digested over so many years about so many troubles and joys, about lives she could never hope to know otherwise. When one of her elderly charges dies, it's a loss, not a tragedy. And when she dies? What will that be?

She's rarely even been sick, yet something about the diagnosis was unsurprising. It's as if she's been waiting all these years. It's not a sense of doom. No. More a sense that everything she experienced and is still experiencing can't be repeated. It's a once-only chance, a once-only choice, a once-only day, month, year. It made her grab and hold onto whatever she could, including Stu.

Gazing at the rocks and ocean below, she remembers asking her father where a minute goes when it's gone. He said it doesn't go anywhere, it gets used up. And she will use up whatever good time is left. After that . . . well . . . the way she sees it now, her loyalty will only be to herself.

Thelma and Louise was a movie she watched years ago. The final scene pissed her off. Two beautiful women driving their car straight off a cliff seemed such a waste. Now, the ending makes sense to her

53.

After two days of repacking suitcases and boxes, she stands in Dory's backyard, idly watching the activity. Zack's busy moving out the items they brought here initially. Rosie's helping Stu pile stuff into the two cars, instructing him on where he should place things. Casey clambers up a short stepladder to adjust a small lamp tied to the top of the car. The children's joyful noises about moving back keeps her silent about the possibilities—none of them good—that continue to take up residence in her head.

The last rage of evening sun bathes the adjacent houses in a golden light, the sky a deepening blue. It'll be dark by the time they get there.

If only she could make a neat package of the past months—leave-taking does that—something to get her arms around and contemplate, but so much remains unknown.

Her eyes flit to Dory, plucking weeds from her flowerbed. "I'm so damn sad," she says, uprooting her friend from a kneeling position.

In black leggings and long green over-blouse, Dory looks tiny, and increasingly fragile.

"You've done an amazing job with the garden. The flowers are gorgeous."

"They are. Strange. I sit here now simply to enjoy them."

"Not so strange," she says half to herself. "All we ever do is rush around and rarely ask why. But you . . . you've been stopped from all that, and way too suddenly."

"It's true." Dory continues to gaze at the flowers. "Actually, I've let go of a lot of stuff, including the chore of loving too much, which leaves me weirdly, happily carefree and able to see, actually see, what's around me in a way I never have before. Sometimes what I see is frightening, sometimes beautiful. Either way, it doesn't matter. That's the carefree part. It's ironic because . . . well, because this can only happen when time is short. Otherwise all of life's traffic would stop to take in the view, and what a pile-up that would be."

She wants to put her arms around Dory, hug her tightly, but it would be more to comfort herself than her friend. "You've both been so good to . . ."

"Stu will miss you."

"What?"

"He's enjoyed having an extended family. Haven't you noticed? He hasn't stopped at a bar after work since you guys moved here. Keep him close when things go south for me."

"Of course we will. We're all family."

"Are you about ready to go?" Dory asks.

"The U-Haul is almost packed. The stuff in storage, I'll let it stay there for a bit, don't you think?"

"The board will let me know their decision tomorrow. If it's a go, you'll be working with me every day for a while. I'll introduce you to my charges, routines, all of it. It's important to develop an honest connection with the people you'll care for."

"I would be over the moon if it wasn't your job."

"Yeah, Lena, well . . . too bad you can't have it all."

"Do I complain a lot?"

"A lot."

"Jesus," she says.

"He can't help."

"We both agree on that."

"How unusual," Dory says.

"Actually, it's not. Growing up we agreed on almost every-thing."

"Except you didn't believe Stu would ever marry me."

"I thought he wasn't the settling-down..." Afraid, though, to meet Dory's searching eyes.

"You were wrong. Say so."

"I was so wrong," she admits quickly, gladly.

"Good, then that's resolved."

54.

The four of them tiptoe into the dark house as if they might wake whoever lives there. Stu and Zack are out back, setting up the generator.

Rosie giggles. "Why are we being so quiet?"

No one responds.

She's worried lights will attract the neighbors. But, of course, they're living here, sort of, not hiding out. When the lights do flicker on, she doesn't move.

"Mom, come on, there's nothing to be afraid of," says Rosie, marching into the living room. She follows her daughter, not quite believing this is happening.

Suddenly everyone's busy. Zack moves past her, carrying air mattresses upstairs, and Dory follows to supervise their placement. Rosie unfolds a card table in the bare living room, then places wine, beer, and soda on it, rewards to come. Stu's already messing with the water in the basement. Casey's down there with him. Dory said Stu knows pipes. Whatever.

Dazed at the flurry of activity under way without her guidance, she takes the bag of paper plates and cold cuts to the kitchen. No one had any dinner to speak of. With a napkin she wipes off Zack's perfectly tiled counter, then begins to prepare sandwiches.

The lemon-yellow walls... She wanted them painted white;

Rosie begged for red; yellow was the compromise. When they first moved in, they bought a kitchen set and lamps. The children investigated each new item as if it were a toy or Christmas decoration. Gossip, arguments, laughter, tears, plans, and so much else went on in this room. If walls could talk . . . She remembers Zack striding through the house like the lord of the manor, and the children, unused to sleeping in separate rooms, visiting each other nightly. None of them knew how to react to the quiet outside.

The first weekend, she recalls the four of them staying indoors, still trying to absorb what was theirs. However unhappy he was with his job, Zack was deeply content in this house. Wasn't she as well? After the newness wore off, it's true that some of her old restlessness returned, but she wasn't unhappy. How easy it's been—too easy—in the past months of misery to obliterate all memory of what went before. At the time, it never occurred to her to savor the pleasure she now looks back on. And she realizes it isn't hindsight but loss that illuminates.

"Hey," Zack calls from the top of the stairs. "Should I hang towels on the bedroom windows?"

"Yes," Rosie replies. "I'm not sleeping with an uncovered window."

"Rosie, do you want to come up and help me?"

"No. I'm waiting in the living room. My friend is on the way over."

She leaves the sandwiches and finds her daughter. "Your friend? At this time of night? Who is it?"

"Mom, you need to chill. Be nice to him, promise."

"Him? You can't invite outsiders. We're doing something illegal."

"Please, get off the illegal crap. It isn't some major heist." Her daughter's studiously scruffy in cargo pants and a T-shirt, her face lovely without makeup.

She takes a deep breath, recalling her decision not to argue with her daughter, or at least not as often. "Who is the man?"

"Not exactly a man, he's eighteen. His name is Siri."

Dory chimes in. "Obviously, Rosie, you've told him all about us, so now it's our chance to meet him. Lena?"

"Did you know about this?"

"Not for a second."

"Oh lord," she mumbles and returns to finish preparing the sandwiches.

"Mom?" Casey stands in the middle of the bare kitchen, looking a bit lost.

"I thought you were in the basement with Stu."

"I was, but turns out water is never really stopped. They just shut off the valves or something. I saw it trickle out in the bathroom, dark brown. Stu left it running."

"Are you okay?"

"Oh, yes, I'm glad. I like being here with everyone."

She puts her arms around his narrow frame, rubs her chin across the top of his curly hair. "I like being here with everyone, too. Help me bring in the sandwiches. We can spread the old green blanket on the floor."

"A nighttime picnic." He sounds approving.

They sit on the floor around a blanket, sandwiches on paper plates, cups filled with liquids of choice. Two bottles of wine already emptied. It's past eleven. They've done what they could to make the house livable, though it's more like camping out— something she won't say, because Rosie will accuse her of being too negative. Siri, in black jeans and a white shirt, seems more at home than she'd ever be in this situation. It's admirable that he came all this way at such an hour to protect his girlfriend.

"The roughing it," Stu says, "something invigorating about it."

"Oh you mean, man sets up abode for clan, then goes back to his modern house for a shower?" she responds, smiling.

"Yeah, something like that. We've all become so wimpy." He wears his usual loose smile, though his eyes have lost their mischief.

"Filled with strange expectations," she murmurs, a bit giddy from the wine.

"Something like that," Stu agrees, and they glance at each other, almost but not quite as they would have before that afternoon.

"Then again, I do like my comforts," she admits. "Though I don't remember thinking about comforts growing up."

"We didn't know what they were," Zack says.

"Once you taste caviar, everything else tastes fishy," Stu declares.

"Did you ever taste caviar?" Rosie asks.

"It is very fishy," Siri tells her earnestly.

"Live and learn," Stu says. "Zack, now he's the guy that led us all here to safety."

"Safety? What have you been drinking?" Rosie asks.

"Wine. And you, girl?"

"Unfortunately, my mother . . ."

"I said you could have a beer." She notices Rosie's hand in Siri's, and notices as well the contentment on Zack's face, some of it the drink, but the rest his beloved house. Her eyes flit to the vestibule where, not so long ago, coats hung and shoes lined the walls, and wonders if that's ever to be again. "It's not our fault, the foreclosure," she suddenly finds herself saying with an awareness that surprises her. "Losing the house, it's not our fault. The banks, the money men, the indifferent ones who sign those foreclosure letters, they're to blame. Not Zack, not me. We tried. They wouldn't give an inch. And for what, to keep another empty house on the street?"

"You just realized this?" asks Dory.

"It didn't register in the way it does now."

Reaching across to squeeze her hand, Zack knocks over a glass of soda. A map of the states spreads bizarrely in the center of the blanket. They all laugh, because who cares? No one tries to do a thing about it, except Zack, who tosses napkins on the spreading wet spot.

"Guess I'm three sheets to the wind," Zack adds, apologetically.

"I'm four," she says.

"You can't be," Stu amends. "You have to own a sailboat, a real schooner to say that. It can't apply to us."

"We should all go sailing someday," Rosie announces.

"On whose boat?" she wonders.

"Strange picnic," Dory says softly.

Lena nudges Casey, sitting beside her. "My love, why so quiet?" But it's Dory who's said almost nothing.

"I like listening."

"When you were two or three and Dory and Stu visited, you'd run around the room touching each person, exclaiming, 'Everyone is here!' Do you remember doing that?"

"I was too young."

"I remember us taking three-year old Rosie for a night so you two could smooch. And she wouldn't sleep. She talked the whole night long," Stu says.

"I can remember back to the crib," Rosie asserts and gets a

sweet smile from Siri, who seems to enjoy anything she says.

"Stu, do you remember me calling you on a winter night? We didn't have Triple-A, and our car had run out of gas on the expressway, baby Rosie strapped in the car seat, Lena outside waving cars past. What a nightmare."

"I drove up, poured gas in the machine from a can I was smart enough to carry."

"I used to watch the children sleep," she begins, refreshing her glass, not a clue as to why this memory came to her now. "I believed nothing bad could happen to them as long as I was watching."

"Mom, maybe you shouldn't have more wine."

"Rosie, maybe you're suffering from a role-reversal problem."

"Funny, funny." Her daughter's tone—thank heavens—is playful.

"Siri, glad to have you on this picnic," Zack says.

"Thank you. It's good being here."

"Yeah, I'll drink to that," Stu empties his wine glass.

"A toast," Zack lifts his cup.

"Do we all have to be quiet?" Casey asks.

"Of course," Stu says. "The leader of the clan is about to talk."

"Okay, shut up, everyone. Dad, go on," Rosie urges.

"My friends, in our year of lack of plenty, I am most grateful to . . ."

The sirens reach them ahead of the blue and red flashing lights that sweep the windows. The silence in the room is sudden and absolute. Then, as if waking from a trance, Stu and Zack rush out, followed by Rosie and Siri. No doubt the neighbors will soon join them. Dory, too, manages to get up and stands by Casey at the open door.

She can hear talking, but not what's being said; no voice is raised, thank god. What if they have to move out tonight? The boxes are still packed. The generator out back, is that a crime? And turning on the water? Are the police going to come in, walk through? Should she go out and plead for extra hours as she did the first time? Eyeing the plates and cups strewn across the blanket, she decides no, what has to be will be. A calmness fills her like the one she felt on first hearing her mother was dead. What she had long expected had happened. Now, too. She never had a doubt it would end this way. Unlike then, though, she has no desire to escape. Not while her family and friends are out in the street, doing whatever they can to make it better.

A few minutes later they file back in. Casey shuts the door. She searches his face. He wears the same alarmed expression she recognizes. He really thought this would work.

Zack murmurs, "Some asshole saw the lights, called the police."

Rosie announces, "They gave us seventy-two hours to vacate."

"Thank Stu," Dory says. "One of the cops recognized him because he did some free welding at his Staten Island house after Hurricane Sandy."

"I didn't know it was a cop house," Stu says defensively.

At the window she watches Stu and Dory drive away in their cars. Stu will drop off Siri at the train station. The children are in their bedrooms. Before turning in, Zack whispered how sorry he was. She assured him his urge to move back was hopeful, not selfish; the best of him, not the worst. It was the right thing to say, even if the past days didn't need to happen. Then again, maybe they did. Maybe they mattered deeply. Maybe they welded the family back together. The strange picnic around the blanket was a bonding as well as a release of sorts. Something is ending. She knows it now for certain. Not her friendship, not her family; but she can feel it, an interruption, a break, a place marker to separate before and after. What that means, she'll have to wait to find out.

Behind her the empty rooms hum with silence. Leaving here for a second time . . . it's not the same. The grief of parting already gone through. She eyes the soiled paper plates and cups on the blanket. Tomorrow. She'll deal with all of it tomorrow. It's after midnight, the navy-blue sky untouched by stars or moon.

55.

The elevated train is crowded with rush-hour riders shuffling for space and balance, trying not to touch one another, such an impossible task. Lena stands, as always, at the window in the train door, watching the passing blur of Bronx buildings. She's on her way to the nursing home to meet Dory's charges. It's how she'll always think of them, even after Dory leaves and the old ones die and new admissions arrive. She'll be the best caretaker. She will. She owes that to Dory.

The packed boxes and suitcases are once again ready to be moved. Stu will pick up the generator after work and turn off the water. It's finished there for all of them, though she and Zack arranged for Casey to travel to his old school until he completes eighth grade. By the look of relief on his face, it was the right choice. With Siri in her life, Rosie seems to care less about where she lives.

This evening, she'll sign a lease for a two-bedroom apartment in an old building she checked out yesterday. They'll move there tomorrow, though no one else in the family has seen it. There's no time to be picky. It's on Valentine Avenue, near Fordham Road, not far from where she grew up. Once more the face of sadness, poverty, and god knows what else will greet her every morning as she leaves and every night as she comes home. Such familiar neighbors. The apartment is small, deprived of natural light, but the super promised to paint it, and there's an eat-in kitchen. She'll bring back the furniture from storage and cheer up each room. She knows how to make it home. Her family is together. That's something. And Zack's ability to believe in miracles will help her navigate the dark moments to come.

The train stalls before entering the tunnel. She gazes at the cloudless blue sky, a gentle sheet over uneven rooftops. As the train lurches forward, an arm of sunlight reaches across buildings to mask the grayness inside.

Acknowledgments

A special note of gratitude to my brilliant friend, Elizabeth Strout, whose wisdom and strength have always been available to me.

Deep appreciation to those who gave generously of their time and support: Jane Lazarre, my talented first reader-editor and constant dear friend, whose devotion to my work never failed to spur me on; Jocelyn Lieu and Jan Clausen, whose detailed and insightful attention to various chapters were more than helpful. For reading through the novel and sharing their comments, my thanks go to Barbara Schneider, whose loving friendship never wavers, and Liz Gewirtzman, who gave unsparingly of her knowledge. For their caring support of my work and more, my profound thanks to: Vicki Brietbart, Prue Glass, Rina Kleege, Wesley Brown, Ellen Siegel, Pat Walters, and Marsha Taubenhaus.

For those who have helped in ways too numerous to describe, I thank Dr. Kristin Robie, Denise Campono, Urszula Kopciuch, Peggy Belenoff, Barbara Gould, and Sam and Yudi Wiggins.

Many thanks to the staff at Haymarket Books and especially Anthony Arnove, Nisha Bolsey, Rory Fanning, Caroline Luft for her incredible copyediting, and Mimi Bark for an amazing cover design; also to Dispatch Books and Tom Engelhardt, extraordinary editor, for his ongoing belief in this project and for being a friend to the end. And, as always, a million thanks to my agent, Melanie Jackson, a national treasure.

To my family for their neverending love and support, I am grateful to Robert and Sam Trestman, Judi Gologorsky Brand, and Dr. Kenneth Trestman for his help and brilliant counsel.

As ever with more than gratitude I thank my beloved, late Charlie Wiggins for his devotion, enthusiasm, constancy, and unfailing belief in what I do. And for always being there, I remain forever grateful to Georgina, Dònal, and Maya, the lights of my life, who make it all matter.